WHAT PEOPLE ARE SAYING ABOUT

LYSANDE[

T0119746

This is a book for anyone who has ev. in love, i.e. most of the world's inhabitants. Julia, the book's heroine, combines wit and intelligence with an agonizing, and all too recognizable, emotional naivety which makes us cry and laugh by turns in recognition. How many of us have, at some time, listened to a friend's rhapsodic account of a burgeoning love affair, knowing even as the words are spoken, that it is all going to end in tears? One squirms for both the hero and the heroine, as we watch them fall in love with the wrong people. But, before it sounds too harrowing, there is plenty of light relief with Jane Myles's genuine laugh-out-loud set pieces. I loved it.
Julian Fellowes, creator of Downton Abbey

Jane Myles captures the spirit of the times and the poignancy of a doomed romance, at the same time exploring the shifting sands of sexuality. The perfect lesson in how to fall in love with the wrong person. The painful honesty of both the central characters and the strong sense of time and place (mostly the seventies) makes this the perfect read for people of 'a certain age'.
William Nicholson, writer of Shadowlands and Gladiator

A great piece of sun-lounger 'hen'-lit for those who are beyond chick-lit qualifying age and who need a break from a surfeit of Hilary Mantel. Despite being a touching tale of 'requited but not requited enough' love, there is a seam of self-deprecating humour which makes one really care about the central characters' voyage of emotional discovery.
Sir Christopher Meyer, former British Ambassador to the US

From as young an age as I can remember, my mother, Jane Myles, is the BEST story teller I have ever known. I hope she inspires you as much as she has always inspired me.

Sophia Myles, actress

Lysander's
Legs

Lysander's
Legs

Jane Myles

Winchester, UK
Washington, USA

First published by Roundfire Books, 2013
Roundfire Books is an imprint of John Hunt Publishing Ltd., Laurel House, Station Approach,
Alresford, Hants, SO24 9JH, UK
office1@jhpbooks.net
www.johnhuntpublishing.com
www.roundfire-books.com

For distributor details and how to order please visit the 'Ordering' section on our website.

Text copyright: Jane Myles 2013

ISBN: 978 1 78279 263 5

A CIP catalogue record for this book is available from the British Library.

Design: Stuart Davies

Printed in the USA by Edwards Brothers Malloy

We operate a distinctive and ethical publishing philosophy in all
areas of our business, from our global network of authors to
production and worldwide distribution.

For Oli and Sophia

Chapter One

1970

'At last I've found my tribe...' said Julia.

'What tribe? Jules, are you dreaming? Wake up! You're on a bus. It's Tuscany not Botswana; it's *me*, Angie,' said Angie Farr, second-year history student, and Julia McCallum's best friend and confidante on the college drama society trip to Italy.

'Eh? Oh sorry, Ange, I was just thinking aloud. I mean I've found what I want to do; I've found the people I relate to; I've found... I've found "me" I suppose. You know, you sit at a desk in school in some little country village and you feel like an alien, like you're some changeling who's been dropped in the wrong place but you kind of know you'll meet your tribe one day. That's now. It's all of you. I never want it to end. God, I love you all. This trip to the drama festival is icing on the cake, really.'

'Steady on, Jules... Been on the Chianti already? It's not the sixties anymore and you're going a bit far on the old peace and love; anyway, been there, done that,' said Angie, looking back out of the minibus window.

'No, but I mean I have such a bond with everyone, and Mark has been amazing the way he's kept the group so focussed and so together. I really feel our play has got a chance in the Festival. I'm even considering chucking in doing the PGCE after my degree and applying to drama school instead. It's what I just said...I've found my tribe.'

Mark Belmont, their director, was sitting across the aisle of the bus a few seats behind them. Angie glanced back over her shoulder then turned to Julia. 'You know why he's never married, don't you.'

'Not met the right girl?' offered Julia, unimaginatively.

'Well, look at him.'

Julia felt like she was thirteen and back in the maths class and was about to be denounced as an innumerate dunce for not knowing the obvious answer to a quadratic equation after the teacher had spent twenty minutes explaining the formula. She stared at Mark's dark, slightly weasel features, sleek black hair and dark gypsy eyes. He made her think of those sepia photos of Rudolph Valentino who used to make women almost faint with passion when they watched him in gloomy picture palaces. Julia still didn't get it. She could try the 'Oh, I *see* what you mean!' gambit which she had employed to great advantage when Mr Parsons, the maths coach, had come to help her on Wednesday evenings and she didn't understand a word he was talking about. But Angie would catch her out sooner than Mr Parsons. She just looked meaningfully back at Angie and waited for her to elaborate.

'Well, just look at him. I reckon that somewhere back along the line, not too far back that is, there's a bit of mixed race, and he's scared that if he has kids there may be a throw-back and people will realise his secret.'

'But doesn't he come from some village in the Midlands? And isn't that the most racist thing I've ever heard you say? To be honest, I'm surprised at you, Ange. This is the seventies for God's sake!'

'Well I don't care. It's what my gran would have said and would have thought nothing of it. Mark comes from the Midlands now, yes, sure enough, but my theory's got to be the explanation. Look at him; d'you know how old he is?'

'Twenty-five?' ventured Julia, never having given any thought to it before.

'He's nearly *thirty* next birthday,' said Angie, as if being thirty explained the swarthy skin and dark eyes and corroborated everything she had said previously.

'Keep it to yourself, Jules, it's our little sec-ret...geddit.? Sikh...ret'

Julia rolled her eyes heavenward. God, sometimes Angie

could be cornier than her uncle Alf when he'd had a few pints at the Working Men's Club.

However, from then on, throughout all the final rehearsals for the forthcoming drama festival performance, Julia listened to every nuance of speech, every cadence and strange use of a word, and watched closely as Mark Belmont issued stage directions and demonstrated how to deliver some of the lines, hoping to catch, amid the actor's diction, and the faint whiff of Coleshill-speak, a whisper or two from the Punjab.

The Rossigno Festival was only a few days away and they were putting the finishing touches to their student production of *Translations*. As well as directing it, Mark was playing Yolland, the Royal Engineer who falls in love with Maire. Mel, who was a research student at Julia's college, was playing Maire. Julia herself was playing Sarah, a part that required no more than a few grunts with the occasional burst of speech since her character is considered in the play to be dumb. For this reason, although she was required to be on stage a lot of the time, she had plenty of chances to observe the others without having to worry about what her next line was going to be.

'This moment when Manus takes Sarah's hands in his is extraordinarily powerful,' Mark said to them all over his shoulder as he knelt before Julia and took her hands in his, demonstrating to Gareth how he should do it. He then fell into role, with Gareth looking on and began, 'Come on, one more try. "My name is—" Good girl.'

Mark stared intently into Julia's eyes and still held her.

'Get it, Gareth?' he asked, and Julia was aware that Mark was still holding her hands and that now he was caressing the back of one hand with his thumb. It was like playing footsie with hands. No one else in the room was aware of what was going on. Presently he released her, and the rehearsal continued. Later, she noticed him with his arm lingering on Rob's shoulder slightly longer than was necessary, and, as this was quietly registering, saw him wink at Andrea as she was offering to fetch everyone a cup of tea.

The man is an incorrigible flirt, she thought to herself. *This stuff about Sikh skeletons in the ancestral Belmont cupboard was a load of crap. He's having too much of a good time touching everyone up to settle down and be faithful to one person. That's the obvious answer. I wouldn't touch him with a bargepole myself.*

The trouble was, Julia was always looking for a second Mr Broadhurst.

Gethin Broadhurst had been her English teacher at school. In fact he had been a prefect the year she had started at the grammar school and he then went off to university and returned a fully-fledged teacher in time to teach her A-level English group. He had been nothing to look at, in fact he could have won a Dylan Thomas lookalike contest, but then that would have been a plus to Julia. She and her friend Liz had been completely smitten by him as he was one of the only teachers who treated them like adults and they "loved his mind". He was passionate about poetry and new drama and regularly mentioned that he was going to this play or that: Pinter, Beckett, Osborne, and would anyone in the English group like to go along too. Often it was just Julia and Liz sitting in Gethin's old banger on their way to Bath or Cardiff or Stratford where they, too, were set alight by these new plays even though, half the time, they hadn't got a clue what they were about.

Julia and Liz had gone, for once without Gethin, to the first night of Pinter's *The Homecoming* in Cardiff in its pre-London try-out (mainly to impress Gethin of course). When they found themselves walking behind Pinter himself and the actor Ian Holm on the way down the road after the performance, they knew this was a chance to score maximum points with Gethin the following day at school. They raced along, hyperventilating, and stopped the two rather surprised men in their tracks and asked them to autograph their programmes. This is all where it fell apart. Harold Pinter asked Julia how she had enjoyed the play. As sixteen-year-old Julia hadn't had a clue what it was about, she grinned inanely and just said, 'Er...very nice; very interesting,' and they skipped away giggling and grabbing each other's arms as if they had just met John Lennon.

It had the desired effect and from then on Gethin began treating them as equals, as if they had just been admitted to some literary élite coterie. Julia used to think up topics of clever conversation for the long theatre outings in Gethin's car. If it was Liz's turn to sit in the front seat, Julia would sit in the back secretly scrutinizing a little crib sheet of conversation starters which she kept rolled up in her pocket. Every now and then she would come out with, 'I see Arnold Wesker's got a new play coming out. Are you a great fan of Wesker, Mr Broadhurst?' However, it was like knowing a few get-by phrases in another language. You could ask a simple question but were in no position to give an elaborate answer yourself if the conversation turned round.

When it was announced that there was to be a school trip in the Easter holidays to Barcelona, Julia beseeched her parents to let her go. By then she was sending herself to sleep every night fantasizing about various romantic scenarios all with herself and Gethin Broadhurst as the romantic hero and heroine. Only Alessandra, her other good friend, was going on the trip from their year. Others were either too busy revising for the coming A-levels or else had parents whose budgets couldn't stretch that far. Alessandra, despite having an exotic name, had lived in Wales since she was four and spoke with as much of a Welsh accent as the rest of them. Her immigrant Italian family ran a little café in one of the small towns further up the valley from the school. Alessandra had been quite a podgy teenager but was now beginning to lose her puppy fat. She was slightly bemused by the

"Gethin fan club" with its two members, namely Julia and Liz, but humoured their endless deconstructions of the drama outings ('Did you see him smile at me when he let me look at his programme?' 'I think his hand might have touched my elbow when I opened the door!' and so forth). Alessandra and Julia had applied to the same university and had both been accepted and had already agreed that they would share a room in Hall.

The school trip proved, for Julia, to be a massive compendium of "Gethin moments". When they were back at school and starting the exam term, Julia spent the first few days graphically describing each special incident to Liz and anyone else who would listen, flushed with excitement at her "special relationship" with Gethin.

About one week into term, Alessandra pulled her to one side in the school library.

'Jules, I need to talk to you. You know when we were coming back on the night ferry and you were sleeping on that long bench in the bar down below deck?'

'Yeah?' said Julia, wondering uneasily what on earth was coming.

'Well, he said to me "Yes?" or "No"? So I said, "Yes!" and that's when he kissed me. And we've been going out together in secret ever since. He told me he loves me and he's prepared to wait three years till I've finished university.'

'Hang on, Ali, you've lost me. Who the heck are you talking about? Stephen Marriot? Rollo? God, not Chris Tonkin! Promise me it's not him! Crikey, you dark horse, you!'

'No, *Gethin*, of course!' said Alessandra, looking suddenly like a smug 25-year-old.

Julia looked at her like a dog that had just heard its master's whistle in the distance, but was baffled as to which direction it was coming from. She cocked her head on one side uncomprehendingly. Her fantasies of the past eighteen months had just come crashing down. She suddenly felt small, childish, stupid and betrayed. She didn't know what was worse: her humiliation in front of all those to whom she had boasted about her inconsequential moments with Gethin during the school trip, or the realisation that she was about to spend three years sharing a bedroom with the person who was the orchestrator of the destruction of her dreams. Even worse than that, she realised, she would be forced to play gooseberry when he drove up to visit Alessandra on his free weekends and there would be no escape apart from failing her A-levels and not taking up her place and going to some other university the following year.

But of course, she said to herself, *it's no surprise, I'm not pretty enough, not foreign and interesting like her; I don't have a fancy name and a "secret smile"... But I'm funnier, cleverer, more sensible...why can't he see that? She's just bewitched him. She doesn't understand Harold Pinter like I do! IT'S NOT FAIR!*

Chapter Two

Julia had carried that feeling with her like an albatross tied to her neck most of the way through university. Of course, Gethin hadn't lasted long with the siren Alessandra. She dumped him after six weeks at university because she had most of the male population of the modern languages faculty falling at her feet.

But now was different. It was 1970. This felt like a new era: the era of Julia the actress, Julia the independent traveller, Julia the popular one, Julia the confident linguist, Julia the winner. So here at last, at about four o'clock in the afternoon, their minibus was crawling up the meandering Tuscan road, passing grimly determined sun-tanned cyclists in leather helmets, jaws gritted in concentration, pedalling as if their lives depended on it to the summit of the mountain. In order to get to where they now were they had already pedalled up the equivalent of a small Alp. *And they do this for pleasure...*mused Julia, *they must be barmy.*

The bus swung in through a pair of wrought iron gates and snaked its way down the twisting dust track to the Villa Marcella.

'There it is!' Julia called across to Mel who was on the other side of the aisle. She pointed out of the right-hand side of the minibus to a small complex of buildings with a pool at the rear. Two swarthy-looking children splashed about in the pool in the heavy afternoon heat. A donkey stood under a nearby tree, head hanging low, as if trying to remember an enigmatic mathematical formula, or else recovering from hearing bad news. It was a bit disappointing, not a bit romantic or Quattrocento, just a little farmhouse thing really, with two dusty Fiats parked outside. But then Julia suddenly realised that their minibus was winding on further down the track. This had not been it, simply a group of outbuildings, maybe somewhere for the Villa Marcella staff or an annexe for guests less fortunate than the Oliver Goldsmith University Drama Group.

By now the view across the valley was stunning and reached

right across to the tiny hill village of Rossigno, with its medieval baptistry and terracotta pantiled roofs perched one above the other like a tower of wooden children's bricks. Remove one and the whole village would tumble down over the precipice in a shower of red dust. On Mel's side of the bus there were a few very skinny horses nuzzling one another and shuffling about under an olive tree trying to commandeer a little patch of shadow while the flies buzzed round their heads causing them to twitch their necks, shiver, and flick their tails, all to no avail. It reminded Julia of bits of newsreel of starving Biafran babies who were too weak and weary to knock the flies away from their eyes.

Up on the left was also a tennis court full of weeds with a net dangling feebly across the middle, almost touching the ground. Then, all of a sudden she saw it: the most serene Tuscan country mansion nestling at the bottom of the gravel drive, festooned in bougainvillea, shimmering in the last spasm of daytime heat.

'Hey, check out the guy on the scooter!' called Rob from the front of the bus. Julia craned to see what he was looking at, and gasped as the vision passed right beneath her window. A vast aristocratic man of about fifty sat astride a Vespa. He wore an elegant Panama hat, a pristine white shirt and outrageous lime green trousers, trousers more appropriate in colour for Beppo the circus clown, or a kids' TV presenter barely out of drama school. His blond straight hair was chin length. He stared ahead, not even acknowledging the presence on the track of the minibus. His aquiline nose made him look like a Roman emperor. And then she saw it.

'Oh bless! Mel, look at him!' she cried out, without taking her eyes from the window of the bus. 'Isn't he wonderful?!' For next to the Roman emperor sat some kind of hunting dog, a pointer maybe, perfectly still, balancing on the footrest of the scooter next to his master's legs, also staring ahead unperturbed, head held high, nostrils slightly twitching. But it wasn't a party trick. It was quite obvious that the two had been travelling seriously about their business in this way for years. Once they had gone past and their ensuing cloud of white dust had settled, Julia turned to Mel saying, 'Guess what "Vespa" means in Italian. It means…' But before she got to "a wasp", her voice dried up as her eyes caught Mel's hands entwined with Mark's, and saw Mel and Mark, blissfully unaware of the other occupants of the bus, quickly kissing one another. This was no 'Mwah, darling' air kissing; this was no 'There, there' placatory kiss. This was full-on nanosecond passion. *Shit*, she thought to herself as she visualised Mel's husband of six months sitting at home in Muswell Hill innocently getting on with his latest watercolour, *Poor Deke*.

But at this point the bus had come to a halt. Mark, the director, and the thirteen members of the Oliver Goldsmith Drama Group bundled out of the bus clutching their half-drunk bottles of aqua minerale naturale into the deafening symphony of cicadas. Two more dogs, more ancient-looking than the Vespa rider, eased themselves to their feet in a fenced-off compound under a few more trees, stretched, but couldn't be bothered to bark. A little way down to the left was another pool with a few half-glimpsed bodies lolling on loungers under sun umbrellas. Vittorio, the minibus driver, was unloading the bags onto the gravel and Julia, claiming hers, picked up one end and dragged it towards the courtyard where she guessed there would be some kind of entrance. She wanted to put her head in the sand; avoid seeing any more of what she had just witnessed and then maybe it would go away. Maybe it had never happened. Maybe it was the heat of the day getting to her brain.

As she rounded the corner of the small palazzo, she heard an anxious 'Guarda signorina!' A man with the head of a Renaissance prince and the embroidered golden brocade waistcoat of a waiter rushed across the flagstones of the terrace and started waving his witch's broom frantically at her feet.

'What on earth's going on?' she demanded, as autocratically and as Lady Bracknell-like as she could manage.

'A snake in the grass, signorina,' he replied, then, camply turning on his Cuban heel, he recommenced sweeping under the pink table-clothed tables on the dining terrace and limply indicated the main entrance to the Villa Marcella, calling out, 'Sono arrivati!' to someone unseen in the dark entrance hall.

After about ten minutes the whole group had assembled around the giant circular walnut table in the almost pitch dark vestibule of the large house. As her eyes became more accustomed to the contrast between the intense sun outside and now the almost dank and dark interior, Julia started to notice the effortless grand manner style of the decoration: the enormous bowls of flowers, the ancient portraits, the book shelves full of pale brown leather-bound books with gold lettering on their spines, the baroque sofas with chubby gilded legs, and something which looked like an enormous dull silver cabbage (actual size) in need of polishing. Was it an ornament? A tureen? A sculpture? There was the aroma of sandalwood: either an unseen candle burning somewhere or else some scented beeswax polish. And then there was the ornate staircase winding up around the corner. And of course there was Antonella.

'Good day and welcome to Villa Marcella; I am Antonella, the proprietor.' She had a husky, Italian-accented voice, exquisitely expensive golden sandals, long blonde hair, the kind of honey-blonde that only northern Italians have, combined with olive skin, a few pieces of jewellery that looked like they belonged on a little plinth in a pricey modern art and craft gallery, and the obligatory streamlined day dress with the designer jumper dangling about her shoulders, sleeves knotted loosely on her chest. All of the girls in the group felt shabby, dirty, unkempt and fashion failures. *How do these Italian women do it?* wondered Julia. *Even if I took all the time in the world I could never look like that, especially on a sweltering day like this. She obviously keeps out of the sun. Probably thinks it's common as hell to lie in it.*

'We 'ave in oll forty-hate guests 'ere at present,' continued

Antonella. 'Twenty-four in the main 'ouse, some in the stable apartaments over the courtyard, and some in the smaller villas down there near the pool. You have come to the Festival, yes? I wish you success. Giacomo will give you your keys and take the baggages to the rooms. You 'ave already indicated who will share with whom and how many people to each room, this is right?' There was a bit of a clatter as Giacomo scuttled across to the little shelf where all the keys were hanging.

'Four ladies, room ten,' he began. 'Two gentlemen, room six,'

'Two fat ladies, eighty-eight, twenty-one key of the door,' sniggered Rob, as he and Josh picked up their rucksacks and went up the winding staircase.

'How come we're here anyway?' continued Rob.

'Someone Mark knows apparently. I dunno, maybe he knows the people who own it, some connection that I never really picked up on. I think that's what Mel said.'

It wasn't long before Mel and Julia were also on their way up to the next floor. Angie was sharing what was nicknamed "the dorm" with three other girls as it was the biggest room in the palazzo. In the dark of the upstairs corridor they made out a large polished circular table with a giant bowl of peonies sitting in the middle and a couple of Italian fashion magazines scattered around, a bit like a Harley Street doctor's waiting room. Along one wall was a ridiculously outsize black wooden high-backed sofa.

'Look at that thing, Mel. What d'you call it? Sofa? Pew?'

'Settle maybe,' said Mel, not really concentrating.

'It looks like something Alice in Wonderland would have seen as she was shrinking. I'm sure if we sat on it our legs would dangle.'

But Mel was already following Giacomo down to the shadowy part of the corridor and rattling away at the lock. Their room, like all the others on that corridor, looked out across the plunging garden of the estate and over the valley towards Rossigno. Once they threw the shutters open the room flooded with light. Everything was opulent and airy: big windows, golden counterpane, golden curtains, and, the best bit, the bathroom leading off from a door near the windows meaning that its windows also overlooked the terrace and the valley. Most toilets and bathrooms that Julia had encountered were airless little boxes often without windows, just a whirring Vent-Axia which swung into action as one turned on the light. This bathroom was like a veritable *piano nobile*. One could lie in the bath with the sounds of guests dining on the terrace below, or, at the dawn, with the sound of donkeys braying in the distance. She imagined that at night, they would hear Giacomo's heels clonking industriously back and forth over the flagstones, trays laden with tiny iced glasses of Limoncello or café corretto. Café corretto made Julia smile. Only the Italians would feel that coffee was "correct" or "right' if it had strong alcohol added to it; by implication, therefore, it was "wrong" to drink an espresso all on its own. The morning sun would be pouring in from seven; the air would be redolent of jasmine; purple bougainvillea tumbling down over the shutters. This bathroom was one of the most luxurious rooms she had ever known. As she looked out across the valley the towers of Rossigno had now turned cinnamon-orange.

By now Mel was running a bath. Because this was essentially a grand but old house, the fittings were reminiscent of rather over-the-hill English country houses. The enormous bath fittings looked like the kind of taps and levers required to adjust the pressure in engines on the *Titanic*. Julia was therefore unsurprised to hear Mel's 'Oh God! Yuk!' as the bath immediately started to fill with rusty brown water with red bits in it.

'Don't worry, Mel,' Julia called from the bed where she was now spread-eagled. 'It's OK. At least it's hot and wet, talking of which, what on earth was going on with Mark?'

'Uh, going on when, what d'you mean?'

'Well, back there in the bus. Were you kissing him for a bet or was it mouth to mouth resuscitation after a swoon?'

There was no answer. Julia heaved herself up and wandered hesitantly over to the adjoining bathroom and stuck her head round the corner. Mel was sitting in a few inches of slightly orange water, arms round her knees, body hunched, head down. As Julia took in the scene, she saw the faint plop of a tear scuttling down Mel's face and hitting the water.

'Oh, Mel, sorry, I didn't mean to joke. It's just…it's just…'

'I know, it's just that I'm bloody married to Deke and now my stomach lurches every time Mark comes into the room. It's a "grand passion" Jules. We can't help it. It started before we ever came to Italy, you know, during those early rehearsals in that church hall in Gospel Oak. He's almost got a gypsy-like quality about him. That slow smile. He seems to be able to read my soul.'

'But Mel, Deke's sitting home there in the flat, innocently painting, so pleased for you that you've been able to come out here; he even sold a painting to help fund the trip, and he could have held that back for his exhibition. Not only that, there's his poor old mum that he's got to see to. That Alzheimers thing is going to get worse by the day you know.'

'I know. I'm a cow. I'm in such turmoil.' Mel sighed. 'I don't know if I love him any more…well, I sort of love him, but he's not the one who makes me feel like I've got a butcher's hook churning my innards around. I married Deke because he was a good, lovely person, someone who would take care of me forever. He was my pal, my soul mate, someone I could imagine sitting next to me in the maternity ward, sponging my face and helping me through labour.'

'And Mark?' asked Julia, raising an eyebrow.

'He just exudes sexuality; if I'm near him it's like I'm possessed. It's like, it's like Rasputin and the Tsarina. If he asked me to climb up one of those towers over there in Rossigno and jump off, I'm almost afraid I might do it.'

'And what about if he asked you to leave your darling artist husband?'

'At this moment, I'd just walk to the ends of the earth with him, but he's not the marrying kind. There's something about him. It's like he's a big tiger prowling about, never being part of a family group. He's always got people falling at his feet; he'd be a fool to get married. He's in love with himself, or his mother, or his "art"; God, I don't know, it's just that I feel powerless to resist this affair, but at the same time I know I haven't quite clinched the deal. He's interested; he makes me feel like I'm the most special person who has ever entered his life, but I have a kind of suspicious feeling that he's been there before, that he's said the lines, been in the play. Know what I mean?'

'You can say that again,' said Julia. 'He's the most talented actor I've ever met; I can't understand why he didn't try to make a professional career out of it. That's the whole point. He's just playing a part. He loves himself too much to surrender himself to you. So what are you going to do about Deke?'

Mel sighed and looked away.

'God only knows, Julia, God only knows. But I suppose a bend in the road is not the end of the road unless you fail to turn.'

'Come on, let's go down, Mrs Dalai Lama,' said Julia, suddenly changing the subject. She wandered over and leaned out of the window, peering down at the large purple parasols which were now in the closed position and looked for all the world like giant furled flags. Mel pulled out the plug and the drain emitted a loud gurgle as the rusty water left the bath exceedingly slowly as if it was navigating a brand new route to a pond somewhere out there in the distance. She wriggled into a skimpy shift dress, pushed her feet into the mules waiting by the bath, and twisted her hair up into a knot with her fingers and stuck a little fawn-coloured elasticated band round the tennis-ball of blonde hair which now sat closely into the nape of her neck.

There was the slight chink of glasses and low murmur of conversation. Guests were arriving for a pre-dinner drink on the terrace, looking scrubbed and glowing from their day out in the sun followed by a shower. Their collective eau de toilette and aftershave mingled with the scent of jasmine and stephanotis which was beginning to crank into action in the evening air. Everyone had the languorous 'I'm on holiday and about as chilled as I can get' look.

When the two women emerged from the dark of the house to the pinkish glow of the setting Tuscan sun, the first thing they noticed was the "lord of the manor" and the lady Antonella sitting at a little table nearest to the door with a small reserved sign on it. Julia glanced away, gazing across at the silhouette of Rossigno across the valley, musing to herself, *God, that's the guy from the motor scooter. He must be the husband. Blimey, he's donkey's years older than her. She must be a gold-digger, but then she said she was the proprietor. Well, obviously he bought it for her; it's a toy. Just look at his extraordinary clothes; who but a clown would wear rose-pink trousers and have shoulder-length hair when they are the wrong side of fifty and well over six feet tall? She adores him though; look at the way she's staring right into his face, never leaving his gaze, and he's got the side of his foot up against her calf, gently rubbing it up and down while he swirls that gargantuan goblet of red wine round and round; he's hanging onto every word she's saying.*

Occasionally, they would break off from their intent lovers' conversation and Antonella would call out to one of the girls waiting at table, 'Claudia, table seven, don't forget to light their candle, and tell Giacomo to start serving the *insalata tricolore*.'

Giacomo came out from the house a few seconds later, plates all the way up his arm, brandishing a lighter in his right hand and minced with a toss of the head over to table seven, distributing plates of antipasto as he made his royal progress back through the crush of diners.

'Signorine, please accommodate yourselves. Table eleven over in the corner, and choose which of the main courses you would like.' And with that, Giacomo was off, the reflected candle-light flashing and twinkling on the shiny brocade of his waistcoat, an oily black Disraeli-esque curl falling from his main mop of hair onto his temple, and he, delighted with how it made him look busy and under pressure, tossed his head just gently enough to move it back a fraction, but not enough to banish it.

'Ah, Signora Cartei!' exclaimed Antonella, once again breaking her diner à deux with the Viking lookalike "lord of the manor" to welcome a couple who looked as if they had just arrived that day. 'So wonderful to welcome you once again to Villa Marcella, and also to see the magnificent Davide!'

Mel and Julia looked at the round-shouldered, greying, rather cowed little man following behind Signora Cartei and thought Antonella had taken leave of her senses. No one would describe him as magnificent unless they were being ironic. Then, suddenly, they saw what she meant. Lolloping nobly behind the grey-haired old man was the world's biggest, tallest dog; a sleek Great Dane who was not only waist high to Signor Cartei, but he was also table-high when it came to his huge elegant doggy face. Signora Cartei handed some kind of covered plastic container to Eleonora who, in turn, handed it back to Giacomo who was coming behind her. He turned briskly on his Cuban heel and retreated to the kitchen with the package. The Carteis progressed slowly between the tables to their own which was right over on the perimeter of the terrace so that the magnificent Davide would not offend the other diners. He followed, head aloof, then, in a flash, when he thought no one was looking, his head spun to the left and his vast jaws clamped tightly over a bread roll sitting in a basket on table eight. The meek little couple pirouetted, bellowing his name in mock rage as the old man wrenched the bread from the dog's maw, but you could tell by the tone of their voices that they were really saying, 'That's my boy!' as proudly as if he was their son who had scored a goal for the school football team. They settled down at their table, and, before they themselves were served, Giacomo and Graziella from the Villa's kitchen team, processed to the table bearing one large pewter dog bowl full of some kind of mysterious mash, and another earthenware vessel holding enough water to fill a camel's belly at a desert oasis.

'Giacomo!'

Antonella's rather stern and stentorian cry rang out as she had obviously noticed yet another small detail which he had overlooked but which she thought was essential to the wellbeing of the guests.

'Poor old Giacomo,' murmured Mel to Julia, 'they treat him like dirt and he works so hard. Just look at him rushing around. I wouldn't stand for it if I were him. They'd be lost if he walked out. He's butler, waiter, gardener, receptionist. That's money for you. They're a pair of control freaks. I hate it the way that people with money feel they can treat everyone else so badly.'

While Mel was saying this, she and Julia sat at one of the two larger tables that had obviously been laid up especially for the drama group. In dribs and drabs the others came down with various tales of the sumptuous furnishings and paintings in their rooms.

The "lord of the manor" and Antonella continued to sample the evening's menu, an astute move because it kept the staff on their toes.

'God, you could set a novel in this place,' gabbled Andrea, awestruck. 'And look at sex on a stick over there,' she added for good measure, nodding her head in the direction of the "lord of the manor" and his Antonella. 'Every woman on the terrace would swap places with her. He's the Incredible Hulk.'

'Well, he's got the lurid trousers,' added Josh with a smirk, 'but it won't look too good with the Hulk's green chest when he does the transformation scene.

'But isn't he transformed already?' asked Rob, joining in the male banter which had the opposite effect of diminishing the female consensus on the "lord of the manor".

'Yeah,' giggled Gareth, holding a pretend microphone. 'And Antonella, what actually first attracted you to your millionaire husband?'

In fact it showed up most of the males at the drama group table as sad, jealous little boys, envious of a man who ostensibly had it all: the trophy wife half his age, the vast villa in the Tuscan hills, not forgetting a pile of money the size of Mount Etna. Josh suddenly remembered that they were staying at the Villa Marcella because of some connection of Mark's and realised that they were a bit out of order criticising someone who actually might be a family friend. He whispered a word of caution to Rob.

'Whatever you say about him,' Andrea struck up, 'he's a complete martinet. I bet all the staff are petrified of him. I would hate to get on the wrong side of him. I think he's probably got a terrible temper. But that's partly why he's so sexy.'

'Oh here we go again, Darcy-fever hits town,' said Rob caustically.

'And he's such a macho kind of bloke it must drive him nuts having Giacomo preening and pouting all over the place,' added Andrea.

'Even if he had nothing he would still be attractive; it's just the way he looks at women,' mused Julia, but because she was gazing in the direction of the aristocratic pair she failed to notice Mark's hand slide under the table and fit snugly into the warm groove just above Mel's knees. Once there it gently stroked the inside of her thigh until Mel looked as if she was going to faint from pleasure. Giacomo's arrival put a stop to the pleasure, or maybe rescued her from moaning orgasmically in front of the entire clientelle.

'We 'ave tonight a small white truffle risotto to begin. These truffles they are so precious that special 'unters with dogs go to find them in secret places in the forest. They can only be found between September and December. They are a true delicacy. Then the cingiale, the wild boar that is, to follow, or maybe an omelette made with the flowers of the zucchini plant for those people who 'ave not the stomach for the meat.'

Because there was a take it or leave it menu, the decisions were made quite quickly and he danced off to the kitchen, only to return with a rather coquettish pout and flaring of the nostrils as he poured the wine for Mark to taste. Mark dutifully sniffed, thought about it, and then nodded. Giacomo waited a few more seconds, then Mark glanced up at him and gave him the now-famous wink, a little smile, and began to pour the Montepulciano into everyone's glasses.

Andrea couldn't resist a dig at poor camp Giacomo's expense. 'Mark, you'd flirt with a bloody Madame Tussaud's dummy if you had a chance!' They all laughed and Mark grinned back. He was swirling his wine glass between his fingers while his hand lay flat against the wooden armrest on his chair and one or two of the group were impressed by the fact that he obviously knew some special technique to make the bouquet of his wine rise more powerfully than theirs. Then, suddenly, there was an 'Oh, shit!' He almost knocked his glass over in his haste to scrutinize the palm of that same hand.

'Splinter!' he announced.

'Serves you right,' chorused Mel and Julia roaring with laughter, and with that they all chinked glasses and settled down to await the truffle-fest.

By the time the iced Limoncello and the espressos arrived, darkness had fallen and what had been a murmur of voices had become many decibels louder with occasional roars from the drama gang as the jokes, fuelled by the wine, got sillier and sillier.

'Oh, I've got a good one,' announced Paul. 'Have you heard the one about the three-legged dog who went into the bar?'

'This is going to be dreadful but tell us anyway,' offered Julia.

'No, what about him?'

'Well, he went into the bar and d'you know what the first thing he said was?'

'How about a double Limoncello?' volunteered Andrea.

'Hang on,' said Paul. 'I've got to get into my cowboy accent here, "No", he said "I'm looking for the man who shot my paw".'

There was a collective groan and a preliminary scraping of chairs as they all made to get up. Giacomo and Eleonora had been beavering about clearing the emptied tables all around and were obviously waiting to go to bed.

'OK, everyone,' Mark reminded them, 'breakfast at eight thirty and we've got to be over in Rossigno for a rehearsal at ten. They've given us a back room in one of the restaurants.'

Later that night Julia lay in the airy *piano nobile* listening to the silence and then the unmistakeable sound of snuffling down on the terrace. She sat bolt upright and listened again. In the distance a dog barked and the snuffling stopped momentarily and then began again. She tiptoed across the room and opened the mesh-covered inner windows and then gingerly pushed open one of the shutters. Down below on the terrace she could just make out the shadow of a wild boar shuffling around in the flower beds around the dining terrace. The stars were unbelievably bright and she could discern one or two low-grade twinkles of light in the little houses in Rossigno. Just then, she heard a low moan of a female voice coming from somewhere above in one of the rooms on the next floor. It built in little waves and Julia froze, intrigued, but at the same time realised she was now hearing the unmistakeably muffled female audio-orgasm going full tilt.

'Mel,' she whispered to her sleeping room-mate. 'Mel, are you awake? Listen to that!' Mel was still fast asleep. Julia looked back to the bed, now that her eyes were accustomed to the darkness.

'Mel?'

And it was then that she saw that where Mel's body had once

been there was just a jumble of bedclothes and an empty space.

'Oh Mel, Oh Mel!' she said to herself, sadly, closing the shutters, and realising that Mark's bedroom was directly overhead and it was Mel that she had been listening to. She walked quietly back to her side of the bed and pulled the soft damask sheet over her head and went into a coma-like sleep.

It was the cockerel crowing that woke Julia, or maybe it was Mel sliding surreptitiously back into the bed, but as she opened her eyes she saw thin lines of sun, like laser beams, piercing the elongated slit where she hadn't quite closed the shutters during her sortie to investigate the wild boar. She reached down onto the marble floor and fumbled around with her hand until she found her paperback novel, a pen and her dream notebook and tiptoed around the bed and into the bathroom clutching all three. She closed the door as quietly as possible and settled down on the seat of the toilet and tried to concentrate hard on where she had been in her head a few minutes ago. She could just catch little wisps of the last dream…something about being on a bus, some dark hedges.

'Damn. Lost it!' she said to herself. Her only hope now was the next night. It never ceased to amaze her how clever the subconscious was. You forgot your dream completely then lay down to go to sleep the next night, and sometimes quite intricate details of the previous night's dream would suddenly flash up into the brain.

She opened the shutters and incredibly bright light flooded the airy little bathroom. There was already a little scuttling activity of the staff below on the terrace as they prepared the tables for breakfast. It was a bit too early to go down and she didn't want to disturb Mel by yanking open the big wardrobe to look for her clothes or rustling around in her rucksack so she sat on the little stool which had been home to their two wash bags and read a few pages of her book. To Julia a book was like a comfort blanket. Her worst nightmare was to find herself on a long train journey minus a paperback. Once she got to the end of the chapter, she washed quickly, brushed her hair and added a dab of perfume and put her head round the door back to the bedroom. Mel was making that kind of snuffly noise that people do just before they wake up.

'Mel!' she called in a stage whisper. 'We've got to make a move. You sure you're awake because I want to go down and explore the garden before breakfast. Don't go back to sleep for heaven's sake.'

Mel groaned, but it was an affirmative groan. Thus satisfied, Julia pulled on a t-shirt and shorts and wandered off downstairs and out into the morning sun. There was a strong aromatic smell of herbs, mainly thyme with its wonderful buttery quality to it. The cicadas were just beginning to chirrup and small high-speed insects were whizzing through the air. Giacomo was rushing around returning the large cushions to the wrought iron chairs after the chill of the night. Although it was only September, there was always the risk of storms up in the mountains. Indeed, once Fer'agosta, the Feast of the Assumption, had passed on August 15th, most Italians made their way back to the cities, convinced that summer was over. From then on, the summer's heat gradually cooled as the *temporale,* the big late-summer thunderstorms, came once every few weeks.

'Good morning, signorina, I hope you 'ave sleep well.'

'*Benissimo!*' she called back.

He was in a hurry, but as she was one of the only people around she continued to chat while he tossed the cushions onto the chairs and onto the stone banquette along the wall.

'Giacomo, who exactly are Antonella and her husband? Has the family lived here for hundreds of years or what?'

Giacomo gave a little pout. 'You 'ave 'eard of course of the famous Lombardini family?'

'What, the ones that are in the gossip columns and all that? The old guy had some relationship with someone in the British royal family a while back... And wasn't there some awful accident too, a plane crash? A helicopter?'

'Precisely. Well Gaspare, Antonella's 'usband, 'e is the youngest son of old Roberto Lombardini. 'e is nobleman, "Count" I think you say in English. The Lombardinis 'ave been a ruling family in Toscana for 'undreds of years, but the family is rich too from all the aeroplanes that they make since the War, but many tragedies 'appen as you know. It is the curse of money. Gaspare's oldest brother committed suicide after Natale was killed in the plane crash. The mother she never recover from this. And then there is the problem with the other brother and the drugs. It is terrible. Gaspare, the Count, and Antonella, 'is wife, they love it at Villa Marcella because is peaceful and safe.'

'But what about you, Giacomo? Do you live here all the time?'

'No, signorina, I close the 'ouse in Novembre; it is not good to stay alone. It make me sad. They go to the Caribbean to stay with friends. I go to see my mother in Rome. My dream is to open a restaurant of my own in Rome. But you will excuse me now, because I 'ave to 'elp Graziella as we 'ave many guests today.'

'Oh, *mi scusi*, Giacomo, I got so carried away with your story,' replied Julia, and with that she wandered on down a little track to a large vegetable patch which was festooned with giant nets to stop all manner of beasts from raiding the plants.

Well, just fancy that! And poor old Giacomo, she thought. He seemed so put upon and a tiny bit resentful at having to be the general factotum when obviously he saw himself as a kind of Malvolio. It's crazy that he has to water the geraniums and sweep the terrace, and some of the foreign guests treat him like rubbish, ordering him around and keeping him up till all hours.

Although most of the ground seemed parched and arid, there were fresh puddles at the base of the basil and tomato plants and some rudimentary irrigation system had already done its daily task. Julia watched carefully where she was putting her feet. Little geckos fascinated her, but the idea of a snake slithering across her bare foot filled her with horror. A rather wizened-looking old man was fumbling with some secateurs, pruning a bush just the other side of the zucchini, and the horses that she had seen the day before were taking up position under the trees once more to avoid the heat of the day, but this time they were munching their breakfasts.

Hmm, time for me to eat too, she thought to herself, and worked out a series of paths that would take her round the perimeter of the garden and up to the terrace from the opposite side. Once up there she put her sunglasses down on one of the smaller tables and wondered what to do. Giacomo came to her aid and instructed her to go and collect what she wanted to eat from the buffet whilst he or Eleonora would bring her coffee. She went into the cool house once more, wondering if she should quickly nip up to see if Mel was up, but hunger got the better of her and she made her way instead to the dining-room.

What is it about these foreign places that they just can't manage to make passable toast? she thought to herself. An extraordinary contraption stood in the corner of the room; it had to be a toaster. Whatever else? A Victorian machine for counterfeiting bank notes?! There was a basket of artificial-looking white squares of bread and some weird mesh containers into which one was supposed to put the bread and then stand for what seemed like eternity while it transmogrified into toast, but in fact all it seemed to do was make the white square hard and crispy, and the mesh baskets also seemed destined to burn your fingers as you fiddled around trying to see if the toast was actually done. There was a slightly more space-age machine in the other corner, but it looked as if you needed a one-week induction course to learn how to operate it and Julia didn't want to make a fool of herself so she picked up a yoghurt, a hunk of rustic Tuscan bread, a few figs and a couple of slices of prosciutto and went back to her little table. A few more people had emerged, but none of the drama group were up yet. Count Lombardini was sitting a few tables away wearing peppermint-green trousers and engrossed in *Il Tirreno*.

Julia made a start on the ham and figs and broke the bread into a few chunks. There was still no coffee pot on her table, and she was beginning to feel the bread sticking to the inside of her mouth and would have welcomed a drink, but was aware that if she complained to Giacomo within earshot of the Count, it may induce another invective from him. As she was thinking these very thoughts, Giacomo swooped past her with a jug of water in his left hand, heading for a table in the far corner of the terrace. To get there he had to pass not only Julia, but also the Count. As he did so, his right hand flashed up, stroked the back of Count Lombardini's head and softly followed an imaginary track down the nape of his neck and along his left shoulder, and with that he was gone to deliver the water to Signor and Signora Cartei.

It had all happened so quickly that Julia at first thought she had imagined it, but knew that it had been real. What was so bizarre was that Count Lombardini had continued reading the newspaper, as if this kind of intimate caress was something utterly familiar; it was as if a much-loved cat had just pressed itself against his leg on its journey across a room. He had no need to look up to find out what on earth was going on or who had done it. He knew from the first flicker of Giacomo's fingers that it was he, and accepted this most private of gestures without the slightest twitch. That instant had spoken volumes about their relationship and probably only Julia had seen it, in the way that only a minute percentage of the population catch a subliminal image cut into a television programme or film. So the Count wasn't just infatuated with his wife...

'Blimey, you look hung over, Jules.' It was Josh standing with a plate, a hunk of bread and a little baby pot of apricot jam.

'No – I – er, it's – it's just my face in repose. When I walk past a building site back home the builders shout, "Cheer up love, it might never happen!" Little do they know it's my normal face.

God knows what I look like when I really *have* got a problem.'

This little speech had given her the time to come back to earth enough to shake herself out of the reverie about her astonishing revelation.

'Giacomo, can we have a jug of coffee, please,' called Josh as Giacomo hurried past once more with an accommodating, 'Subito!'

'I see the "lord of the manor" is up bright and early.' Josh nodded his head in the direction of the Count.

Julia smiled and went on dissecting her figs, thinking, but not saying, *There's only one person here who wields supreme power, and it's the camp clown carrying the café latte to our table. I can't believe I felt sorry for him half an hour ago. How naive am I? I will never ever make that same mistake again.*

Chapter Three

1975

When Robin Forester first arrived in the staff room at Haverstock College he stood in the doorway next to the South America poster, turned his hand into a pretend gun, pointed it at the Amazonian parrot and announced, 'Make me feel welcome or the bird gets it.' Immediately there gathered a little coterie of amused colleagues around him as he introduced himself and made one self-deprecating joke after another. The first was about his interview and how the board of governors had made him sit on a tiny stool so that he looked like he was about to milk a cow, then he told them about his journey to the college and how he had rescued a woman with PMT who said she was wanting to throw herself in the river, then progressed onto his search for a flat in the area.

Julia McCallum looked up from a lesson she had been preparing and craned her neck to see what all the fuss was about. It was the beginning of her second term as junior lecturer in the modern languages department. She had flirted temporarily with the idea of abandoning the teaching dream and trying her hand as an actress, but the more she talked to acquaintances who were just out of drama school and struggling, she realised that she was not cut out for the constant rejection, nor did she have the slightest interest in following the "casting couch" route. More than that, she didn't have some secret trust fund behind her or parents who would bail her out forever if need be. It was time to grow up and get back into the real world. Teaching, ironically, was supposed to be this real world.

Robin's arrival was massive respite from the dreary routine of the staff room. She had been expecting to get an amazing buzz from teaching, and instead could not quite believe how, even in this day and age, the whole place still managed to be so stereotypically sexist. The domestic science and home economics teachers always seemed to be discussing new ways to pickle eggs, make a Madeira cake or hang wallpaper. A few of the old boffin blokes were permanently hunched over students' project books doing a bit of marking, whilst lazier males of a certain age gathered in a smoky corner deciding which horse to back in the 2.30 at Kempton Park.

It didn't take her long to realise that people liked the newcomer because (a) he was very funny and (b) by telling this kind of story he wasn't a threat. However, it didn't have the effect of making everyone sorry for him; it did the opposite. People wanted to be around him because he was clever and amusing. Amongst the "poor little me" stories were references to Sisyphus, the quoting of a line of line from *Tosca* in the original Italian, the description of the action in the bottom left-hand corner of a Richard Dadd fairy painting, the mention of the Marmeladov family (rather than Raskolnikov) in *Crime and Punishment* and detailed knowledge of the Treaty of Versailles. OK, so he hadn't played the rocket science card (although he knew that a guy called Mitchell had invented the Spitfire), but this was certainly someone who could beat her in the "Humanities Olympics", and there weren't many of those. Then again, he was a little older than her. She realised very soon that at last someone from her true tribe had arrived. But she needed to play a long game. She sat up, took note, and realised that the only way to engage his attention was going to be through humour. And this, of course, was exactly what everyone else was doing, unselfconsciously or otherwise. The staff-room suddenly became wittier than the offices of *Private Eye*. People were vying with one another to come out with the punchiest, pithiest one-liners. Robin loved it; they all loved it. It seemed that since he arrived, a light had been punched on and all the shop-window dummies had come to life. They were all, by some strange woodland magic, turning into stand-up comedians.

Martin Cox, the deputy head, known to the students as "Fish" as his family had kept a fish and chip shop in the area for about sixty years, steered Robin across the room making a few introductions.

'And this, Robin, is our baby, Julia. She was our newest addition at Haverstock – until your arrival, that is. Julia's been here for a term teaching Italian and running a couple of English classes with the adult education unit that's attached to the College. Julia, this is Robin Forester who's going to be teaching French and English and a bit of philosophy.'

'Hi, Robin,' she grinned. 'I don't suppose you have a teething ring or a couple of rusks in your pocket, do you? I was hoping to disguise my extreme youth and inexperience but I guess I've been outed by Martin, here.'

'Oh, it's OK,' quipped Robin. 'I can see beneath the make-up and the well-fitting wig that you are actually sixty-five but your secret's safe with me. I'm actually eighty-four but the rescue remedy is working a treat on the crow's feet. See you around, eh? Take care.'

And with that, he was moving on to Donna Kilpatrick who had been teaching music at the college for the past ten years.

It became quite apparent to Julia over the next couple of weeks that Robin had marked her out as a kindred spirit. He frequently came and threw himself down dramatically in a chair next to her and chatted about films he had seen the previous night, restaurants he had eaten in, or students who were either appallingly bad or destined for great things.

'Did you have to spend a year in Italy as part of your course?' he asked her one morning.

'Yes, I was attached to the university in Pisa; I loved it. I chose it partly because I had been to Tuscany with a drama group I was in, and you're so near the coast there as well. I just feel that it's a kind of spiritual home for me, as if I was born there and lived there in another life. I think if I was abroad somewhere else in the world and someone told me England had been wiped out by a nuclear attack or a meteorite or something, then I would be quite happy to think to myself, "Oh, then I'll go and live in Italy". I just feel so easy there.'

'That's a great coincidence. I knew someone who did all that drama stuff in Italy too. He adored it...' Robin seemed to defocus for a moment as if lost in his own private thoughts. 'I'm almost glad in a way I never went there. Knowing me I would probably be serving ravioli for a living in a place called something like "Bar Cristallo" in Poggibonsi by now if I had.'

'Don't knock Poggibonsi,' said Julia, nudging him, 'it's like Clapham Junction; everyone goes there in order to get somewhere else.'

'Well not everyone, exactly,' said Robin. 'As far as Clapham is concerned I actually lived there for a while and when people asked me where I lived I would say, "Clapham-oh" because I knew that if I just said "Clapham" they would say "Oh..." so I just put the "oh" on the end for them to save the bother.'

'Clapham's not too bad,' said Julia, smiling. 'A whole load of people I know who work in TV live there, and a few people who work on *Private Eye* who are old mates of someone I know from university.'

She watched him absorbing this bit of extra information, storing it away, liking her a bit more with each little exchange.

So this is what they mean by sexual chemistry, she thought to herself, and realised that what made him attractive to her was simply his power to make her laugh. But it was mutual. They had met their match in each other.

'But getting back to Italy, why didn't you stay on out there?' asked Robin, looking puzzled that anyone in their right mind would choose Haverstock College over a life of Botticelli, fritatta and spaghetti alla vongole.

'Well, I thought about it, to be honest,' answered Julia. 'But after two years out of England I realised I was beginning to miss all my friends; everyone lives in London or passes through, and however well you speak another language you never really get down to all the nuances, the puns, the humour, the cultural allusions. You are in a perpetual world of basic language. You can't suddenly come out with a line from *Round the Horne* or *Monty Python*. They'd think you were mad. A friend of mine lived in Scandinavia for a while and apparently when they showed *Monty Python* with sub-titles the announcer would warn, completely seriously, before the programme started, that it had nothing to do with pythons or flying!'

'I know what you mean...language is a weird thing. I found the same when I did my year in Toulouse,' added Robin. 'A mate of mine teaches in a language school and he has loads of Japanese students in his classes. You know how they love t-shirts with bits of English on them. Well, one of the girls in his beginners' class – she could only have been about fourteen – came innocently into class one day with a new t-shirt that she had obviously been flogged by some guy in a dodgy souvenir shop saying, "There's a party in my pants and you're all invited to come". Poor old Nick had to take her to one side and explain that it might be a good idea not to wear it!'

'Oh my God!' shrieked Julia. 'Imagine! Thank God it wasn't me who had to do it! It's like telling someone they've got body odour.'

'I know!' he said. 'And thank God it wasn't me either.'

'I love those bad English things. It's a bit like a sign a pal of mine saw in Bangkok,' added Julia. 'It was outside a dry cleaner's and it said "Drop your trousers here for best results".'

'Well how about this?' asked Robin. 'When I lived in Toulouse for a bit as part of my course: it said "Please leave your values at the front desk" on a sign in my room, and, wait for it, a girl who was also doing the year abroad with me saw a sign at a fashion boutique saying, "Dresses for street walking" and there was another—'

He was laughing so much he couldn't continue. Julia was shrieking and actually wiping tears from her cheeks.

'—it said,' he tried, but had to stop as he was laughing again, 'it said, "ladies may have a fit upstairs"!'

'Oh, you win!' said Julia, as Robin suddenly looked at the clock. He jumped up and grabbed a pile of papers from the table.

'Blimey, dereliction of duty! I've got my poetry group right over in the new block and I'm supposed to be doing the Mersey sound with them,' he said, frantically looking at his watch and flicking through the papers in search of the vital Roger McGough poem. With that he was gone.

Julia thought long and hard about how to stage manage a date as he seemed more than happy to babble on about films or plays he had seen but showed no inclination to involve her in subsequent outings. She realised that she had to do something out of the ordinary to get onto his radar.

A few days later she sent him the following note:

You are invited to dinner
at 15 Beauchamp Gardens, the chambers of Ms Julia McCallum
– dress informal –
on Friday April 16th.
Assuming that you are free on that evening, tick which of the
following you would like as your dinner companions: Harpo
Marx, The Pope, Trotsky, Sean Connery, Basil Fawlty, Her Majesty
The Queen Mother.
RSVP.

'I was tickled, intrigued and curious,' he said the following week. 'The line-up was irresistible so I ticked all the boxes.'

'So you're definitely coming?' she asked, unable to believe her luck.

'How could I possibly resist?' he said, winking as he dashed off to another class.

On the appointed Friday he rang the bell of the basement flat in Beauchamp Gardens. She took his coat and gestured him into the room nearest the front door where there was a table perfectly set for a formal dinner for eight people. Although she had sent him the joke invitation, she realised from the way he surveyed the table that he had obviously secretly hoped it would be just the two of them. The sight of the table made him realise that there were actually other guests, although not the ones on her list.

She had given him clues from the brief conversations she had had with him, that she was quite well-connected in the media world via ex-college friends, and she could tell that he was wondering rather apprehensively who his fellow dining companions might be. She had already mentioned that she had pals who worked in TV and on *Private Eye.*

'White wine or white wine?' she yelled from the kitchen.

He smiled.

'Umm, well maybe I'll have the white wine if you're sure you have any,' he shouted back.

'OK, I'll just get—' but she never finished her sentence because the phone at his elbow had suddenly started to ring.

'Could you be an angel and answer that?' she shouted. 'I'm having trouble with the corkscrew.'

She smiled as she heard him pick up the phone and a little camply announce, 'Miss Julia McCallum's residence.'

A heavily-accented male eastern European voice (Russian? Polish?) at the other end said, 'Mr Fawreester? Pliz geev message to Mees McCallum. I kent to be present at deener. I must to my obligations in other place. So sawry.'

Thinking that it was a distant McCallum, Robin looked like he was embarrassed that he had answered the phone in such an outrageous way and his tone became more polite and deferential.

'Who should I say is calling?' he enquired.

'Eez Meester Trotsky here. She call me Leon.'

And there was a click as Trotsky replaced his receiver. "Oh

no!" squawked Robin as he suddenly realised that it was an elaborately set-up joke. Julia popped her head round the door with his white wine in her right hand.

'Who was that?' she said, completely straight-faced.

'Oh, Mr Trotsky,' said Robin, going along with the joke. 'He's had to cancel. He sends his apologies.'

'Oh bugger, then I'll have to take his things away,' she said, rapidly scooping up a place setting from the table. She scuttled away to the kitchen again, shouting back over her shoulder

'I'll just fetch my wine; it's out here on the table.'

With that, the phone went again.

'Could you get it for me?' she called out.

Delighted that this was now a game, he complied. Connery muttered his apologies, as, a little later, did the Pope. Basil Fawlty barked rudely and shouted something incoherent about his intended absence; Harpo spoke through a messenger, and Her Majesty explained that one's dinner was already in the oven and the staff would be so disappointed if one went out for the evening. With each call, Julia, sighing and tut-tutting, took away another place setting until there were just two places at the table, his and hers. As they settled down with the wine and a bowl of big dark-purple calamata olives she explained that she had inveigled some friends into assisting with the plot. She could see that the fact that she had friends who would, and could, do that at the drop of a hat, let alone that she had thought the whole thing up, obviously delighted and captivated him. She looked at him and felt like an angler who could feel a large fish on the end of the line.

The night that he left her flat after that first dinner he had said goodnight cheerily and said that he hoped next time Meester Trotsky would be able to make it, but had held her eyes with his just that bit longer than people normally do in casual situations, and eventually she had glanced down, unable to continue. In fact that gaze had been more powerful than if he had grabbed her and put his tongue down her throat. The fact that he hadn't even made a big move to kiss her was even more tantalising. He was giving off every signal possible that he fancied her, that she made him laugh, that he was intrigued and impressed by the quality of her mind, but here he was kissing her on both cheeks like he was some visiting French cousin. Her earlier feeling of being in the driving seat suddenly fell away. In one rapier-like look, he had turned her to Play-doh. Her heart was thumping away in her chest as she waved him off down the dark street and walked back down into her basement. What had been a dullish little one-person flat was now the enchanted domain. He had been here. He had sat there. He had picked up that photo of Julia's grandma on the mantelpiece and scrutinised it. He had sniffed those freesias and professed them to be second only to sweet peas, her own favourite flowers. That bit of Leonard Cohen had become "their tune". He had drunk out of that wine glass. Suddenly she was fourteen. Control had passed from her to the puppeteer. This time it wasn't a crush. They were two consenting adults...but what would they be consenting to? And how many others in that staffroom had exactly the same designs on him? But that polite and restrained display of kissing on the cheeks like a well-brought-up grateful dinner guest still left her a tiny bit confused and wanting more. Maybe he was just a natural flirt. He was popular and funny. The staff liked him; the students all got on with him. It was charisma city whenever he was there, so maybe she was just one of many. The years of low sexual self-esteem which had always dogged her throughout university reared their ugly head now. She took the dishes through to the small kitchen, cleaned up the flat and got ready for bed. Just as she was brushing her teeth, the phone rang in the sitting room and she ran the length of the corridor, thinking it must be bad news from home. No one ever rang that late. There was just a little too much urgency in her voice as she simply said her number into the receiver. A foreign voice replied, 'Hello, eez Meester Trotsky here. I voz wondering if you would like to theatre go on Saturday to see *Doll's House*. Eez late but verry sawrry eef you were sleepink.'

'That would be an honour, Mr Trotsky,' she replied, grinning from ear to ear.

And then in his own voice Robin added, 'Night night, Sweet Pea. It was a delicious evening. Sleep tight. See you tomorrow.'

'You too,' she added. And the phone clicked off at the other end.

Pure textbook; at last I am embarked upon the Big One, she mused to herself as she wandered back to the bedroom putting off the lights as she went.

But there was a little "no esteem" demon inside who managed to pop into action as her head was on the pillow. *So why has he got two tickets for Saturday? Was he going to take someone else? That production of* The Dolls' House *has been sold out for weeks. If I hadn't invited him to dinner tonight who would he have asked to go with him on Saturday? OK, he'd had a nice meal and a bit of a laugh, but this was probably a bit of a flash in the pan; there were lots of people in his address book and he was usually turning things down and moaning about overbooking and double booking.*

No, remember how he looked at you, came another voice. *Remember that he has just got back through his front door and he has called you. He could easily have left that till tomorrow.*

Yeah, thought Julia. Bet *he does this to all the girls...* and with that she drifted off to sleep.

She dreamed that night that she was walking down the hill near her house and she came to a high privet hedge. As she got close to it she realised that little windows like portholes had been cut into the hedge. She bent her knees and peered in through the dark green foliage and saw an aged couple bent over luxuriant and vividly coloured plants, all of which were in flower. They were both working away, concentrating hard on the weeding. While Julia watched them, someone suddenly appeared at her right shoulder and she turned round to see a strange man standing at her side.

'Do you like it?' he asked, smiling wryly.

'Oh, it's the most beautiful garden I've ever, ever seen,' she panted.

'Well, I can fix for you to have one like that.'

He produced a little card and she read his name and the sub-title: landscape gardener.

'You see, it's what I do for a living, but although I can set it all out for you, you have to realise that it's the most monumental amount of work involved in maintaining it. It's a huge commitment. Take those two up there, for example.'

Julia's eyes followed the direction of his gesturing arm and looked back at the elderly couple not unlike her own parents still pulling out the weeds from between the clumps of red hot pokers and lupins.

'They spend about twelve hours a day working on that garden,' he continued. 'It's a full-time job and you can never decide to stop or have a bit of time off. It's forever.'

'I – I – er, I don't absolutely know for sure right now if I can commit that much time…can I just take your card and get back to you?' Julia bleated.

'No problem, he said. 'You know where you will be able to find me.'

With that he was gone. The dream had such an intensity that it woke Julia up; not just that dreamy in-between-dreams-awakeness, but that totally wide-eyed "I'll-never-go-back-to-sleep" feeling. The trouble was, she knew this wasn't just a dream born of looking at too many junk-mail seed catalogues; this nascent relationship was a big one. Her vital organs did a passable impression of a washing machine on the fifty degree wash cycle whenever she thought about him. And that was how she spent the rest of the night, having written the dream down in her little notebook, noting the dawn chorus, the first plane roaring into London air space, and, bizarrely, a barking fox in a nearby garden shouting for its mate.

It had taken a long time but at last she was the one with the glittering prize and she wasn't going to let this one autodestruct if she could help it. It was extraordinarily empowering knowing that someone was attracted to you, and, of course, sexy. What had always intrigued Julia was the way how knowing some people fancied you made them repugnant and pathetic, whilst being aware (or being made aware by a third party) that others fancied you suddenly made them seem attractive in a way which had never been apparent before. It was the latter at work that evening with Robin.

Chapter Four

By the time Saturday came, Julia was doing a pretty passable impersonation of a 16-year-old. She had subjected her body to a ludicrous concoction of unguents, essences and fragrances. Her legs and armpits had the texture of a glass-topped coffee table, except for the few places where she had lost her concentration with the Ladyshave and nicked the skin, so that in fact she had metamorphosed from hairy to scabby. Debating which of the two was worse reminded her of those playground debates where kids asked you whether you would prefer to be buried alive or burned alive. It was seriously no-win.

She had even contemplated going to the hairdresser: big mistake. Julia's hair had very little body, but was curly where it shouldn't be and straight where a few curls would have been essential. It always reminded her of the plant which she used to see growing in the hedgerows on the way home from school. It was called "old man's beard", at least that was what it was known as by the children. It probably had some huge Latin name such as *barbaricus vecchionae* or something daft, but it would always be "old man's beard" to Julia. Her hair simply waved about as if some giant magnet were suspended over her head attracting the hair upwards, but instead of shooting straight up, it waved and twisted in slow motion completely unsure of where to go next. The hairdresser would either slick it down unnaturally so that she would look like some fifties teddy boy, or else attempt to cut it into a short manageable style so that she looked, as one of her friends joked, like a nun from an order where they've gone modern and just been allowed to stop wearing wimples and veils: sensible, functional, severe. So the hair had to stay as it was, although it had been washed, teased, rollered, gelled and perfumed.

She had bought herself a new blouse, but as usual that turned into a *House That Jack Built* project, meaning that the blouse was great, but it actually needed a different-shaped skirt from the one she had been intending to wear. She managed to find just the right one, but her black shoes looked a bit weird with the skirt so she had become insane for an hour or so and convinced herself that the perfect accompaniment would be boots, which she duly bought. The effect of the boots and the long calf-length skirt made the bare neck of the blouse seem rather unbalanced: the bottom half said 'winter' while the top half said 'summer' so she had found an amazing little tangerine-coloured long silk scarf which was brilliant, but the usual earrings didn't look quite right any more. By the time she was holding out her hand for the change from the purchase of the new earrings she was wondering how many months of working as an all-night security guard in addition to her daytime lecturing job she would have to do to pay off the debt; or maybe she could rob a bank; then again, she could simply get more overdrawn.

By the time she was walking down Shaftesbury Avenue to the theatre, her cheeks were glowing like little red apples and her face was set into a crazy rictus. She glimpsed herself in a reflection in a shop window and thought, *God, I look like someone deranged. I must just stop this smiling.* But she couldn't, and, when she saw him in the foyer, she recognised a complete mirror image of her own expression.

'I thought you wouldn't come,' he said rather sheepishly.

'Why on earth would I do that?'

'Well, I couldn't believe that you had actually said yes.'

Hang on a minute, thought Julia. *Here he is sounding like I am the unobtainable siren beloved by all and granting the occasional favour to one fortunate suitor. Little does he know I would have run barefoot from Putney to Penzance if he had suggested that it might be a good idea.* But she managed not to dispel the myth, and smiled back quizzically as if not turning up actually may have been a possibility.

'Come on, let's find our seats.' He took her hand and led her through the crowd.

Please God, just put your finger on the pause button right at this moment, she said, in a silent and private impassioned plea to her Maker, *Please let someone I know see us together. Please let someone who knows him see us together.* People always used say that the truly happy moments in your life are the times when you are unaware of being happy, because you are so busy enjoying yourself. You only see them in retrospect. This wasn't so for Julia. She wanted never, ever to forget this perfect moment, the moment they were a couple, out in public, and both obviously totally taken with one another. It was uninterrupted blue sky and bright, warm sun, full of promise, before clouds had even been invented or drifted into view. There is nothing quite so magical as the virginal early moments of a love affair.

'What an exquisite little scarf that is,' he said as he glanced back at her, forging ahead through the throng.

She quelled the urge to say, *Yes, I bought it to go with the boots because I'd just bought them to go with the skirt because I had to buy the skirt to go with the blouse and I had to buy the blouse because I was about to go out on the most important date of my whole life.* She merely said, 'Yeah, tangerine's the new black.'

'How did you manage to get tickets for this?' she ventured. 'According to all the listings I've seen this has been completely sold out for ages.'

'An old pal of mine works as an ASM and he can occasionally get tickets at short notice,' he replied. 'We can go round afterwards; he insisted that we drop in.'

'Great! Does he have much to do with the actors socially, I mean the big star names?'

'It depends who they are; he's quite pally with some of them, has meals out and all that; a few of the others are a bit up their own bums, just like life really.'

And with that the lights dimmed.

The play was stunning: absorbing, moving, intense; in fact all the things that plays in the West End are often not. They wandered down to the bar in the interval, agreeing on the brilliance of the production. Robin observed, 'Why do so many actors today sound like they are impersonating a member of Mr Crummles' Victorian theatrical troup from *Nicholas Nickleby*? Why do they bellow and roar at one another, as if they are shouting to a farmer in the next field?'

'I know what you mean.' She laughed. 'But then I've probably been guilty of it myself. I used to do a lot of acting when I was a student. There were a few times when I even thought I might try to do it as a profession, but I think I couldn't have coped with the fallout of my dad's rage at having to fund me through drama school when he had already coughed up for a first degree plus a year abroad and then a teaching diploma.'

'So you're not a wealthy heiress then?' he quipped.

When she shook her head he, with a dramatic flourish, let go of her hand which he had been holding and said with mock hauteur, 'In that case I shall not continue to pursue you!'

'Oh, I think I'll allow you to chase me until I catch you,' she giggled. 'Come on, let's get back to the paupers' seats otherwise we'll miss the next act.'

Once the play finished, they shuffled down from the upper circle with everyone else and wandered round to the stage door. At the front of the theatre the roar of the middle classes braying and guffawing as they exited from the brightly lit, glittery foyer filled the air. The immediate side-street was another story, with scrofulous beggars, blankets over one shoulder and dogs on strings lurching around trying to locate another of their drug dealers or approach one of the theatre-goers for a bit of small change. Robin led the way to the stage door with Julia in tow.

'Jeremy Thaxton, please,' he announced to the doorman who then directed them down a series of twisting passages resembling badly maintained public lavatories to the backstage area where a very nimble curly-haired blond man of about thirty was orchestrating a team of minions in the post-performance clearing up process.

'Robin! Absolute heaven!' he squealed camply and hurried over.

'Evening, goose pimple!' answered Robin, giving him a hug. 'This is Julia.'

He then gestured to Jeremy. 'And Julia, this is the great Jeremy Thaxton, without whom the entire West End theatre industry would collapse.'

Julia and Jeremy beamed at one another but almost immediately they both looked back at Robin.

'Well, any excuse for a drink,' said Jeremy. 'Just give me ten minutes to lick this lot into shape. There's a little bar across the road that most of the cast go to called Arlecchino. Tell Lorna, that's the red-haired Australian barmaid, that you're with me. They sometimes let us take over the little room up the stairs on the left of the bar if it isn't hired out for a private do. Introduce yourselves and I'll be over as soon as I can.'

'Terrific.' Robin grinned. 'Come on Julia, walk this way!' And, with typical Robin panache, he marched back down the corridor to the street in front of her doing a gorilla walk impression. She giggled and said, 'Now I didn't think even you would sink to doing old Marx Brothers jokes.'

'Welcome to *Mastermind*, and your special subject is "The history of comedy", starting now! Is there *anything* you don't know, Julia McCallum?'

'Well, my quantum physics is a bit rusty, but I suppose I can just about get by,' she answered. 'Uh, are we going over for long to the bar?'

'Oh, I just thought it would be fun to have a drink with them and then we can have a late supper if that's OK with you. I hope you don't have a pressing appointment at 7 am. It'll make it quite a late night.'

'I think I can give my two-hour circuit-training a miss just this once,' she said, just convincingly enough for him to do a double take and look at her quite seriously for a split second.

'You don't, do you? I mean circuit train?'

'I try to fit it in with the New Testament Greek classes, the plumbing for beginners and the orienteering,' she retorted.

And his face registered that she had wrong-footed him for an instant.

Over at Arlecchino Robin held court, absolutely revelling in the banter, the show-business gossip, and the thrill of meeting new people. Julia sat next to him drifting in and out of her own private reverie. How strange, she mused, that all she wanted to do in the world as they walked out of the theatre was be on her own with him, and yet he on the other hand was so excited by the idea of seeking out company. Straight away she realised how different they both were. Was he just doing something that brought him complete pleasure or was he doing it because he would rather surround himself with people, even strangers (although some of them were familiar from the TV or stage) than elect to slope off with Julia to an intimate little bistro supper. Even thinking that made her realise that she was caring too much already about being with him, about being special to him. She resented sharing him with a multitude and yet this was the Robin package. Would there ever be anyone special enough for Robin to forsake the magnet of an audience? Perhaps he should have gone into the theatre himself as a profession. He certainly had the talent. He was a brilliant raconteur; he was funny; he was confident.

She cringed when she thought of the many examples of crippling shyness that had dogged her own life. Once when she had just started school, her teacher, Miss Spicer, had instructed them all to ask their mothers for tins, bottles and packets to stock the little pretend shop in the corner of the classroom. She had dutifully told her mother who assembled a collection of five or six tins and put them into a small leather satchel which an aunt had bought for her a few months earlier. Of course, what self-respecting streetwise five-year-old went to school with a leather satchel? She died at the very idea of walking to school with the dreaded bag. There was worse to come. It was one of those that you wore on your back, like a rucksack. She looked like an illustration from a Ladybird book circa 1954 when "saddled up" in the satchel. Next morning her mother had loaded it onto her back and she had clink-clanked her way to the village school, dying with embarrassment at every step, trying to pretend it was not there, and hoping no one would see or hear it. Once in class she was too shy to ask for help to take it off. Once the register was called, Miss Spicer asked if anyone had remembered to bring in the stuff for the play shop. As the hideous realisation that she was the only one who had bothered to do so dawned on her, she started to go red and hot from her chest up to her forehead. She could hear her own heart thumping, and no words would come. To admit that she alone was the class goody-goody was more awful than being part of the mass telling-off for being collectively negligent and forgetful. She sat there awkwardly, unable to lean back in her seat because of the clunky metal burden on her back, pretending that there was nothing unusual at all about her appearance, and, therefore, hoping no one would notice she had a large leather bag strapped to her body which made a noise like Alpine cow bells each time she turned to the left or to the right. Miss Spicer was interrupted by the arrival at the classroom door of an eight-year-old from another class bearing a dinner register passed on from another teacher, and so the day wore on. Julia had returned home that afternoon (no one had asked her why she had the satchel on her back all day because she was too shy to make friends) and said, placidly, 'Miss Spicer didn't want them after all so I brought them home again.' Her mother tutted and fussed and unstrapped the satchel and no one ever thought any more of it again, except Julia of course, who could never pass a tin of baking powder without being reminded of her shame.

'Come on, Sweet Pea, time to get us something to eat!'

Julia came to herself with a start and realised that members of the group were looking at them with an 'Oh, must you really, we've only just started' expression, but with that, Robin grabbed her and led her determinedly down the rickety staircase to the hubbub of the general bar below.

'Tell you what,' he said. 'Let's just go and make an omelette at home or something. We're only ten minutes walk away and it seems daft to spend a fortune and wait for ages to get served.'

'Sounds brilliant,' she agreed, and they set off towards his flat near the British Museum.

'Have you always been like you are now?' she asked.

For a moment he seemed disconcerted, then, after a moment's hesitation, joked, 'What do you mean, have I always been talented, wonderful, urbane, intellectual. You bet! Um, actually, to be honest, no. I think I had quite an inferiority complex as a teenager, but then isn't that what happens to all teenagers? You think you are the only one with the agony that no one else in the whole history of the universe has ever felt, but that's how it is for everyone. But I think I've tried hard to make my life what it is. I've certainly felt loved, almost to the point of worshipped, by my parents. In fact, if I turned into a serial killer I think my mum would still support me. People who talk about destiny are talking rubbish.'

Julia was taken aback by this. 'So you mean it wasn't my destiny to meet you?'

'No,' replied Robin, suddenly becoming much more earnest than the anecdote-telling entertainer she had witnessed twenty minutes earlier. 'No, destiny is not a matter of chance. I believe it's a matter of choice. It's not something to be waited for; it's a thing to be achieved.'

'So what's your destiny then?' asked Julia, intrigued.

'To be united with—' and here he paused and her heart stopped. 'To be united with,' he continued, 'a mushroom omelette, a bottle of chilled Pouilly Fuissé and a green salad, and to have you to keep me company for supper.'

She thumped him playfully on the shoulder, and they strode on, discussing the performances of the two stars of the play, and sharing theatre memories.

Before long they reached Robin's street. His flat was above a little second-hand bookshop and had its doorway to the right of it. Once in through the slightly shabby hallway, they made their way up a rather drunken, wooden staircase to the top floor. The flat was very Scandinavian; lots of stripped pine floor, bookcases which went right up to the ceiling; wicker furniture; footstools; a few catalogues from recent London art exhibitions; nothing very cosy, no sofas to sink back into; no television visible anywhere.

He took her coat and bustled off to the kitchen, talking over his shoulder as he went.

'What would you like to listen to? After the Ibsen I think we ought to put on something to cheer ourselves up, don't you?' She glanced over at the music collection thinking that he might mean *Beach Boys Greatest Hits* or something of that ilk. 'There's the Scott Joplin or there's something called *Renaissance Dance Band Music*. It's not too intrusive and you can imagine all the Capulets and the Montagues bopping around to it.' She chose the Scott Joplin. As the *Maple Leaf Rag* plink-plonked into action she wandered after him.

'What can I do?' she asked.

'Here are the mushrooms; they'll need a bit of a peel, and you can do the salad. I'll open the wine. It's a thigh job I'm afraid.' Robin was wrestling with the bottle and the corkscrew.

The wine glasses were tall, thin, and expensive.

They ate on the their knees sitting opposite one another across the coffee table, she now talking about the summer school she had attended a few years previously in San Diego.

'They've got these fantastic rickshaw-type things,' she told him. 'I was out one evening after a meal overlooking the water, and this guy who called himself "Bike Man" stopped and tried to persuade me to have a little trip in his rickshaw. It was ridiculous. I didn't really have the money, and I didn't need to do the trip, but he was such a one-off guy and talked about himself only in the third person and it meant you had to do the same, so if I wanted to say "Is this your only job?" for example, I would have to ask a question like, "Does Bike Man have another job apart from this?"'

'And did he?' asked Robin. 'Actually, don't tell me, let me guess, he was writing the Great American Novel.'

'Well, almost, he was a lecturer at the university.'

'No! Well there's hope for you and me. We could operate a tandem rickshaw!'

'I couldn't possibly do that; I don't know you well enough,' she said, semi-jokingly.

'You don't know how true that is,' said Robin, looking just so slightly uncomfortable. And then a long pause.

'Let me tell you about me,' said Robin all of a sudden, which rather took her aback as he now had gone in a trice from funny to "I mean business". Then, absolutely out of nowhere he said, 'The most important relationship of my life was with a man.' It was as if he couldn't keep this fact to himself any longer and it had just burst from him despite his best efforts to suppress it.

She thought to herself *God, what on earth am I supposed to say to this?* She realised that he was looking back with a slightly manic, anxious smile on his face. Saying the first thing that came into her head, she replied, 'Well, as long as you were faithful that's great, and better a man than a mountain gorilla, eh?' But he wasn't laughing. He obviously wanted to talk about it.

She settled back, as much as the wicker sofa allowed, and tried to look at him in as grown-up a way as she could, with a voice inside her going, *Oh shit! Oh shit! Oh shit!* He leaned over and filled her glass, then filled his own.

Chapter Five

'I remember my fifteenth birthday like it was yesterday,' Robin began. 'When I got downstairs I laid out my birthday presents on the floor in the lounge, and propped up my new *Buddy Holly* album behind them against the couch, like a themed backdrop to the display: new jeans, jacket, giant Toblerone bar, *Guinness Book of Records* from Mum and Dad; *Frankenstein* Airfix kit (with head, hands and scars which glow in the dark) from my younger brother Rory, and a Chelsea scarf and goalie gloves from my grandma. She never did give up on hoping I would be a sporting hero. What a disappointment I've been to her! Fifteen did feel different but I couldn't say why.

'"Here, Robin, you haven't opened this card yet," Mum said as she handed me a card which had been resting next to the toaster. The card was from Marcus. I'd been saving it.

'I opened it as I sat down on the top deck of the bus ten minutes later. It was warm inside and the windows were all steamed up. It was raining hard outside, and it was still quite dark; you know the sort of day: the world stumbling its way into another winter.

'The front of the card was a gaudy scarlet block of colour with the words *I'd like to send you something naughty for your birthday*, and below it a keyhole cut out of the card. Through the keyhole you could see what looked certain to be a sexy cleavage. But when I opened the card, what had looked liked naked breasts was in fact a giant bare backside. I was excited to get it but embarrassed about it too because inside, in Marcus's handwriting it continued: *but instead YOU CAN KISS MY ARSE!!.* Tattooed on the left buttock was the word "Happy" and on the right was "Birthday". It was like getting some sort of pornographic card. His writing was distinctive – a disturbing chaos of flicks, strokes and crossings out; barely legible in fact. I can still remember what it said.

'Now you are an old fart. Meet me at the wreck after school. Marcus
'As always, he had done the M with a flurry of two small arrows at the base of each of the M's vertical lines. I was never quite sure what the significance of this was, and Marcus never told me. Hooks? Spears? Portcullis? Devil's tails? Strange Marcus. Clever Marcus. A boy signing off with spikes.'

'So did you meet him after school or what?' Julia interjected. She really didn't want to know any of this, but somehow the desperate desire to sound accepting, interested and signalling that it was no big deal was already in place, while in her heart of hearts she was wanting to stick this Marcus on a bonfire like a guy and put a match to him.

'Well, yes, in the end, but it was a weird kind of day because Marcus didn't turn up at school. No explanation. Old Giggsy, his form master, asked me if I knew why Marcus wasn't at school because he knew I hung out with him but I said I didn't know. He was a bit older than me but we were the only two who lived over in Saddlewood. The teachers assumed we were mates just because they saw us queuing for the same bus every day. Giggsy just sighed, marked him absent and assumed it was simply Marcus's incurable habit.

'At four o'clock when the bell rang, I went over to the bike sheds, unlocked my bike and made my way to the river. It was dark again – the day had never really had a chance – and there was another cloudburst as I reached the woods. I got off the bike and eased it through the clearing in the hedge and got back on to the small track which led through to the river on the other side. I remember that it was muddy and I was hard-pressed to keep my balance. My face was soaked from the trees dripping on me but as I got further into the wood the trees were denser and it made the rain seem lighter. As the mud slowed me down, my dynamo offered less for his lights. As I stood on the pedals to push on uphill through the track, the light could only manage a tired orange glow. When I reached the wreck the lights dimmed to nothing.'

'What was the wreck?' asked Julia.

'Oh, it was a rusty, burnt-out Ford Anglia at the end of an old disused lane. The lane had overgrown with weeds and bushes and no car could make it down there and no passing driver would know it had ever been a place to turn into.'

'God, it sounds like the perfect spot for a murder!' she said.

'You're right. I suppose it was a miracle we weren't clubbed to death by some nutter and buried in shallow graves, but in those days you just didn't seem to have murders going on every day of the week like now. We felt quite easy about wandering off to deserted woods. We were so sure that we were the only people who went there that we had even fitted the car with bits of carpet, boxes to sit on, and some canvas to keep out the wind and rain.'

'So was Marcus there when you arrived?' she asked.

'Yes, of course he was. He was my friend. Well, he was more than that...he was my hero...there was something dangerous about him and it aroused I don't know what inside me. I just wanted to be around him but I felt rationed with his attention. The torch was on inside and I could smell cooking. His first words were, "Hey, Birthday Boy! You took your time."

'He wasn't looking up, He was kneeling over an upturned biscuit tin where he'd made a little fire and was cooking sausages and bacon on the upturned lid. I remember helping him punch a few holes in it a few weeks before so we could use it as a little rudimentary stove. Pitiful really. We actually thought we were such brave SAS survival types!

'He handed me some fried bread and his hands were filthy. When I thanked him for the *Buddy Holly* LP he made some joke about only buying it to save me borrowing his all the time. He seemed agitated. Irritable. That's when I saw a large army grip, full, wedged under the dashboard. It was so full the zip was having a hard time holding on. When I asked him what it was he just said, "My stuff." I must have looked a bit puzzled because then he said, "All my stuff." That's when he told me.'

'Told you what?'

'Told me he was leaving. When I asked him where he was going he just said, "Stop asking me stupid fucking questions. I don't know. I'm off tonight." I felt my stomach do a full turn. I can actually remember wanting to run away and tell someone so they'd make him stay.'

'But was there anything, well, you know, anything between you?'

'What, romantically you mean? God no! We were just really close friends, mates, you know the way blokes can be: bonding and all that. But it was all unspoken. I just couldn't believe he was going. I'd never felt closer to anyone in my life. He didn't even seem to be too bothered about money.'

'I asked him again, "Are you really leaving?" but he gave me a look and I knew it was true. I tried to get used to the idea. I can hear my voice now, quivering a bit but trying to sound brave asking how would I be able to reach him. He was so...so handsome, mysterious and grown-up. I just wanted not to be near him but to *be* him.

'He simply said, "You won't." When I insisted that he'd write or phone or something, he just shrugged and said, "Course not." I started to panic and worry about what his parents would say, but he just seemed to think it would be a relief to them. Actually, deep down, knowing them and knowing him, I believed him.'

'So did he just walk off into the sunset with his bag?' asked Julia.

'No, he suddenly said, "You'd better go." When I refused he shouted at me, "Go on. Piss off back to your nice house with your mummy and daddy and little brother."

'I was in a whirl. I didn't know what was happening; how what had been a bit of a laugh, a pathetic attempt at Boy Scout campfire stuff in the wreck had turned into the stuff of nightmares. I told him he was a cold bastard, that he may have had a shitty life, but it wasn't all shitty, and he just swung his foot round and struck the hot biscuit tin, which bounced out and hit me. Some fat splashed out and burnt us both. The fire was out in an instant. The torch fell from its fastening on the steering wheel below us and I stood up and banged my head on the car. I felt Marcus lunging in the dark, kicking, throwing punches. By the time I'd scrambled out onto the river bank I was actually crying. Real teenage angst. I could just about make out Marcus's silhouette thrashing inside the car, pulling up the carpet, kicking the tin, swearing. I picked up my bike, slid on to the muddy track into the trees and pedalled off into the dark. I turned once to see his distant shape standing by the car. Because it was dark I couldn't work out if he was standing still, looking back at me, or facing the river.'

There was a long pause. Robin got up and went over to the wine bottle and refilled both their glasses. Julia was mystified, thinking to herself *So what's the big deal?* She'd been expecting some gruesome, salacious confessional details like something from a James Baldwin novel and it had just been a bit of an Enid Blyton with attitude so far. But she could see that it was seriously formative in Robin's story, and that to make some kind of cheap joke was utterly not on. But that was how she felt: elated and relieved. What was all the fuss about? One minute all the hope and optimism had been smashed; now it seemed like what he had confessed was ridiculously trivial and had no adverse effect whatsoever on how she now saw him. In fact it was quite sweet, very "new man".

'Robin, thank you for telling me that,' she said quietly, smiling benignly whilst inside a little fist was punching the air above her head and a voice was shouting, 'Yes! Yes!'

'Oh darling, that's just the prelude!' he yelped, rather too camply for her liking, but it was as if he couldn't quite sustain the serious emotional energy level for too long at a time and had to break the mood in order to pretend, for both of them, that this unburdening was not a big deal. But it was evidently time to continue.

'So did you ever go back there?' she asked.

'It made me almost sick to return to the wreck after that. One night I dreamed that I had gone back in spring when the ferns were waist-high, green, waxy and tightly curled. It was early evening and summer time and the air was heavy with midges, gnats and silent high-speed flying, teeming insects. In the field leading down to the woods there were dried, cracked cowpats, all these details, and suddenly the dream just disappeared and although I woke with a deep ache in my throat, I couldn't catch the end of the dream. I couldn't find out if I ever discovered Marcus in the wreck, if it was empty and overgrown or if it simply wasn't there. For years afterwards it became a kind of major icon in my dream life, a symbol of the energy, excitement and danger of coming of age, and a heavy air of unfinished business hung over it.'

Robin leaned across and clicked on another little low lamp on a table next to him.

'I keep remembering little incidents from my much earlier childhood. Little vignettes just pop into my head.'

'Well that happens to us all,' said Julia, trying to take the spotlight from the Marcus story. 'What are the most vivid things you remember?'

'Me running across the field near the farmhouse on holiday, determined to be the one to find the missing cricket ball and to impress the older boys and then suddenly feeling my legs sinking into the thick mud which was the semi-dried-up pond. I remember the squelching as I tried to struggle out, the pounding in my chest, the nausea of fear and one of the lads shrieking my name and then the whole circus of people running from every direction, pulling me out of the mud by the arms with a loud plopping and sucking sound, and then carrying me to the farmhouse kitchen sink, standing me there on the wooden draining board, ripping off my clothes and sluicing me down with tap water.'

'You make it sound as if you were a shy little loner. And you're one of the most extrovert, entertaining people I've ever come across,' volunteered Julia.

'Oh, but I wasn't always like this,' replied Robin. 'You should have known me at nursery school. I was too shy to speak in the school nativity play, and the following year they made me take the part of the donkey so that I could hide under the giant papier mâché ass's head with none of the "no room at the inn" dialogue, just a bit of nodding and braying now and again.'

Julia knew that this was simply putting off the inevitable question which she had to ask sooner or later.

'So, did you ever see him again?'

He sighed and looked away at his groaning shelves of books.

'Oh, well, I've gone this far and so I need to tell you the rest of it I suppose.'

'I'm all ears,' she said, and tried to smile reassuringly and look as if it was the story she had been looking forward to for the last six months.

'Well, I left home to go up to university a few years later. Being a first-generation undergraduate, I had to be subjected to the over-anxious mother treatment. It was as if I was a six-year-old preparing for a five-year expedition to Vladivostok.

'"You'll need a new toothbrush, some more pants, oh, and where did you put your green belt? And d'you want to take your tracksuit bottoms with you? They'll be useful if you have to go down the corridor to the toilet at night."' Robin winced at the memory.

'"Oh Mum, for God's sake," I would say repeatedly, "just let me pack, will you?" But she couldn't let it rest. She was scuttling up and down the landing at battle speed.

'"And what about needles and cotton?" she would run back

and add.

'I can remember myself screaming at her, "For goodness sake, Mum, they sell needles in bloody London. I'm not going to Tristan da Cunha!"

'"Tristan, did you say? A lovely name! Who's Tristan? Did you meet him when you went for the interview?" It never stopped. Maybe she was just dying inside because I was going away and she couldn't stop babbling. God forbid, did she have Alzheimer's or was she just plain stupid? I would just put my head in my hands then turn up the volume on the record player and close my eyes. I don't know the actual moment when she ceased to be the adored mother and turned into this figure of fun with embarrassing gaps in her un-well-read knowledge of the world. All I know is it happened. The time left remaining for Mum, Dad and my brother to be "a family" was down to days, not weeks or months. And all I could do was patronise her, whilst all she could do to me was nag. I so longed to be in the kind of confident, secure family where they joshed, joked, held each other by the shoulders, had eye contact and told each other they loved one another, had "dinner" at 8 pm rather than 1 pm; where they shared intelligent anecdotes and snippets of film criticism interspersed with little pithy political comments, and where the dad and the son hugged and even kissed one another on the cheek when they said hello or goodbye. But my mum had had a lifetime of making sure the apple was in the lunch box, the swimming trunks were in the satchel on Fridays, that I had enough money for the occasional school trip, that I had done my history revision or handed in my graphics project on time. She was too bogged down in the minutiae of being the servicer of our needs, the washer of clothes, the person who made sure my toothbrush was not too curly and worn-down, to see the bigger picture. The picture was so big that she couldn't really look at it at all. What would she do once my brother and I had left home? She was terrified and lost. I really understand it now and feel deeply ashamed of how abrasive I was. The burden of being the elder son; the burden of being the first-generation university student. It just made me crawl with embarrassment. I couldn't handle the enormity of it any more than she could. She compensated by fussing; my way was to be offhand, churlish and to affect total nonchalance about the whole thing while secretly pooing my pants.'

'I shouldn't let it bother you,' said Julia. 'It was the same for me. It's just what growing up is about.'

'I know; I kind of understand it now,' he said. 'I had applied to UCL because it was the biggest college. There had to be someone there who fancied me I reasoned. Life in my grotty little provincial town made me feel that life was perpetually being lived in other universes.

'"I feel like a character in the *Three Fucking Sisters*," I wrote in my diary one night. I longed for a proper, adult relationship, instead of the hideous fumblings and stammerings which had so far not added up to much. The girls I knew were either unobtainable goddesses, spotty slappers or quite witty, intelligent but sexless chums. They were girls who, ten years on, I might meet at a party somewhere and who would perhaps be managing a pension fund, having exchanged the glasses for contacts and having invested in highlights and spot cream. They may possibly appear on late-night book programmes on Radio 4 for all I know, but then, when I was just eighteen, they were swots, and nothing about them made me tingle. It just didn't happen for me and I suppose I thought I was a late developer; that once I met the right person everything would click into place.

'Those first few months at university I felt like an eight-year-old who had somehow hoodwinked the authorities into letting me go there. Any day, I was expecting to be called out of a lecture and told to come back when I had grown up. But outside, when I strolled past gaggles of tourists trailing along to the British

Museum, I became soigné Robin Forester, urbane, witty, man-about-town, city intellectual, the guy who was off to a lecture on T. S. Eliot's *Four Quartets* – in my head, anyway.'

'Didn't you have any friends?' asked Julia.

'Oh yes, I had the people who were living on my corridor in Hall and there were a few people in my tutorial group that I used to have a laugh with in the Common Room or the student bar. My best friend was a chap called Geraint Stevens. He was Welsh, like you, but really seriously Welsh from the depths of the Valleys. I think they might have even spoken Welsh at home. I can remember one day he said to me, "Have you got one?"

'"Got one what?" I asked.

'"An invitation to Rawlings' drinks thingy," he said.

'Geraint and I were in Dr Rawlings' tutor group for eighteenth-century European literature and were on the same corridor in the Hall of residence. He was a good laugh and he had a really dry sense of humour.

'"Yeah. You going?" I replied. I had nothing better to do. How sad is that when you go to your tutor's flat to a drinks party on a Friday night?

'"Well, we might as well. Free drinks, maybe a few new faces. You never know your luck," said Geraint. He was always one for free drink. It must have been his rugby playing days which had trained him to sniff out free alcohol like a bloodhound. I told him, "My luck's a debatable thing right now, since Sasha dumped me in the sixth form there's been nothing special. I wouldn't come too close – what I've got might be catching." It was meant to sound like a joke, but the hint of "relationship despair" was pretty transparent behind my weak attempt at raising a laugh. Sasha was a beautiful creature but she had been way out of my league and we had both been very young anyway. Geraint had had a bit more luck in the girl department since the beginning of that term, but Nicole had suddenly turned from angel of mercy to bitch of the year with no apparent warning and so he found himself on the pull once more. Geraint's self-esteem had been dented but not crushed totally out of shape.

'"Make sure you don't wear the Eau de Courier," Geraint said to me as he was opening the door to leave.

'"Who's Courier? Fashion designer or what?" I enquired. I can't believe I was so stupid.

'Geraint said in his ultra-Welsh voice, "Only joking, boyo." Then added, "You know that thing when you're up in a tall building and a bike courier gets in the lift with you, in all the leathers and the big dome on his head with all the crackly message shit broadcasting, and then he gets out before you get to the ground floor and the lift smells like a leopard has just had a piss in it and the doors open: da – daa! and about five people look at you as if you've just made that smell while you've been coming down…well, that's Eau de Courier. Just put the old Brut on tonight boyo, and we're both going to be in luck. See you about six. We'll miss supper. Bound to be stuff up at Rawlings' place to eat. If not we can pick up a curry on the way back."

'A few hours and one failed essay plan later, we set out for the Tube, both of us not having much idea of where on earth we were heading. Belsize Park was pretty much the frozen north for us two rather green boys from out of town. We'd both swotted up the A-Z hoping to bluff to the other that we were well-travelled metropolis types though. Up on Haverstock Hill – not far from Haverstock College, ironically – there was a distinct chill in the air after the muggy swamps of Bloomsbury. We set off purposefully, each lost in our own thoughts. A couple of salubrious avenues later and we were on the doorstep of Dr Rawlings' flat. A stunningly beautiful young man opened the door and I immediately started my socially immature blather along the lines of was it was the right evening and was his flat-mate at home, and nice place you've got here, et cetera, when the side of Geraint's right foot jabbed me on the ankle. My heart sank as I heard the nightmare prompt from his stage whisper, "Waiter, dickhead." But in moments, coats were taken, long-stemmed glasses of very superior Australian wine were pressed into our hands and we joined the drawing-room roar. The sight that greeted us astonished me. I will never forget it. I suppose that's why I've got such clear recall about it all. I had been expecting an approximate replica of the Junior Common Room from College with a couple of tutors and staff thrown in. In fact I had assumed that Rawlings had been deputed to put on a bit of a social thing to make the department seem a bit more student-friendly; a confidence trick to make us feel we were "ladies and gentlemen" rather than "girls and lads". And anyway, whatever the motive, we had made the decision to go there because it was pastures new and free alcohol. For all our provincialism, I realised immediately that this was somewhere where I was going to have to raise my social game – hugely.'

Julia smiled as she gazed at Robin who was now in full flow, obviously miles away, back in that party so many years away, a lifetime away. She was waiting, however, for the great reveal.

'The first face that caught my eye was one of the guys from *Coronation Street*. I was amazed at how little and ordinary he really was. Even better, from my point of view as I drank in every detail, I noticed he had a pretty unpleasant zit on his forehead but of course, media fame being the aphrodisiac it is, he was surrounded nevertheless by some of the best-looking women in the room. The room seemed to be rather scarily empty of fellow students and rather diarrhoea-makingly full of moderately famous people from the film and TV world. Since I didn't know anyone apart from Dr Rawlings and Geraint, I began to examine the invitation cards on the elegant marble mantelpiece: invitations to a private view in the Francis Kyle gallery off Regent Street, an invitation to High Table in an Oxford college, an invitation to the wedding of one of BBC 2's most famous talking heads with a reception in the Peers' dining-room in the House of Lords; an invitation to a book launch in the British Library; a

charity ball programme for an extravaganza in the Savoy in aid of
abducted children. Suddenly all I wanted was a mantelpiece full
of invitations just like these rather than a dralon sofa with a copy
of the *TV Times* and a box of *Quality Street*. I was contemplating
this particular coup de foudre about my own small life and what
my new self-image was when a sultry female voice spoke so close
to my ear that I felt her warm breath ruffle my hair. The combination of the wine, the warmth of the room, the proximity of a
strange mix of patchouli and sandalwood, the sexual charge of
having someone blow in my ear made me almost faint with
pleasure. She may as well have been talking Sanskrit for all I had
understood of what she said. I spun round, almost grazing
against her cheek with the side of my face and found myself
staring into the most amazing pair of pale blue, almost wisteria-
coloured eyes with very small pupils like dots. The rest was the
predictable drop-dead-gorgeous combination of great cheek-
bones, ash-blonde dead straight slinky hair, little black dress
covering one sun-tanned shoulder and completely off the other.
God, shoulders are sexy was all I could think of, during the
pregnant pause equal to an elephant's gestation period. After a
while the noise of the braying literati cut back in and I realised it
was my turn to speak.

'"Oh, I'm so sorry,"' I stammered. "I was miles away... Have
you come far?"

'God almighty, why did I have to come out with that bloody
Prince Philip-type thing when this was the nearest I had ever got
to a total goddess in the flesh in my entire life?'

Julia smiled as she listened. He told the tale with such self-
deprecating candour, but so far all it seemed to be was about
heterosexual longings, so where did the "relationship with a
man" thing come in? She was still feeling relieved as nothing so
far, except the uneasy look on Robin's face every now and again,
gave her cause for concern.

'What's the matter?' asked Robin. 'Are you bored? Do you

want to go home?'

'Of course not,' replied Julia. 'I've got a feeling you're about to come to the good bit. What did she say?'

'"Well," she said, "you've got to be joking. I'm the lodger. I live in Warren's basement. I can get as pissed as I like tonight. My boyfriend and I can just stumble down the stairs and collapse in a heap. Brilliant, eh?"

'Boyfriend. OK. Exocet safely embedded in target. Building has been totally demolished. But I somehow regained my composure. In fact now that the heat was off having to do chat-up lines, I relaxed a bit and started to be a bit more Robin Forester and less stammering new boy at school.

'"So you live downstairs. Dr Rawl...I mean, Warren (I felt so cool saying that!) seems to lead a pretty interesting social life. I've seen posters for the exhibitions at the Francis Kyle. I've even got one on my wall in my room; they seem to have an eye for choosing modern artists who do stuff that you want on your walls rather than the kind of stuff you buy for an investment but you can't make out what it's all about, or worse, the kind of stuff that makes you want to top yourself," I said, or something like that – you get the drift – I was just so excited to be having a grown-up arts and culture conversation in a posh flat in north London and pretending not to be a total turnip, that I was getting a touch of the verbal diarrhoea.

'"I couldn't agree more," she responded. "My boyfriend likes all that avant-garde stuff, you know shocking stuff, dead animals as art kind of thing. That's about as sad as having 'I love Elvis' tattooed on your arm. Can you imagine the nurses undressing you for your bath in the nursing home fifty years later and saying how sweet it is, and the skin all wrinkled up and saggy."

'She made me laugh. Nice sense of humour. Sharp. How old was she? In fact, as I mellowed out a bit and got the confidence to watch her while she was speaking, I realised that she wasn't much older than I was. Girls have that irritating thing of being able to look thirty when they're only eighteen.'

Robin stopped to sip his wine.

'But then it has its downside,' added Julia. 'You get pervy grandads in pressed jeans and desert boots in the film and TV business thinking it's par for the course and that these waifs are suitable bed partners for men of sixty-five. But sorry, I'm interrupting the story. Do go on.'

'By this time,' Robin took up his story once more, ' I had her in total eye contact and felt at last I was winning my drinks party spurs. Over her shoulder I now spotted the director of the film that Geraint and I had seen the week before in one of the London Film Festival previews in the NFT. Across the room Warren Rawlings was introducing Geraint to Jonathan Miller. This was fucking surreal!'

'God, amazing,' said Julia. 'So what did you do next?'

'I remember saying to her, "And your boyfriend? Is he here now?"

'"Coming any minute," she shouted over the cacophony of clever talk vibrating all around them. "That's what they all say! Oops, I think I'm getting a bit tipsy. Sorry. He's been on a shoot for four days in Morocco. He should be on his way back from the airport right now. He's a model. I'll introduce him when he arrives. What do you do?"

'Oh – oh,' said Robin to Julia. 'At this point should I have said I was an investment banker, no, way too young. A rich kid? Not posh enough. Writer? No, couldn't bluff it for long enough.'

'So what *did* you say,' asked Julia.

'I stumbled out, "I-I'm a student, one of Dr Raw—, one of Warren's students. French and Russian, joint honours. You?"'

'"Oh I'm a student too," she said. "Well, officially. I manage to get the minimum couple of essays done and turn up now and again, but I've got an agent and I've done a couple of films and I've got the bug I'm afraid. Hello Paramount! Goodbye Wittgenstein! You know the kind of thing."'

As Robin went to get more wine from the fridge he continued over his shoulder to Julia, 'Thank God I hadn't told her I was a barrister or some other nonsense! The hired caterers were moving about with vast platters of devils-on-horseback and exquisitely sculpted little unidentifiable puff pastry mouthfuls and I was in need of more wine. I offered to refill her glass and then, stupidly, realised I didn't know her name.'

'"Sorry, I'm sorry I've been extremely rude. I didn't ask your name," I said.

'"It's Eloise. Eloise Lascelles."

'Something started whirring in my grey matter database taking me right back to my Mum's "I Love the Royal Family" bookshelf collection and rang a bell. Something deep in the cul-de-sacs of my memory told me that this was a surname shared with distant cousins of the royals. *God, if Mum could see me now!* I thought to myself. Not only was Eloise beautiful, she was aristocratic too.

'By the time I returned, Eloise was in an animated exchange with an arty and arch old lady with a beaky nose, teeth like garden implements, and a voluminous, droopy hand-embroidered knitted jacket. They were talking about a mutual friend and I felt I had lost the will to live on that one. I handed her the replenished glass, and edged sideways through the crowd to find Geraint. Geraint was looking like he had just died and gone to heaven.

'"Fucking Harold Pinter, boyo!" he bawled in my ear, tapping me on the shoulder and gesticulating with the wine-glass hand to England's greatest living playwright who was now chatting amiably to Warren Rawlings and Jonathan Miller over near the French windows.'

Julia smiled when she remembered her own embarrassing encounter with Pinter when she was an impressionable sixteen-year-old.

'What's wrong?' asked Robin.

'Nothing,' she said. 'It's just reminded me of something funny. Remind me to tell you later. Don't stop, please.'

'OK,' he said. 'Well just then, two cool, long-fingered hands with their perfumed palms clasped my eyes and Eloise's unmistakable voice purred in my ear. "Surprise!" she said.

'As my head turned ahead of my body to face her, I saw that she was reaching out with one hand to grab a dark, sun-tanned man by the hand and was pulling him into our circle. His face was partly obscured by her head – she was almost as tall as me, and also Mr Boyfriend was looking the opposite way from the direction his body was going, trying to greet a few familiar faces as he was pulled into our orbit.

'"Robin – meet Marcus. Marcus – this is Robin, my new best friend," she said.

'Marcus's smile went into slow motion. His eyes twinkled and crinkled, and then he let out a huge guffaw and threw his arms round me shouting, "I don't bloody well believe it!" It was Marcus, *my Marcus,* from back home! The guy who had run away never to be seen again. The guy who had been my role model and childhood hero now completely reinvented as a hot young male model!

'I simply gaped and stood speechless and dazed. By this time Eloise and Geraint, and even Warren had all been caught up in the hysteria of the moment. Warren touched my shoulder, and muttered camply, "So how come you know our resident hunk of the month?" and as he said it he winked at Marcus. Marcus, to Robin's astonishment, mouthed "Fuck off" back at Dr Rawlings – yes, at Dr Rawlings! – but the genial expression on his face belied his words. It was said in playful flirtatious friendship, and this coming from the pseudo gangster of my youth; this was Marcus being teased by Britain's leading authority on the poetry of Baudelaire. And this was Marcus being so cheeky and familiar back to someone who still had the power to put the academic fear of God into me. Marcus, it seemed, was lighting up the room. It was as if Jay Gatsby had just walked in.

'"We've got some catching up to do, my friend," said Marcus, and put his arm around my shoulder and steered me to a quieter corner of the room near a large table laden with dressed crab, canapés, blini, smoked salmon, quails' eggs, lumpfish caviar and sour cream. I know what it was now, but I didn't recognise half of it back then. At our house salmon had always been pink and came in a tin. It was the Sunday afternoon treat. There was a vast damask tablecloth hanging right down to the floor. Marcus patted the seat next to him and started helping himself to food. What was this mockney accent? This wasn't the accent of our origin. Marcus had actually had a bit of a Scottish accent when we were kids because he'd spent a lot of his early childhood there. He was like a chameleon. He could turn himself into anything and obviously had a good ear. In fact, with his brooding dark good looks he probably could have been an actor. I sat there, dazed, and, by that time, slowly metamorphosing into a stewed owl courtesy of Hunter Valley Riesling.'

Julia started looking down at the edge of her seat and began playing with a stray small thread of cotton coming from the cuff of her new blouse. She was getting a bit of a premonition about what was coming.

'"But how long has all this been happening to you?" I heard myself saying.

'"Well, difficult to say," Marcus began. "But things were shit for a couple of months after I disappeared out of your orbit and then I got stopped in the street in Knightsbridge one day, model agency scout, and it was better than stacking shelves in Tesco, so I toddled off to find my crock of gold."

'"And did you find it?" I asked, intrigued not only by his new-found wealth, but also his demeanour, his new way of talking, his knowledge of gourmet food and good wine and the way he seemed to ooze confidence and charisma, and, I might as well say it, sex. It was that heady mix of danger, glamour, a thin seam of earthy geezer running just beneath the surface, money, and a way of looking at people as if they were the only people in the world at that moment. I couldn't believe my luck that I had him all to himself for a while.'

Julia was starting to feel uneasy. She could sense where this was leading. Robin's face had completely changed now that he had got to this point in the narrative.

'So he was rich, then, was he?' she asked.

'I think he said something like, "Well let's say, think crock and multiply it to the power of ten."

'While I was digesting these facts he said, "Come on," quietly, serving me as well as himself with a few spoons of poached salmon and freshly-made mayonnaise, "I'm just a pretty face with no A-levels. Tell me about you. What are you doing here? Did Warren hand-pick you from the multitude too? He has a knack, you know. He can spot potential ten blocks away."

'*Blocks.* Imagine talking like that back in the wreck. We would have pissed ourselves laughing at this image of the two of us sitting there with the great and the good of the Hampstead glitterati. This was turning out to be one of the best evenings of my life. How could I possibly contemplate the mundanity of life back in a Hall of Residence, subsidised student meals in the refectory and the slog back home at the end of term via Victoria coach station? This was where I wanted to be. Forever. I think I remember coming to my senses and realised Marcus was smiling at me, waiting for an answer.

'"I'm just a student," I said. "Nothing special. Kept my head down after you left; studying modern languages at UCL. I get back home now and ag—"

'But as I began the final word of my sentence I suddenly felt the pressure of the sole of a foot in its expensive Christian Dior sock caressing the side of my leg just above my ankle. I glanced down nervously first of all and realised that both my own and Marcus's feet were safely hidden from view under the tablecloth, and that the room was in full literary cry and no one was looking in our direction. Compared with how I had felt when Eloise had put her hands over my eyes this was completely in a different league of…of…'

'Seduction?' volunteered Julia.

'Well, yes, I suppose so,' said Robin. 'I had never felt so excited by anything in my life. And terrified. And bewildered. For a moment I thought it was perhaps an accident, but I glanced at him and could see him looking at me with a slight smile playing at the corner of his mouth. It was as if he had flicked a switch inside me. I was hoping and at the same time fearing that this gesture was as important for him as it was for me; that he wasn't just some kind of drugged celebrity tart who was happy with anyone as long as he had taken enough of the substance on offer.

'"Come to dinner with me and Eloise," said Marcus casually. "How about next Wednesday? Actually why don't we make that Friday? She's off for a few days doing some little cameo part in a costume drama and we've got years to catch up on. We can get a curry delivered, open a bottle of wine. It'll be a gas."

'I realised that I was blushing for the first time since I was about thirteen. My mouth was dry.

'"Yep, why not?" I replied. "What time do you want me?"

'"Eightish?" he said.

'"Cool" was all I could manage.

'Then I remember hearing, "Marcus, darling! Over here!" Eloise's voice broke in like an alarm clock waking me out of a deep and vivid dream on a day when I had to get up for school. I realised I would be coming back to this house the following week.'

Chapter Six

Julia felt sick but at the same time transfixed by this story. It was like driving along a motorway seeing the flashing display lights telling all cars to slow down and realising everything was coming to a halt. An accident ahead...ambulances rushing along the hard shoulder, sirens. The dread that maybe one would see carnage, and yet craning one's neck nevertheless for a sight of it, macabrely hoping it might be dramatic and on one's own side of the road. Would Robin ever tell someone the tale of how he first met *her* with such a radiant glow on his face, or was this just going to dissolve into "Let's just be good friends"? In a weird way, what he was telling her was not acting as aversion therapy. Instead, she realised that he would not be going into such intimate detail unless he cared about her and needed her to know it before they could move on. But then again, maybe it was just the prelude to "So you see why this can't go further"? She was in utter confusion.

'Are you OK?' asked Robin, hesitantly. 'It's ridiculously late.'

'Well, yes,' replied Julia. 'But if you give me any more wine and don't give me something to soak it up, I'll be on the floor.'

Robin popped into the kitchen and returned with a baguette, a little block of Normandy butter and some Brie.

'If the cheese doesn't give you nightmares, the rest of my life story will,' he said, again, nervously as he wasn't sure how she was taking this.

'Don't worry,' she replied, 'I'm saving it for my novel. They say use your own voice and write about what you know, so it's just as well you're giving me some new material.'

Robin grinned at her, realising that while she was still making jokes, it was safe for him to continue.

'So quite a night back in Belsize Park then, eh?' said Julia, signalling that it was time to continue now that they had the bread and cheese on their laps.

'Are you sitting comfortably?' asked Robin. 'Well, here goes... Later that night Geraint and I sat on the almost deserted platform at Belsize Park waiting for the last southbound train. Geraint was slumped forward, silent, with his head in his hands. I was on another planet and would not have noticed if Geraint had been reciting *Beowolf* at that point, but gradually I was aware that he had sat upright and was leaning back on the designer-torture seat, resting his head on a poster advertising *Juliet of the Spirits* at the Hampstead Cinema, and laughing to himself, shaking his head back and forth in slightly too much slow motion to be anywhere near sober.

'"Harold Pinter. To think, three years ago I was writing essays about his stuff for my exams, and tonight there I was"—he held up two fingers on each hand to signify quotation marks—"sharing a joke" as they say in the old *Tatler* captions to those knobby photos. Trouble was, I was so full of old Rawlings' Riesling that I showed myself up to be the complete tit that I am. Why couldn't I have come out with something more memorable than, 'We did one of your plays for A-level'?"

'Geraint always made me laugh. I remember laughing and nudging him with my shoulder, and saying, "That's because you *are* a tit," and both of us began smirking in lazy but helpless fits.'

'You seem to remember a lot of this in quite some detail,' said Julia.

'Well, it was, as I said earlier, one of the important evenings of my life,' countered Robin.

'I can even remember that a small dark grey mouse ran along the side of the track below us, up and down, up and down, and when my eyes became more focussed on its implausibly high-speed scuttlings, I realised that there were four or five more of them down there. Imagine what else comes out at night when all the trains stop running, more mice, bigger mice, rats, bigger rats, whopping great mammoth rats. Imagine working down there at night, sticking up posters, sweeping the platforms, wandering through the tunnels carrying spanners and lamps, and sluicing down the disgustingly piddly corridors and tunnels.'

'I thought you were telling me a story of love and lust?' prompted Julia. 'Even though this prolonged meditation on the nocturnal wildlife system of the London underground is intriguing.'

'Actually, all I could think about as we waited for that train, was the place on my leg where Marcus's unshod foot had rested for a moment then gently moved up and down,' said Robin. 'All the time Marcus had watched me quizzically, like some kind of hypnotist, amused and slightly supercilious, intent, examining me like a scientist watching for an anticipated auto-response. He was smiling to himself as if he had a secret but wasn't sharing it. And then there was Eloise...' he added. 'I began to wonder if I was part of some pre-planned game they were both into. Was this the way they got their kicks maybe? Was it some kind of kinky honey-trap? I started to get scared and tried to replay the exchanges again and again, and although I didn't want to admit it to myself, I decided Eloise had been quite ignorant of the secret life of Marcus's foot. But then again, she was an actress. Maybe. The slightly smutty, foetid wind, the distant rumble, and the movement of other tired and bored Tube travellers moving their shoulders away from chocolate dispensing machines and graffitied underground maps where they had been reading and re-reading their eight-hour-old copies of the day's *Standard* signalled an end to the reverie and the speculation. We clambered into the carriage and rattled back to Bloomsbury.

'I sort of couldn't think about anything else,' continued Robin. 'I closed my eyes and let the cacophony of the rattling carriages wash over me. Who was this person I had now become, attending fancy drinks parties? What would my gran back home have made of the evening? She died ages ago. She'd just died quietly in her bed early one morning and had just been there, still and cold when the home help had called to get her up. What about you?

Are your grandparents still alive?'

Julia shifted her position on the sofa and resettled as she answered him, relieved to have a bit of respite from the slow-burning homoerotica.

'Years ago, when I was about eight, my grandad had his first "turn" as the family referred to his massive heart attack. The bed was moved down to the little cramped Welsh front room which housed nothing except the three-piece suite and the glass cabinet full of useless cheap ornaments bought by me and my cousins as little children on our first holidays. The Tower of Pisa was dwarfed by a seal glued to a chunk of rock emblazoned with its name: "Newquay", and they were nothing compared to the massive shiny china dolphin leaping on its little pedestal over the static wave behind them. A small carved and painted wooden sailor stood jauntily next to the dolphin, making it look like a minke whale, and a little white marble statue of Moses sat just behind. That was one of mine. I was determined to buy a Greek god for Gran and I had chosen it carefully because it looked so "classical". It probably was made in China and cost a penny to produce. My parents never had the heart to break it to me that it said "Moses" on its bottom; it wasn't Neptune after all. Jumbled in amongst all this was a little Perspex photo cube which held me and my cousins frozen as perpetual toddlers. "When I go you can all have back whatever you've given me," Gran always told us. For years I awaited the return of my treasures, even Moses, feeling slightly guilty that reparation involved the gruesome demise of Gran. But of course, Grandad had gone first and this had been my first encounter with death.'

'Did you see him when he was dead?' asked Robin, relieved to be having a bit of a break from his own confessions.

'Grandad had spent his declining years in the bed in what Gran had always called "the room" with only his huge black oxygen tank for company,' said Julia.

'Often when we visited he would look mournfully at us from

over the top of his mask, moving just his eyes and inhaling pitifully, having had one of his myriad of minor turns. I could only have been about ten at the time of his death and we all went to the house the next night to meet up with the gaggle of aunties. My cousins and I solemnly followed Dad into "the room" to say our goodbyes. Because no one I knew had ever died before I sort of didn't know what to expect of the evening. Somehow the reality of what I was about to see had never ever occurred to me. Instead of the focal point being the bed over in the corner, there was just a bare mattress, and the oxygen tank had gone. But the room was completely full, full of Grandad. He had been a tall man, and when I was small he used to pick me up and hold me aloft then throw me so that I could touch the ceiling if I reached out in the midst of all the terrified but ambivalent hysterical shrieking of "Stop, stop, I hate it…do it again, Grandad". And now there was this long giant man-shape under a white sheet inside a coffin that seemed to go from the fireplace to the opposite wall. The first thing that struck me was the total chill in there. Gran's house didn't have central heating and each room had a little fire permanently glowing. "The room" before Grandad's "turn", had usually been cold and unlived-in, opened up for Christmas and the occasional family get-together, but then, throughout Grandad's illness, the fire had been kept going like a sanctuary lamp in a temple. And now it was freezing. We shuffled round the foot end of the coffin to make room for a few more of my younger cousins to squeeze in. My dad lifted the hankie-thing off Grandad's face, and there he was, yellowy white and utterly serious, as if he was having a particularly stern dream, and his yellow hands with their liver spots were folded over his chest. His nails were a bit long. We stood looking down for what seemed like an age, and I remember saying, without turning, to my cousin Colin, "Like alabaster, isn't he?" But there was no answer. Colin and his sister had zoomed out of "the room" and were back in the kitchen with Auntie Beryl and I was on my own with the corpse. I wished again and again that I had never seen Grandad like that and knew that it was an image that was going to haunt me in the middle of the night for years and years to come.'

'Remind me not to take you to any horror films,' joked Robin. 'You may have to be taken out screaming after ten minutes.'

'So you were on the Tube then...?' said Julia, smiling and changing the subject.

'Yes, I realised that if we weren't careful we would miss our stop. I remember glancing out of window as the doors where closing at another stop. We had no idea how many we had missed already. But it was OK. It was Warren Street. We could walk from Goodge Street to our Hall of Residence.'

'"D'you get her number then?" asked Geraint, assuming that I had achieved at least that after investing so much time talking to Eloise. Of course I could hardly tell him what had really happened.

'"Uh, sort of," I replied, my left leg crossed over the right knee, left foot jigging as I looked away, giving all the body language about not wanting to talk about it.

'"Well, what's that supposed to mean?" Geraint asked me. "Did she give it you in Braille, or crossword clues, or did she write it in lemon juice so that you've got to hold it up to the fire to read it?"

'"Her boyfriend gave me the number. I used to know him," I explained.

'Geraint backed off, losing interest in what was turning out to be just an old mates' reunion, not the promise of a hot date which he could enjoy vicariously. We stumbled off the train at the next stop and strode across Tottenham Court Road in silence and walked, shoulders hunched against the cold, towards bed. We had gone from giggly drunk to sad, tired and "I'd pay twenty pounds if someone offered to take me by magic to my bed right this instant."

'I tried not to dwell too much on the events of the evening,' continued Robin, 'since I knew I would probably have plenty of time for that around four thirty, that bewitched time when people racked with problems or anxiety find themselves staring wide-eyed into the blackness, unable to get back into the cocoon of rapid eye movement sleep. However tired I was at that moment, I knew that I would feel like Judy Garland on 1930s-style medication designed to keep her awake and "up" to complete punishing film schedules and only allowed to rest when the next downer was handed to her with a glass of warm milk. But no downer for me that night. Too much had changed. Forever.'

Chapter Seven

Robin's great confession to Julia was still not finished. He seemed to be reluctant to cut to the real business now and yet, having started on the saga, he had to finish it.

'And so you went back a week later,' said Julia quietly and without emotion. Robin was looking at her anxiously now. He was exhausted from both the length of time he had been talking and also the slow-motion reliving of his life. Julia by turns was exhilarated and flattered that he was giving so much personal stuff away, and felt that surely if he was telling her all this, it was not to warn her, but because the relationship they seemed to be tentatively embarking on was important enough to warrant this total confession. There were not to be secrets between them. He respected her too much for that. However, he who had been so ebullient and confident a few hours before in Arlecchino was now darting rapid glances at her as he spoke, and she could tell that he was occasionally employing humorous voices in the telling of bits of the story to cover up his rabbit-in-the-headlamps fear that she would just pick up her coat and race from the flat, never to return. He was, Julia could see, exhilarated by telling the story, but it was interlaced with panic. She didn't even dare look at her watch and she could see no clock in the room but she was aware that it must by now be the early hours of the morning. She was also aware that it may be one of the most seminal conversations of her life. If they could get this out of the way there may be a future for them.

'Yes, I went back,' said Robin, now a hint of deadly seriousness in his voice.

'And was Eloise there?' asked Julia, surprising herself at the familiarity with which she asked the question. It was as if she had known this motley dramatis personae all her life.

'No. I didn't know quite what to expect. It seemed so strange, the two of us acting like men about town when it only seemed like yesterday that we'd been sitting in that old wreck in the woods cooking sausages on a biscuit tin, both of us real plebs, and there years later taking canapés off trays borne aloft by hired catering staff at an academic drinks party. Surreal. But he was much more grown up than me. He'd worked, been part of a very glamorous set, travelled to exotic places, lived in London in a flat, whereas I was still an overgrown schoolboy really. I was bluffing my way in the adult world, still dependent on being fed in the refectory every night and having no clue about how to run a home of my own, take out home insurance, budget for weekly food shopping, buy a TV licence, and all that other grown-up stuff. The flat was amazing. It was like a cross between a Moroccan prince's palace and some kind of Edwardian bordello. Everything seemed draped in quilts and coverlets; there were cushions of every dimension scattered all over the place, some covered in dark brocade, some in velvet, some in satin; little sequins twinkled here and there on the edges of the cushions or on the borders of a throw. There were wall-hangings and a huge chaise longue near an old-fashioned open fire. There were little blackamoor statuettes, figurines, beautiful hand-painted pottery, and masses of bric-à-brac. It was like a kind of enchanted grotto. The whole place smelt of some sort of exotic scented candle, frangipani, sandalwood, patchouli. I don't know what it was. And yet, for all the antique stuff it felt very modern, very considered, very much like it had been decorated by some theatrical designer. And it had, of course, as I later found out. Before Marcus had met Eloise he had been living with a costume designer who had been nominated for an Oscar for his work on various period dramas. Because of this, Marcus had even considered getting into the acting business himself. He had seen it at close quarters and liked what he saw, and of course, even though he left school and ran away, he was no fool. More than that, he was drop-dead gorgeous. As I said, people were just staring at him at Rawlings' party. The camera loved him.'

'It seems such a massive leap. How on earth had he gone from Marcus, the council house boy, going on the run with just one bag of world belongings to Marcus, the smooth man-about-town?' asked Julia, intrigued.

'God knows,' replied Robin. 'Probably by way of the international catwalk, the celeb circuit, a bit of Arab money, sleeping with the right people, who knows? I didn't ever ask. All I knew when I walked down the steps into that basement flat was that I had my toothbrush in my pocket.'

Julia felt both excited and horrified to know that she was being allowed into the intimate gay centre of this story. Still, a huge speech bubble with the word "Why?" was going round and round her head like a child's kite on a blustery day at Kensington Round Pond. But all she knew at this point was whether it was midnight, 2 am or time to get up the next day, this confession was unstoppable. Part of her was nauseated, while a much bigger part was flattered that she mattered enough for him to unburden himself in this way. For a third time she asked herself was she supposed to believe by this that he was wiping the slate clean? Or was he giving her as full as possible an account of why a relationship in the real sense was never going to happen? For now she didn't know. All she did know was that it was a major night in her life and that after it things would not be the same again.

'So, do you want or need to tell me what happened that night?' she asked, suddenly feeling more in control than she had earlier. In that second, she experienced a flash of power; she was in control over what he would or would not tell her, and at the same time it was as if she, or the telling of the story, had put him into some kind of trance. She was assured of some kind of chemistry between them, which was the same magic which was forcing him to crawl through the slurry of painful confession. Had he not met her he could have gone on, dancing the superficial tightrope of conversational stardom like the *Cabaret* compère, everyone guessing he was flirting with them, but no one quite sure. She had given him a metaphorical truth drug and he was unable to stop. She also realised that she "knew too much" and that he was instinctively trusting her with his confession.

'He offered me a drink and I said, "Dry Martini" because even I knew it was that bit more sophisticated than a glass of Mateus Rosé which was the acme of alcoholic beverages in those days. Of course I was too stupid to know that the real dry Martinis were made with gin, so when I started gulping it down like it was a box of Kia-Ora from the girl with the heavy tray round her neck in the Gaumont, I was anybody's. Because I'd had no lunch I was almost unconscious from about halfway down the glass. I remember something about pasta, red wine, a big bowl of salad, but to be honest, all I really have a fix on is his hand reaching for my knee and sliding up my thigh, and feeling my erection about to break the material of my trousers and burst out into the night. And the worst thing is I didn't care. All I wanted was for him to kiss me and take me to bed.'

And then there was a long silence.

Too much information.

Did she want to know any more? No. But he was going to tell her anyway.

'Well, we did. Go to bed that is. And for four years I was in love with him and I would have gone under an express train for him. It was the first time I had ever felt so alive like that, and by that I mean having the entire ground of my being wrenched from me and reconstructed according to someone else's world. We were very discreet of course. Eloise was given her marching orders but I think she managed to find a rich and elderly director quite soon afterwards. I've even seen her in a few films playing the glamorous thin blonde who always seems to say, "Look out, he's got a gun!" but Marcus was by then quite successful and worked abroad often. It wasn't as if we were a woosome twosome living out of each others' pockets – or each others' flies – as you have probably gathered from the way I have just described that first sexual encounter.

'So, if you'd like me to call you a cab, Julia, I quite understand. It's just that if we were to progress anywhere beyond where we were tonight I owe it to you. We could have stayed at the "Robin the clown" moment and we could have spent months on theatre trips, wine bars and other nonsense, but I...it's just...er, I haven't...'

Julia felt at this moment she just wanted to be violently sick. However, she stayed silent, staring at the intricate patterns of wickerwork in the arm of her chair, and then looked up at him. There he was, positively squirming with embarrassment but looking at her like a King Charles spaniel who had just been told off for pissing on the best Wilton rug.

'You were about to say?' she ventured.

He took a deep breath then began again.

'I haven't felt like this inside myself since Marcus. I know this is disgraceful; I shouldn't say it; it's too revealing, it's against all the rules but bugger the rules. I just feel like there is something between you and me and I want to explore it more than anything else. I read somewhere that although not everything that is faced can be altered, nothing can be altered until it is faced. God knows where I got that... From a cracker? Was it in a horoscope? A gypsy? Who bloody cares?'

With that he got up and came across to the empty place next to her on the sofa and took both her hands.

'My dearest, sweetest little butterfly,' he began. 'Don't look so scared and worried. We are on a preposterous little journey together and if we are brave it can be the most magical thing. Are you willing to walk some of that way with me? I don't know where it's going, but I've not met a woman like you before, ever, and I'm terrified. I'm terrified of you going and I'm terrified of you staying, and I just had to unburden myself otherwise I would have gone mad.'

Completely buoyed up by his eloquence and the expression in his eyes as he looked into her face for what seemed like eternity, she just smiled and leaned forward and kissed him excruciatingly delicately on his mouth and then put her arms round him and stayed quietly intertwined with him. When at last they drew apart they both knew that what had gone on was too special and too precious to do any more.

'It's time for the pumpkin coach I think,' she whispered, but he knew from the way that she said it that she wasn't leaving a golden slipper behind and that he would not have to search the kingdom looking for her.

'Can we meet on Saturday?' he asked quietly, humbled at last after the bravado of six hours previously.

'You say when, where, how,' she replied, thinking that she was the luckiest girl in the world, convinced that destiny was not a matter of chance but a matter of choice. It was a not a thing to be waited for but a thing to be achieved.

'The Tate. Three o'clock? Then cinema? Then supper?'

'As long as we don't have to sit and listen to an Edmund White story on Radio 4 Book at Bedtime and drop into the Coleherne for a gin and tonic en route,' she joked.

With that he suddenly dropped his pitiful "gay confessional" persona and metamorphosed into Mr Masterful.

'Prince Florizel at your service, and Oscar Wilde had their marching orders,' he said with a low bow, and then, from his lowly position, took her hand and kissed it in courtly fashion, his lips still pressed to the back of her hand whilst looking up intently into her eyes.

'Blimey, no wonder they all fall in love with Mr Darcy,' she said, almost willing herself to break the mood otherwise the whole thing was too emotionally laden to bear. Either way, the only way to re-enter reality was to plunge out onto the cold street and jump into a cab which would take her home.

As she clattered down his drunken wooden staircase to the door she heard him shout after her,

'Julia!'

'Yes, what?' and she turned her head back to see him standing like a little boy lost at the top of the stairs.

'This is special.'

'I know that,' she said hoarsely, and opened the door to the street where a fine misty rain was swirling in no discernable direction. Her hair stood on end and she knew that an umbrella would be no protection. However, a pumpkin taxi swished up beside her in no time.

Once back in her flat she lay on her bed with a stupid grin on her face. It was now 4.15 am. There was work the next day and she was nowhere near sleep, but she had been hit by such a thunderbolt that the only thing to do was to fumble frantically through poetry books amid the muddle of novels and old A-level textbooks on her shelves and search out metaphysical love poems. John Donne, ironically, was the only person who could articulate what she was now feeling. And of course, like all lovers who have been hit by the dreaded arrow, she thought she was the first one in the world to feel like this. Just her and John Donne, that is.

She somehow nodded off and had about three hours of sleep before the alarm woke her and she sat bolt upright thinking that the hours of conversation with Robin had been a dream, but it only took a few seconds for the wave of reality to hit her and for her to remember the enormity of the past evening. She spun around the flat getting ready for work in that weird, slightly light-headed way that only too much alcohol can induce, when one is experiencing the illusion of being totally in control, and yet to the outsider, one is 100 per cent pissed and putting on an Oscar-winning performance of being OK.

Being naive is like having Alzheimer's. Everyone can do the worrying for you while you live in the cocoon of your own mind.

Julia floated to work unable to think about anything except the intimacy of the confessional of the previous night and of the intense new bond that existed between her and Robin. They had crossed the Rubicon and there was no doubt in her mind as to the intensity of what he felt for her. She had felt his heart thumping when he had hugged her, but whether it was nervousness or passion she would have to wait to find out. His eyes, when they lingered upon hers, held her gaze for so long that it was like looking into the sun and she had eventually to look away. It was as if he could not get enough of simply looking at her, unable, just like her, to believe his good fortune in finding what the Spanish quaintly call "the other half of your orange". They simply fitted together. She had found her soul mate.

At two thirty she was in the staff room when he rushed in. He was much better than she was at concealing any of the drama and intrigue between them; she was waiting for discreet displays of intimacy but there was nothing. It was as if everything from the previous night had not existed. She suddenly felt sick as if she had had a very vivid dream in which she had done some naughty sex stuff with him, and that nothing had really happened except her massive projected nocturnal mountain of feelings about him. When she next looked up he had gone out of the room and disappeared down D corridor towards the staircase. Feeling abject and disappointed, she returned to the place where she had dropped her bag and her books and noticed a little beige envelope in her pigeon hole. Inside was a little postcard of Seurat's *Bathers at Asnières*. Coming from the head of the man in the bowler hat who was gazing out at the river along with his little spaniel was a stuck-on thinks bubble. In Robin's unmistakable handwriting it said: 'I hope she doesn't forget about the Tate on Saturday.' Later that day Julia went out to Dillons and bought a reproduction of Seurat's *Sunday afternoon on the Ile de la Grande Jatte* and from the mouth of the lady with the big bust and bustle she wrote a little speech bubble saying, to the man walking alongside her, 'Non

Auguste, c'est impossible. I have to be at the Tate at three o'clock on Saturday so I can't elope with you.' She popped it into Robin's pigeon hole as she was leaving at six o'clock.

'What are you smiling at?' asked Maurice Cunningham, the German lecturer.

'Nothing, ' she replied. 'Just me being daft.'

And she went home for an early night.

Chapter Eight

When Saturday afternoon finally arrived, Robin crossed Vauxhall Bridge and walked along Millbank towards the Tate and bounded up to her.

'Well, fancy seeing you here!' she said, with the intention of teasing him, but the delight on her face at seeing him gave too much away. He didn't mind; he felt exactly the same.

'I saw you before you noticed me,' he said. 'You were standing on the steps looking anxiously down the river towards Westminster. The wind was blowing from behind you. You looked like an Afghan with a problem hairdo.'

'Thanks for the compliment,' replied Julia. 'On windy days like this I look like I've just stuck my fingers in an electric socket.'

They strolled around arm in arm past Turner sunsets, Turner sunrises, and lingered in front of the Matisse snail, not really concentrating too hard on the paintings, and after about an hour called a truce to the pursuit of art and went and sat in the café.

'After the cinema we can go home to my place if that's OK with you. We can pick up a pizza from across the road and there's a big bag of herbs and leaves and stuff to go with it,' said Robin, then adding, 'Oh, and a friend of mine is using the flat for a few hours to have a clandestine tryst with his mistress but I'm sure they'll have left before we get back. She's married so it's all a bit cloak and dagger. I shouldn't encourage him really, but he's incurable I'm afraid and they've nowhere else to go.'

Julia was intrigued and secretly hoped that they would still be there so that she could see what these fornicators looked like.

'Got any more four-hour stories to tell me?' joked Julia, but then felt embarrassed that she was making light of something deeply important. He smiled wanly and she knew she had upset him. She stared at her Tate plate for a moment and started to jabber crazily about how anything called a gateau in England is a guaranteed disappointment just as anything called a cup of tea anywhere south or east of Dover is the same.

'I remember once when Marcus and I were in a restaurant in Madrid,' he contributed, 'we had one of those wonderful foreign menus where they translate everything badly and I spotted "Jake Fish" in the pescatorial section.'

She grinned. 'But I suppose that's just how they would say it. Talking of which, my Italian friend Constanza was once raving to me about some pop concert she wanted to take me to back in the sixties. I saw a poster of this rather racy-looking bunch of macho pop stars with a stupid name underneath: the Rokes. I said it over and over to myself, rhyming it of course with "blokes", but then the penny suddenly dropped and I realised Constanza was taking me to see "the Rockers" because that's how they would have written the word down in Italian. She was brilliant but God she was moody. If it was hot weather she would be complaining it was too hot; if it was a fresh spring day she would be shivering and saying "too cold, too cold". I wonder what happened to her.'

'I'd love to take you to Italy with me one day,' said Robin suddenly, looking disconcertingly serious.

'Bags are packed, plus three tubes of mosquito cream, two pairs of sandals, straw gondola hat with a red ribbon and my passport,' she beamed, all the while just with a little inner voice going, "OhmyGod!OhmyGod!OhmyGod!" but at the same time it all felt absolutely right.

They wandered out of the gallery and hopped on a bus up to Trafalgar Square, feeling like two children on a school outing.

'Oh, please, please let's see the new Rohmer film!' he squealed as he suddenly saw an advert for it on the side of another bus. She would have been happy enough at this point to have watched a black and white film called "Knitting Patterns Made Easy" or "Spot-welding for OAPs" but the fact that they went to see *Le Genou de Claire* and both adored it made it the perfect day.

When they arrived back at Robin's flat he led the way once more up the squeaky staircase and opened the door into the main living area. It felt like she had never been away.

'Still here?' he bellowed, and another voice, female, and eerily familiar to Julia, responded with a cheery, 'Hi!'

Julia composed herself ready to meet Robin's two friends and then, to her total disbelief, out of the kitchen walked Mel and Mark. The two girls screamed and rushed up to each other, hugging and doing repeated choruses of "I don't believe it!" Mark leaned forward and kissed her on both cheeks and looked decidedly uncomfortable but made a big effort to cover his confusion with charm and bonhomie. Robin was intrigued and slightly disconcerted to find out how they all knew one another and they explained about the student drama festival from many moons back. Julia was astonished that Mel and Mark were still a kind of an item and she felt a dreadful pang for poor old Deke. *Maybe,* she thought to herself, *they've just arrived at some kind of modus operandi which leaves them space to have their own separate adventures.* Mark's shiny dark hair flopped seductively down over one eye and Julia noticed how Mel darted him glances like an adoring gun-dog, just waiting for a signal from its master. Robin was busying himself with a bottle of Frascati and an obstinate cork.

'We've just seen a heavenly film,' he said. 'Don't you just love French films? They're so subtle, so simple, and yet there's absolutely oodles of sub-text which is just how it is in real life I suppose. Why has Hollywood got to give us everything on a plate and spell it all out? Can nothing be left unsaid?'

Julia felt he was speaking for much more than Claire's knee but filed this away to think about later.

Mark, charming as ever, trained his megawatt smile on her and held an empty wine glass out to Robin, while Julia, seeing that both men had their backs turned away from her, mouthed to Mel, 'How's Deke?' Mel just shook her head in an over-desperate 'Don't even try to mention his name here' mime and frantically tried to signal with her eyes that it was total taboo to ask in front of Mark.

'So how on earth did you two meet one another?' asked Mark.

'I work with "Hulia"' said Robin with a twinkle in her direction, alluding to their own little jokes about "Jake/hake fish" earlier on in the day, in a way which made her feel he was trying to set up a private alliance with her against the waves of suave charm emanating from Mark. Julia decided to help him out. 'Yes, I met Sir Baceous Gland, here, when he came bursting into the College and terrorised the entire Senior Common Room.'

'Hey, guess what I learned today!' said Robin, getting excited by the idea that the four of them were all together in his flat. Julia marvelled at his manic ability to think on his feet and change the subject in a fraction of a second. 'If you lift your right foot off the floor and make clockwise circles like this...'He demonstrated with his own foot.'...Go on Mark, I want to see you doing it! While doing this, you draw the number "six" in the air with your right hand and your foot will change direction.'

They all tried it with various degrees of "Ooh!" and "Oh damn!"

Egged on by this, Robin clapped his hands, 'Now here's another one for you all. Who is the most bumptious of all the saints? You especially, should know this, Julia, since we've been to see a French film this evening.'

'No, give up!' they all chanted.

'Coquille St Jacques!'

But they were all three of them groaning and making as if to throw the cushions at him so he scuttled off to the kitchen, laughing and excusing his sad pun by saying,

'I think it's the lack of food getting to my head. Have you two eaten anything?'

Mark and Mel grinned sheepishly at one another, and Julia wanted to be anywhere rather than there, witnessing this.

'No, we weren't too hungry,' said Mark, looking rather smugly satisfied with himself. 'But if you were going to offer us something, Robin... What time are you supposed to be back home, Mel?'

'I've got a late pass tonight,' she replied, 'so I don't have to get back until well after midnight.'

'Well let's just pop over to *Pizza Express* and bring some pizzas back here,' suggested Robin. 'We've got the wine; got the knives and forks. What else could anyone wish for?'

'There's the small matter of the gateau as long as you are prepared to run across the Channel for it!' added Julia, and she received the sweetest smile in return.

'Come on, Belmont, make yourself useful!' said Robin, pulling Mark out through the door by the sleeve. 'And girls, don't drink all the Frascati! We'll only be about twenty minutes at the most.'

Once their noisy clump-clumping footsteps quietened down as the two men reached the downstairs front door, Julia and Mel fell upon one another, inundating one another with questions.

'Are you two going out together or what?' asked Mel.

'Well, yes, I suppose so, but we've hardly had more than a couple of dates, but it feels very good, very promising, I can barely believe it but we seem so compatible it's not true.'

'Oh, Julia, I'm so pleased for you. If only things were as simple as that for me and Mark.'

'But you've been together for a long time now. How long is it exactly?'

'To be honest, I can't remember, but the whole thing is so bloody cloak and dagger it's killing me. I should leave Deke I suppose, but you know the awful thing is, even though Mark and I have got this incredible, passionate thing together and we can never keep our hands off one another, if I suddenly became totally available I think he might run a mile. The fact that I am unobtainable is part of the thrill for him. And I never know if I am just a compartmentalised bit of his life or if there are others like me in the "Secret Kingdom". And in an odd sort of way, I love Deke. We're comfortable together; I know if anything dreadful happened to me he would always be there. If I had to spend my life in a wheelchair or some nightmarish thing like that, I think Mark would be off like a shot, but that still doesn't stop me feeling like I'm going to be sick when I see him walk into a room.'

'Me too,' said Julia.

Seeing Mel suddenly looking oddly at her, she added, 'Not because of Mark, because of Robin, you donkey!'

'Are you sleeping with him?' asked Mel.

'God no! I told you. We've only been out together a few times. It's all very gentle and very sweet. It's not some heavy sexual grope. We – I know this sounds ridiculous – we get such pleasure from just looking at one another. I've never known anything so disarming in my life. It's not that I don't want to, of course, but it's so overwhelming that we're just taking things slowly. He's been talking today of going to Italy together. It makes me faint just thinking about it. I've had so many examples of relation-ships, or non-relationships to be precise, where I have yearned for someone but they haven't been even fractionally as interested in me, and I've had my share of impassioned aardvarks sending me Valentines or who want to see me again after what is so obviously the most boring date of the century that I can't believe what's happening here…that he likes me, or seems to, as much as I like him. I have to pinch myself.'

'Jules, be careful, won't you? It sounds like you're about fifteen and having a crush on the maths teacher! It makes you very, very vulnerable. I don't want to put a dampener on it but it's approaching triple-critical.'

With that, the door burst open and Robin rushed through it, one arm behind his back, hand in a fist, the other stretched up and forward like Mighty Mouse, singing the cartoon catch phrase, 'Here I come to save the day!' Mark was coming behind, clutching the pizza boxes and a little paper carrier bag with the dough balls.

'Knives! Forks! Plates! Come on, chop! chop! What have you

two been *doing* all this time!?' yelled Robin, and they all scuttled about creating the instant dinner table, refilled all the glasses and settled down to a happy, raucous meal.

'This is such a weird coincidence, us all meeting like this!' said Julia. 'Let's drink to us!'

They all clinked glasses but no one added anything to the toast and there was a short silence.

'The angel has passed over,' said Robin.

'What do you mean?' asked Mel.

'That's what the Russians say when it goes quiet in a room and no one speaks for a moment or two.'

'That's such a lovely thought,' said Julia. 'Trust the Russians to come up with something like that. Russian was one of your subjects wasn't it, Robin?'

'Yeah, but I was better at French,' he said. 'Don't get me started! But I told you about my ghastly New Year's Eve experience, didn't I?'

They all looked blank.

'I've told *you*, haven't I, Mark?' said Robin.

Mark merely shook his head saying, 'It was probably so riveting that I forgot it!'

'Pig!' replied Robin, slapping him over the head with a napkin, and launched into his Russia story.

'It was a couple of years ago, no, more than that, and I had been mad about Sasha Featherstonehaugh who…'

'Featherstonehaugh!?' they all screamed.

'I didn't know people existed who were called that,' said Mel. 'I thought it was a made up name for Cluedo or something.'

'Well, they do. Shut up, I'm losing my thread,' said Robin. 'Now where was I? Oh yes, she was in the sixth form with me at school. We were in the school choir plus the orchestra and did a Gilbert and Sullivan opera together.'

'Sasha? I thought that was a bloke's name,' said Mel. 'Like Sasha Distel.'

'Well, loads of English people don't know any better and they think it sounds like a girl's name, and so she was called Sasha. Even the Featherstonehaughs can get things wrong sometimes. Anyway, we'd been in a youth orchestra together and she was stunningly well-connected, witty, very intelligent, and fabulously rich. Music's a great leveller, you know. I was from quite a humble family, but every time I went to stay the weekend at her family place it was as if there was a never-ending house-party going on. I particularly remember one Sunday when we were all sitting around after Sunday lunch. I think her sister and two brothers were both there for the weekend too. Sasha's mother clapped her hands and announced that we should make a movie to give us something to do with our afternoon. All my own parents would have been doing at the same hour would have been reading the *Sunday Express*! Suddenly it was all hands on deck: an old-fashioned cine camera was produced, and Alexandra and her brother Caspar—'

'Caspar!?' they all shouted in mock disbelief.

'Yes, Caspar; now shut up and listen to my story. Caspar began roughing out a script and Sasha's mother bustled about moving props here and there as the two boys fed her the main story line, "You'll be needing a couple of jugs of water on the kitchen table for that bit, and I'll go down and get the big axe Daddy uses for chopping firewood from the shed. Oh, and how are you going to do the bit with the seance? Are you going to use the library for that?" Library! I ask you! Back at my house where my mum and dad live we had one small bookshelf with Arthur Mee's *Encyclopaedia for Young Children*, an atlas, a dictionary, Mum's royal family nonsense, and a couple of DIY books apart from all the various schoolbooks I had picked up along the way and all my Billy Bunter and Jennings stuff from when I was a kid. The only library I knew was the one in the town near where we lived and that was where all the old tramps used to go to read the papers and keep warm.'

'Was the library in the Featherstonehaugh stately one of those really gloomy old-fashioned places like a gentlemen's club?' asked Mark, although he wasn't really interested in this tale.

'No, it was quite an attractive room really, with lots of window seats and a big table in the middle with a half-finished jigsaw. Every time I went it was a different one.'

'What's all this got to do with Russia?' asked Mel

'Was her dad a spy?' offered Julia.

'No, wait, wait, I'm coming to that bit. I was completely in love with the whole thing as you can imagine. I'd come from a world where my parents both worked. We had a week's holiday in Bournemouth every summer; I'd never used the word "loo" in my life. It was just a toilet where I came from; we had "dinner" at lunch time and another cooked meal called "tea" at six o'clock and when we had visitors on a Sunday afternoon my dad would open a tin of flabby pink ham in jelly and add it to a bowl of beetroot, spring onions, boiled eggs and Webb's Wonder lettuce. But it was a social nightmare. I bluffed my way left, right and centre in order to pretend I was one of them. My worst moment was when his dad asked me to get a corkscrew from a drawer in the kitchen and I pulled out a grapefruit knife which was lying alongside it and shrieked, "Oh look at this poor old knife! It's all bent!" and I started to try to straighten it out. His dad told me that was because it was a grapefruit knife and it was supposed to be like that. My face must have been almost purple with embarrassment by then, you know, the whole "pink blotches on the chest area" utter, utter blushing with horror. Of course I couldn't stop digging myself into a hole and stupidly added, "Yes I knew that but it's even more bent than they usually are!" Look at me. I'm even blushing now remembering it! I think I even tried bending it back into its curve on my thigh with my other hand.'

'But what's it got to do with the bloody Russians?!' the other three all chanted in unison.

'Well, not long after that awful grapefruit gaffe, she dumped me. I was so miserable I just wanted to jump in the lake. Not really because of her I suppose, but because of that whole magic world that I had become part of. That's what had bewitched me. I was in love with that world but that made me think I was in love with her. Although I had made a fool of myself it was so much more a place where I felt at home than the council estate dump where...' and he looked at Mark for a moment '...where I came from.'

Julia noticed this but couldn't quite understand what it was all about. She merely surmised that it was because Mark and Robin were old pals and maybe Mark had visited Robin at his parents' home at some point.

'So,' continued Robin, 'my friend Nick had done Russian as his degree subject and he'd been over there for a couple of months on some sort of scholarship. I'd done Russian to A-level but was barely able to ask for a bus ticket. When you did Russian in the old days you could dissect a Chekhov play or a Pushkin poem at the drop of a hat but try to ask for an extra dollop of mashed potato in a college refectory and you were stumped and unmasked as a complete fraud. Anyway, he was going over at New Year to see some family that he'd made friends with while he'd been studying and someone had dropped out of the group he was travelling with and he asked me if I wanted to go. I thought it would be a great way to get my Russian up to speed. It wasn't too expensive either, and I think I borrowed a furry hat with ear flaps from a pal of his, and a coat from somewhere else. Anyway, I got the kit, got the ticket, got the visa, and off we went.'

Mark stood up and got another bottle of wine from the kitchen and wandered back to the table and started to uncork it.

'Did you freeze?' asked Mel.

'It was a nightmare if you had to wait ages for a bus,' said Robin, 'but most of the time it was quite exhilarating. When it was very cold, and I mean minus twenty or something, each time you took a breath it felt like someone was stuffing twigs up your nose because all the breath froze as you breathed in. So, where was I? Oh yes, New Year's Eve. Now, I don't know about you but I can't stand New Year's Eve. It seems so soppy and sentimental and you always imagine everyone's having a better time than you are, and that everyone is in some passionate romantic thing and it's all going to be pledging another year of love and looking back smugly on the one just gone, et cetera, but if you haven't got anyone special, you feel like taking off your scarf, putting it round your neck and attaching it to the nearest tree. That was me. And Nick invited me to the little flat where his friend Dmitri lived for a party.

'It was a teeny-weeny little living area, lined with books, things like *Westward Ho!* by Walter Scott, *Dombey and Son* in the original English, and loads of various dictionaries. Dmitri's mum was a lecturer and I don't know where the dad was. Nick said something about the Gulag but I don't know if he was trying to terrify me or whether that was where he actually was. There were a couple of others there when we got there, and Dmitri's mum and younger sister were beetling back and forth from the kitchen to the table absolutely laden with mismatched stuff. Everyone seemed to arrive with something: a bottle of vodka, a cucumber, a loaf, a few chocolates, some mushrooms on a string, more vodka, a tin of sprats, some salami…anything people could lay their hands on really. There were big bowls of buckwheat on the table, sardines, little mini mountains of Russian salad and a great big vat of borsch. Eventually there were about twenty of us all squeezed round this little table. Not one bowl matched any other and we passed this borsch along. Each time it went from one person to another, little red waves of soup lapped up over whoever's thumb was holding the dish, and there was this absolute roar of conversation. Not from me, of course, because no one wanted to hear about the symphonic structure of Turgenev's *Fathers & Sons* in English, they just wanted to know if I'd been to watch an ice hockey match or something. It was all washing over me, and I was getting more and more morbid and maudlin and wishing that Sasha was there. I suppose I'd already had far too much to drink as well. They were pouring out these little thimblefuls of vodka and making speeches and downing them in one every time and I was just going with the flow, not wanting to offend anyone. The guy next to me was this really big mean and moody type who looked like he should have been called Boris, but in fact his name was Alexander. Because I'd had so much to drink my Russian was coming along utterly fluently, as you can imagine. So I asked big butch Alexander what happened when midnight came, since I imagined they weren't all going to open the door to a man in a kilt carrying a lump of coal and playing the bagpipes. So he then started to explain this horrendously complex tradition thing and everyone around me started joining in adding details. Can you imagine what it was like for me? Me with my "My name is Robin and I live in Nuneaton" Russian? They told me how they tuned in the radio to the main station just before midnight to hear the president do his new year speech, then the Kremlin bells chimed and you were supposed to write a wish on a piece of paper, set fire to it, drop the ashes in your champagne and drink it all down and the wish would come true provided that you did it before the twelfth chime. Oh my God! The tension! The stress! I was in such a lather I was almost volunteering to sit on a commode for the duration of the Kremlin chimes. Anyway, I didn't have a pen and someone lent me this emerald green felt pen, and I was there, poised. Of course, working out what you want to wish for is like trying to make up your Oscar acceptance speech in five minutes, and didn't some famous know-all once say, "Be careful what you wish for because it might come true"?'

'I think it might have been John Lennon,' interjected Julia, grinning.

'So,' continued Robin now in full flow. 'The president finished his bit; we all had our glasses refilled with Soviet champagne and I was like a greyhound about to be let out of a trap in a racing stadium. I thought that I ought to write the wish in Russian because it might not work if I wrote in English, it being a Russian custom and all that.'

At this point they were all hysterical. They were leaning over on the couch, clutching at each other and rocking from side to side with amusement.

'How sad are you!? What do you mean it wouldn't work in English?' spluttered Julia when she recovered enough to speak.

'No, I really believed it had to be in Russian because I was so pissed by then that I thought I was as fluent as anyone who'd been brought up alongside the Volga. So I started scribbling away frantically on my paper napkin like I was doing a timed essay in an exam.'

'So what did you write?!' asked Mel.

'Well, obviously because I gave you that huge preamble about Sasha, it was about her. Because I didn't have the language to do some subtle version, for instance, "I would like another chance to make a meaningful relationship with Sasha because I really feel that we are kindred spirits and she's got good breasts and a posh house" I just had to write something quick and simple.'

'Which was?' asked Mark.

'Well, I just wrote in Russian "I want Sasha". I tore the bit off where I'd written my wish and scrunched it up. Already a couple of them had set fire to their wishes so I grabbed a candle off the table and put the flame to my remnant of napkin. I almost burned my fingernails because the paper flared up so fast. I dropped the ashes into the champagne but the trouble was there were no ashes because the napkin hadn't burnt properly and so it all started swelling up once it hit the liquid.'

At this point Robin was laughing so much he could hardly continue telling the story and the others were crying and screaming and beating their hands on the cushions.

'Then what? Did you drink it?' asked Mel, gasping.

'I tried to but I was having to sort of gulp it down like a gannet struggling to swallow a bit of fish. In the end I got it down but it sat like a bunched up rag in my gullet. I sat back exhausted, and as I was just congratulating myself at having managed it, I realised to my total horror that the felt pen had gone right through the absorbent paper napkin and onto the tablecloth. There, in green, it said, "I want Sasha" in Russian! And then, the next thing I noticed, and this bit is even worse, old Boris next to me, otherwise known as Alexander, is transfixed by the tablecloth. And then it hit me. Sasha is short for Alexander in Russian. As I said, in Russian it's a bloke's name. By now he was looking at me in a sinister way. I wasn't sure if he was closet gay and thought that it was his lucky day or whether he was appalled and was about to hit me.'

'And?' said Mark, smiling.

'The former; but he was about as attractive as a grizzly bear, probably less so, and so I spent the entire evening trying to hide in the wardrobe, in the loo, behind any convenient door, just wanting it to be time for Nick to want to leave so that we could get away. I would have got in the fridge if there had been any room in it. I couldn't really speak enough Russian to explain the whole situation to him, and anyway, we were both too drunk by then. And *voilà*! That was my story!'

They all three applauded and whooped and Julia looked so proudly at him like a mother watching her first-born performing in the school nativity play.

'On that note,' said Mel, 'I've got to be back home otherwise it's solitary confinement for me.'

'I'll help you find a cab,' said Mark, and they all started getting up and pushing chairs back noisily.

'I ought to be going too,' added Julia.

Robin took her hand as they walked together to get Julia's coat.

'What about you, will you be alright getting back?' he asked.

For a moment she wondered if this was a veiled hint that she might stay, but said cheerily, 'Oh, I'll be fine.'

'OK, I'll come down and walk with you to the Tube,' he offered, picking up his keys and his jacket as they went. When they got downstairs Mel was standing on the pavement while Mark was flagging down a taxi.

Mel ran up to Robin and kissed him on the cheek.

'Night, Robin, and thank you so much for everything,' she said.

'I'll send the bill to Mark as usual,' joked Robin.

Julia was quite touched by the way that Robin and Mark hugged one another and even kissed on the cheek too, but that was theatre folk for you, thought Julia, remembering how Mark had been such an aspiring luvvie when they were in Rossigno.

Robin and Julia walked on together down the side street. The city was still buzzing with traffic, even though it was, by now, very late.

'See you in college on Friday,' said Robin, giving Julia a little peck on the lips.

'Robin, it's been an incredibly lovely day, and I shall think of you gulping that napkin down your throat all the way home on the Tube and that dreadful thing will happen when one starts grinning all by oneself in a public place and everyone thinks you are totally round the bend.'

'You'll have to dig your fingernails into the palms of your hand or think of your parents' dog dying or whatever people do,' he continued. 'Nightie night, Sweet Pea, and safe journey. Ring me if there's a problem. You should get back quite soon if the train doesn't take too long coming.'

'Robin, are you free a week Friday?' she suddenly asked, knowing that there were only seconds before she should run for the train.

'Don't know! No diary! Think so, why?' he yelled.

'My birthday!' she twinkled, effecting a casual offer of information.

'Count me in, your royal highness!' he shouted.

And with that he was off, and she walked down the steps into the bright and bustling underground station, avoiding the bundles of homeless people already setting up camp for the night in the short tunnel joining the stairs to the concourse.

She remembered how a priest pal of her father's had once said how people often paid him no attention at dinner parties and then, just as the coffee was being poured and he was slightly pissed on Merlot, the lady who had been sitting next to him extolling the virtues of Peter Jones over Debenhams would suddenly turn and ask him whether he believed in the afterlife or what did he think about transubstantiation. This was precisely what she had done to Robin. She so ached to spend her birthday in the most romantic way possible that she had been terrified that he would say no or that he would be busy, so it was best just to have hurled it after him. That way it sounded casual and not laden with all the 'Oh God, oh God, this is so heavy and meaningful and you are the most important thing that has ever happened to me' stuff. And he had said yes.

Chapter Nine

As she sat on the rattling, rolling train heading for home, she played and replayed the day over and over again in her mind. It had been idyllic in so many ways, and yet she just couldn't put her finger on what had left her with the feeling that a small piece of the jigsaw was missing. She had been entirely stunned by running into Mel and Mark, but the hilarious evening had made her warm somewhat to Mark, since he seemed rather less supercilious than he had appeared years ago in Italy. She realised that everyone mellows with age, and it had been a long time ago after all. He obviously cared quite seriously for Mel, and that alone earned him several Brownie points in Julia's book, but she still felt a terrible pang of guilt about Deke. But maybe she was being a bit of an old woman about this. These days marriages failed and people seemed to pick themselves up and move on. It was hardly Mount Etna erupting. On the other hand, if she imagined the same thing happening to her, it would be more than just a volcano sending out a few tons of lava. It would be the end of her world. As she was pondering upon this, a man on crutches whose face was covered entirely in tattoos lurched in through the doors at the stop before hers. He propped himself up against the pole near the door and tried to attract the attention of the sparsely populated carriage by making a speech in a feeble Smike-like voice about needing money for the night in a hostel. Most people just looked down at their *Evening Standards* as if they were high-powered academics studying ancient runes and were on the verge of a major breakthrough. Julia got up and walked swiftly to the end of the carriage, as far away from him as she could get, and hoped that the next stop would be in a few seconds so that she could avoid him altogether. At least her flight from the tattoo man served to wipe her head of her other concerns about the evening.

On her walk home to the flat, she started planning her birthday dinner with Robin.

Julia woke at eight the next morning even though she didn't have to work and the day stretched ahead with nothing planned. She had a bath and for the tenth time re-ran the previous evening's events through her head. Now she was waiting impatiently for the rest of the world to wake up so that she could phone friends to chat about it. Celia was the first person she got hold of.

'OK, so what's he like?'

'Dark, funny, clever, actually make that very, very funny and brilliantly clever, travelled a lot, well-read.'

'Sounds like he's too good to be true,' Celia interrupted. 'So is he married or divorced or what?'

'Um, well, he – er, he's the last one.'

'He's "what"?! What's "what"?' Celia was beginning to sound thoroughly lost.

'He's not married, no,' Julia searched for the way to say it, 'but he has had a pretty serious long-term relationship before.'

'Well, what's wrong with that? Proves he's not a commitment-phobe.'

Julia sucked in her next breath through her teeth, realising that she was going to have to come clean about this.

'This long-term thing… It was with another man.'

'Oh Christ!'

'But he's over it. It was like, er, a kind of experiment and now he's mad about me and it was just a thing like you read about that happens to boys in boys' schools. It doesn't mean anything. I mean, I can tell just by looking into his eyes that he really, really, really feels some incredible connection the same as I do which wipes out everything that has ever gone before. I feel his heart actually beating, thumping that is, when he hugs me. I've met my soul mate, Ceals.'

'OK, you win, but I want to meet him and check him out.'

It was at that moment that the brainwave hit Julia.

'I know. I'm giving a birthday party for myself! He's free; he told me last night he'd spend my birthday with me. Instead of going out to some little restaurant I can introduce him to you, Nat, Francis, Marie-Claire, Angie, Geoff and Sarah and Nigel – they can bring Polly with them. Did you know they'd had the baby?'

'Oh that's great news! I'll send them a postcard! Great name, too. And remind me again. Which day is your birthday?'

'It's a week Friday.'

'Julia, I really hope this is going to work out for you, but be careful, my sweetheart, won't you?'

'Course I will, Ceals, and you will be entranced, I promise you. He tells the funniest stories. He should go on chat shows and do it for a living.'

'Done! And I'll bring a birthday cake so don't go making one!'

'You're on! Now all I have to do is make sure that all the others are free. I'll get back to you if there's a problem.'

Later in the day she managed to contact Marie-Claire and Geoff who both said yes. She left a message on Nat's answering machine and decided that she needed to have a bit of a serious talk with Francis since he had been a boyfriend of hers for a year or two and she had only just been beginning to get over it when she met Robin. This neutron bomb which Robin had dropped on her had suddenly swept all residual longing for Francis away. And what was she going to cook? Oh God, Geoff was a vegetarian but she didn't want to subject everyone to the asparagus tart and the lentil soup. What about duck breast? No, too expensive…and also too much cholesterol and Marie-Claire was on a diet… *I could turn this birthday meal planning into an art form, I can see*, she thought to herself, and went in search of cookery books.

Two days later Julia went out shopping for clothes. Crazy. She had enough to last for the rest of her life, probably, but now was a slave to the "he must see me in something new and stunning" syndrome that comes over women who have just fallen madly for someone. She spent the equivalent of what would have fed a Sudanese family of four for a month on a skirt and top, and then, of course, realised that none of her shoes would look right with them and spent a further sum equalling the national debt of a minor African republic on a pair of pigskin boots. She had already been this way before on the first date, and now was beginning to think it was a new wardrobe, not new clothes, that she really needed. On Friday she put the lot on and sidled into college as if she had been wearing them for years.

'These old things? Oh, I've had them forever!'

When he saw her in the staff room later in the afternoon he gave her a megawatt smile which burned like a laser through the middle of the room. At least that's how it felt to Julia. How could people fail to see and not be dazzled by it? She walked over and together they left the staff room as if just happening to be wandering off to independent lessons which, also by chance, were in the same direction.

Julia had already arranged to go to dinner with Nigel and Sarah, old pals from home who now, by weird coincidence, lived quite close by. They had just had a baby and she had promised to go to coo over the cot and deliver the present.

'At your service,' she said when Robin rang, intending to ring Sarah and Nigel the minute she was free and make an excuse.

'Dinner?'

'Great!'

'You choose!' replied Robin.

'OK. Meet me at South Kensington Tube at seven thirty.'

'Done!'

And with that Robin was off.

Julia managed to get hold of Angie later that day. Angie, a friend from college days who had also been on the drama trip to Italy, was working in a city bank and had really scary responsibilities. She had a love-hate relationship with her job as it consumed most of her waking life, but also funded her burgeoning lavish lifestyle. Angie always seemed to be just returning from the kind of holiday one reads about in the article which appears at the start rather than the end pages of the weekly travel supplement. If she wasn't looking at birds in the Galapagos Islands then she was trekking to a Mayan temple or helping in an orang utan sanctuary. The rest of the time she was slamming her hand down on her alarm clock at 5.45 am every day of her life, lurching android-like onto the Tube, and striding into the bank, hardly taking one breath of exterior air. Despite her exotic itineraries, she, like Julia, had never really managed to hit the jackpot in the reciprocated love stakes and was intrigued to hear about Robin, although she usually went more for the testosterone types. This, too, had its downside in that so often these men assumed that every female they dated would deem it an honour and a privilege to be propositioned after the second vodka and tonic.

Julia knew a tiny little bistro in a side street that she was sure he wouldn't have been to. Their almond and pistachio Charlotte was a pudding to die for. The place was bohemian and the atmosphere was intimate without being elitist and expensive.

That evening, hand in hand, they battled with the wind-tunnel which was the Old Brompton Road and struggled round the corner to *La Perla*. It was still only half full even though it was a Friday. They sat at a tiny table for two next to the wall. As they scraped their chairs closer to the table, Julia said, 'Well, here we are, *little lower than the angels…*'

'*…in the tea shop's inglenook!*' he said triumphantly, 'John Betjeman! Bingo!'

In her head Julia put a tick by yet another compatibility box. *Fancy him knowing the same obscure poems as me*, she thought to herself, but then realised that it was exactly what she secretly suspected. Everything, absolutely everything about this, was right. It was as if she had met her twin.

As they settled into the marvellous process of choosing their food, she glanced up and saw Robin looking round wistfully.

'You won't believe this,' he said, 'but the last time I was here, it was with Mark.'

She smiled back politely, thinking to herself what a coincidence as it was such a tiny hidden little restaurant. And how sensitive and sentimental he was to remember he had eaten here with a pal. She was a bit annoyed that he already knew the restaurant that she had thought was her own little secret. So, he'd been there with Mark; it was no big deal. Even memorable meals with his friends made him dewy-eyed. It was sweet that he was so caring. Maybe he would be like that about her, too, when he talked to his other friends. They lived in London. It was the kind of restaurant people like them would frequent. So then…a little coincidence.

The last time Julia had been there was with her boss at a business lunch but it was hardly worth mentioning in the same lyrical tones. The last time they had had a pizza it had been with Mark and Mel but that was no cause for a sentimental sigh.

She looked back at the menu. Something wasn't right.

'Have you chosen yet? The risotto nero is brilliant here, oh, but of course you've been before.' She was aware of her own voice trailing around in a kind of echoey nowhere. She wanted everything to be right so badly, that she was like an ostrich in a desert pitted with holes, all made by her own head, repeatedly bashing down into the sand. Bonk.

Why's he telling me he had dinner here with Mark? Bonk.

What's so bloody special about Mark? Bonk.

Why's he never kissed me properly? Bonk.

Why has he never suggested that I stay the night at his place? Bonk.

'I feel in a kind of a squid mood tonight,' said Robin suddenly, and they both began to laugh and she thought to herself, *As long as he makes me laugh we'll be all right.*

'We'll probably be just like this when we're old,' he said.

'What? You mean having to eat squid because our teeth aren't sharp enough for the steak au poivre?' she replied.

'No, you little donkey, I mean us, arsing about like this in restaurants and having giggling fits.'

Surely everyone could hear my heart beating, Julia thought to herself; she was almost jumping with each thump. Here he was talking about when they would be old: old together. But then she told herself this was how he was – flippant, funny, expansive. It was only she who was dissecting, analysing, and memorising every phrase and nuance because she was looking for what she needed to find: commitment, love, security. All those wasted evenings with drippy male students with acne or fat lips who were studying things like Japanese or biochemistry and who had nothing in the world in common with her were worth it if this was the reward for patience. Nothing, ever, had prepared her for how this would feel. On the one hand she couldn't wait to be sitting eating one of her favourite meals opposite the man of her dreams; on the other, she knew that the emotional charge was making her feel distinctly nauseous. *Maybe this is what they call "love-sick"*, she thought to herself.

'Are you ready to order?' The waitress's voice suddenly burst in on her thoughts.

'Uh, oh, yes, er – I'll have the insalata tricolore to start and the rack of lamb for the main course,' she said, dragging herself awake and into the practical demands of the present moment.

'Squid to start… And I'll have the sea bass as the main,' added Robin, 'and a bottle of house white please. Oh no, sorry Julia, you're having lamb. D'you prefer red?'

'No, it's fine,' she replied, thinking that if he had said, "Will you be OK with the rancid mare's milk?" she would have said the same thing. She was in danger of losing herself utterly and compromising herself out of existence. But she was a willing victim. And just as she thought she had found the secret of eternal peace, he dropped a little sentence into the conversation which had the equivalent impact of a cluster bomb entering a cave.

'Wasn't it a scream on Saturday?' he said, as he splashed the house white into their glasses. 'I absolutely adore having Mel and Marcus round at the flat.'

'You mean Mark,' she chided.

'Mark, Marcus, whatever he chooses to be on any given day. He's so fickle, that boy, he'll be wanting to be known as Martha next!'

'But you mean...Marcus as in...' Julia stumbled with the words like someone running headlong and falling down a flight of stone steps.

'As in Marcus,' he finished the sentence for her as the waitress put her salad in front of her.

'Oh, squid is something I could die for!' said Robin, completely bound up by the vision on his plate. He squeezed the lemon juice over it, ostentatiously rotated the pepper mill, and said, '*Buon appetito*, my little Sweet Pea!' chirpily as ever.

Julia, meanwhile, was computing a billion flashbacks, tangential thoughts, action replays and every other permutation. It was suddenly like getting to the end of a film with a massive twist and a huge reveal, finding that the people you thought were alive were actually dead all the time and the ones that were the ghosts were the living people. You wanted to watch the whole film again in the light of the revelation. Julia now wanted to re-run most of her life in the light of the realisation that one of her oldest friends was having an affair with a bisexual man who had been the lover of the person that she was now enslaved by. Even Iris Murdoch couldn't have dreamed this one up. And there was Robin rocking around on his chair in a lather of "Oohs" and "Aahs", wiping up little patches of oil and lemon juice from his plate with torn-up chunks of ciabatta, completely oblivious to the hyperactive brain turmoil that she was experiencing.

So, that made sense of all that stuff at the start of the evening about being here before with Mark. He had obviously meant Mark/Marcus had been here with him at the height of their affair when he, Robin, had been as madly in love with Marcus as she herself was, now, with Robin. No wonder he had looked so wistful, and of course the way he said it implied that he assumed she had known that Mark and Marcus were one and the same. And of course a bell rang from ages back when she had been in the drama group. Angie had suggested that the reason Mark wasn't married was because, preposterously, he may have Indian blood and was afraid of being found out when all the while the real reason was that he was bisexual! How bizarre, she thought to herself, that Robin had assumed throughout the whole evening with Mel and Mark that she had already put two and two together and made the requisite four thousand and twenty-eight. So could he possibly think that she would be easy with all this? Did he imagine that by off-loading his most recent sexual history in a confessional, she had taken it all on board and thought nothing of it? Well, in a way, she had, but that was before the clunking reality of who his previous partner actually was had hit her like a piece of granite being hurled by urchins from a motorway bridge and through the driver's windscreen.

God, she thought to herself. *Does Mel know? I can't ask her. I can't tell her. Was Mark having an affair with Mel simultaneously as he was having this thing with Robin? What on earth's going on?!*

And as she tried to absorb the billion possibilities, Robin's voice seemed to come from a million miles away.

'You're quiet this evening, not the usual little twinkling star.'

She looked up and said, 'Uh, oh, it's squid envy.'

'Squid envy?'

'It's one of my little failings. I always want what the other person has ordered, even if I have taken twenty minutes to decide. I've got a dose of it now; I knew I shouldn't have ordered the lamb. It always gets stuck in your teeth for hours afterwards.'

Phew, she thought, *that sounded a very convincing speech.* Or did it? She hoped so since she needed to play for time to assimilate what she had just learned.

'So how was the day?'

'You won't believe this,' said Robin, grabbing her hand.

'I'm all ears,' she answered. 'Just try me!'

And this was an excuse for Julia to sit back and let Robin's "I wanted the ground to swallow me up" story to wash over her while a vision on Mark/Marcus kept floating past her eyes about once every two minutes.

'Well,' began Robin, 'you know how unbelievably boring old Cosgrave is. God knows how he's held that job of Principal for so long. You know he used to teach Classics and then saw the writing was on the wall, so did a couple of Russian evening classes and got an A-level by some miracle and then bluffed his way into teaching Russian instead. A bloody useless teacher he must have been! He once told me that he didn't have time for literature…couldn't see what people saw in it. His actual words were, "I'm more a news and weather forecast man myself". Anyway, he was the person, can you imagine this, who was supposed to be firing up A-level students with a grand passion for Dostoyevsky, Chekhov and Tolstoy. He's such a bore. And what's worse, he's our boss!'

'Couldn't agree more,' said Julia. 'But at least he's not the head of Modern Languages any more now that he's the Principal. That's left to Martin Cox – and he's not much better when it comes to intelligent conversation!'

'I absolutely agree with you there, and I can hardly bring myself to tell you what happened,' he said, almost blushing with embarrassment. 'The thing is, my old friend Tom Mercer used to teach at the college but he's really got his head in the clouds and isn't too good with names. I ran into him at lunchtime over in the White Lion where I'd gone for an hour's peace with the *Times* crossword. He mentioned that he'd actually run into Cosgrave about half an hour earlier and that he was totally boring and had nothing to say for himself, so he was quite relieved when a huge juggernaut had come along. It was so impossibly loud that they couldn't continue with the conversation and so it was an excuse for him to bid him farewell and go on his way. Later that afternoon I was in a finance meeting with both Cosgrave and Martin Cox. Cosgrave went on and on, and really seemed to have no grasp whatsoever of the overview of the college finances. He kept going off on tangents and everyone was almost falling asleep. When we finally broke for a cup of tea in the Senior Common Room I found myself standing behind Martin in the queue and said what a terrible bore Cosgrave was. Martin agreed. I then expanded on it by saying that my old pal Tom had met him in the street just before lunch and had said that he was so boring that he was hugely relieved that a juggernaut had come along thus giving him an excuse to terminate the conversation as they couldn't hear a word the other was saying. And do you know what Martin's next words were?'

Julia shook her head, hunched her shoulders and mimed the "Search me! How should I know?" sign with her hands.

'Martin said…oh, God, I can't bear to say it…Martin said, "No, Robin, that was *me*. *I* met Tom when I was crossing the road on my way to the newsagent to pick up the early edition of the *Standard*."

'Oh no!' shrieked Julia, letting her knife and fork drop as she clutched her face in a pretty passable impression of Edvard Munch's "Scream".

'Oh yes…I am expecting to have my contract terminated any minute. There was nothing I could say. Nothing at all. I knew when to stop digging. I will just have to live with him hating me for the rest of my life.'

'Well I have heard it said that if you tell someone they are boring or have no sense of humour, it's worse than telling them that they are not very good-looking,' said Julia, but this, of course, was not very helpful to Robin who had put his foot, knee, and whole upper body into it.

Robin caught sight of the waiters hovering in the distance and hurried to finish his squid as he hadn't eaten a single mouthful for a while, partly because he was speaking but also because he felt almost ill with embarrassment at his huge social gaffe.

As the main course was delivered to their table, Julia asked, 'Have you ever met Mel's husband, Deke?'

'No, I don't think I have,' he said. 'Deke's some kind of painter, isn't he? How long have they been married?'

'Oh, about seven years, maybe a bit more, but I don't really know what's going on now, to be honest. I had no idea that the thing between Mel and Mark was still going on. How, er – how do you feel about it?'

'Mark is a law unto himself,' said Robin, and looked back down at his plate.

'It's never quite the same eating fish inland, is it? What I would give now to be sitting at a table on the terrace of a little table overlooking a beach on the Mediterranean.'

'You can't beat it,' she sighed. 'What I love about some of those beaches is that you go there one summer, and I'm talking about the ones that the Italians go to, not the touristy ones, and you find big encampments of extended families under their umbrellas, all generations, grannies cuddling their latest baby grandchildren sitting right at the centre of the group in the deepest shade, children shrieking and running back and forth to the water, mums and dads shouting at them not to go too far out, maybe some weird suntanned old Neapolitan guy with some little bagpipe thing who serenades each of the umbrella camps, North African pedlar types selling beads and hairbands and other stuff, old chaps selling chunks of coconuts out of a bucket...'

And she stopped as she was aware that Robin was watching her with a dreamy expression and a half smile on his face.

'And don't even get me started on Venice!' he said.

It was as if the last bit of Italy talk had over-ridden all the earlier revelations. She was beginning to calm down. *No,* she said to herself, *Mark is over and done with. He's with Mel. He's not gay. He's just an opportunist. Forget it.*

'We can't have come here without having the you-know-what,' she joked.

'And to think…we were so busy putting our suntan lotion on and enjoying the sun on your Italian beach we almost forgot about our *Charlottes,'* he quipped. 'I wish I knew how they made them and then we could serve them at dinner parties.'

She noted the 'we'.

'What you really mean is,' said Julia, 'you wish you knew how they made them then you could put on a couple of stone by eating too many of them.'

'Me? I have a sensational body as you will discover,' he replied. And with that, he ordered the espressos.

Julia squirmed with pleasure, and silently scooped up the remaining cream on her plate. She was so hungry for signs that he meant business with this relationship that any small thing said in passing assumed epic proportion. What had been said by him in jest would no doubt be written verbatim in her diary that evening. She would linger over the phrase "sensational body" and the implications thereof. However, she got no nearer to discovering any secrets of the sensational body that evening as he simply kissed her briskly on the lips, stepped back, grinned and locked eyes with her for a few seconds before sending her off into the night.

Later that night, as she was walking down the road to her basement flat, she realised that she needed to get away to think about things. Miranda, a very old school friend whom she had known when she was still young enough to play hopscotch, had married a burly Welshman called Owen. The couple had met on their first day at university. They were living in a stunning but remote farmhouse about twenty miles from Cardiff with only sheep and chickens for company. Julia thought it would be a good idea to have a long weekend and a bit of breathing space if there weren't any other guests at the farmhouse that weekend. Miranda was a great sounding board for relationship stuff. She could have worked as an agony aunt. As Monday mornings were free on Julia's timetable this would be perfect. When she got home she gave them a ring and invited herself to stay.

'That will be magic!' yelled Miranda over the noise of Poppy hurling Lego bricks across the playroom and Ethan hammering his broken fire-engine with a die cast oak tree from the model farm. 'And guess what, I'm pregnant again. The new baby's due on the twins' fourth birthday!'

'Wow! Lucky you,' said Julia. 'How are you feeling? Are you as sick as you were with the twins?'

'Let's just say that as long as I eat a digestive biscuit on the hour, every hour, it's OK this time, but I'm looking like a galleon under full sail at the moment.'

'Rubbish, you're probably radiant.' Julia laughed. 'Anyway, see you Friday night...'

'Actually, can we make that Saturday morning? I've got to clean the flat up a bit and get organised...but I can stay over till Monday morning. I don't have to be in college till first period in the afternoon.'

'Fine. Just let us know when you're getting in and Owen can meet you on his way back from his squash game. He does boys' stuff on Saturday mornings.'

'As long as you get time for girls' stuff too!' said Julia, relieved to have her weekend plans sorted. 'And I've got some lurve news for you as well.'

'Can't wait! Poppy! Excuse me a sec, Jules...Poppy, will you *stop* that at once! Sorry, Julia, got to dash!' And with that the phone clicked dead.

Julia searched up and down the bookshelves to find a suitable novel to see her through the inevitable train delays. *Robertson*

Davies will be fine, she thought. *We could be stuck in the Severn Tunnel for about four days and I still would have something to keep me occupied, but God, it weighs a ton and it's only the paperback. I would've needed a wheelbarrow for the hardback.* So, jeans, a bit of clean underwear, and a couple of jumpers and she was sorted. As long as she had a book, all was well.

A newspaper might well run out before the end of the journey. However, Julia had a nagging suspicion that she was going to be joining the ranks of those people who gaze into the middle distance on long journeys, lost in thought, and having no need of printed distraction. Her head was having to do a lot of processing at present, although her heart was still pulling at her coat and saying, *No, let's just read a few love poems and pretend it's all fine.* Because, of course, in some ways, Julia's life was much more than fine. She was walking a few feet off the ground and even one of her colleagues who knew nothing of her recent dalliance with Robin said that she seemed to be behaving like a 16-year-old.

'Oh God, I'm suffering from Stockholm Syndrome,' she joked in reply. 'I've only been teaching my A-level group for a couple of terms and I've become one of them!' It took all of her inner resolve to resist saying, *Yes, that's because I've fallen in love.*

Next day she went out in search of presents for the twins and managed to find a wonderful plastic suit of armour and all its attendant bits for Ethan and was in a great quandary about what to get Poppy. She was worried that, having bought an aggressive boy toy for Ethan, she would be pandering to sexist instincts by getting a dressing-up doll for Poppy, but then spotted the most magical large pink wand. When you swished it around violently it made a series of bloop-bleep noises and lots of coloured stars flashed on and off on the pointy star bit at the end of the wand. *Oh sod sexism!* she thought to herself. *I don't care. Poppy's going to love this, and I bet even Eeth will fight her for it...and then use it as a lethal weapon! Now...just a bottle of Sauvignon and some chocolates for the grown-ups and I'm done.*

On Saturday morning she got up early and caught the Tube to Paddington, the handle of the long plastic sword poking up strangely out of her hand luggage. What with the wine bottle and the Robertson Davies, her bag felt as if she was going away for two weeks rather than two nights.

The train was already in and she went and found her seat. Most of the train was half empty except for the bit with the reserved seats where the little white flaps stuck out on top of every single seat. She took one look at her reserved place and decided that it would probably be better to go and look for something quieter. Two carriages down she found an empty table and got out her book and popped the offensive weapon bag down in the gap between her seat and the one behind. Shortly before the train pulled out, a girl in her late twenties arrived with a piece of hand luggage and heaved it up onto the rack. A moment later, she stood up again, removed her jacket and popped it up on top alongside the bag. She was wearing a white t-shirt with "Ready to Rock" written across it, and a pair of dark blue jeans with a glittery sequined motif on the left buttock. The blue jacket, which was very well-cut Julia noted, elevated the jeans and t-shirt to extremely smart casual, whereas without it she passed for a mature student on her way to the college library. A third passenger (male) asked them if either of the other two seats were taken, and when assured that they were both free, he sat down next to the other girl so that they were both facing Julia.

The train started its lengthy trundle through Westbourne Park and Acton and by 10.30 they were soon racing through Ealing Broadway and urban sprawl gave way to storage units, gasometers, factory car parks and, eventually, fields. Julia was making quite good progress with *The Deptford Trilogy* and had already got to page 49. This was not such a phenomenal achievement since the book seemed to have about six pages with nothing much on them except the title, a few headings and pithy quotations and therefore really began on page 13.

The drinks trolley made its slow progress through the carriage and about thirty-five minutes into the journey, Julia glanced up to see that the girl opposite was pulling her bag down from the rack, picking up her handbag and smiling at the man next to her to give a signal that she would like to get out. She disappeared down the corridor and out through the sliding door at the end so that she would be in position by the door when the train stopped at Reading in a few more minutes. Julia, by this time, had lost her momentum on her book and started to think once again about Mel and Mark. She now of course had that picture in her head of Robin and Mark together as a couple too and tried not to go there. She wondered how many other people knew about this and were silently laughing at her. The gay world was not known for its compassion and sweetness. Still, Robin had shown such devotion to her during the meal and certainly seemed to be thinking along the lines of a trip to Italy in a couple of months. As her mind once more started on its stream of consciousness through the Tuscan hills, she felt the train judder a little as it started to brake and Reading gaol was visible on the left. The train gradually stopped at platform 4 and there was the usual hustle and bustle of people getting off and on. New passengers shuffled down the aisle past her, carrying their bags at odd angles to negotiate the long narrow space, and anxious parents glanced repeatedly behind to make sure their children were following them on their overbalancing route march down the train.

Julia was just about to look back down at her book when she noticed up above her, the jacket belonging to the girl who had been in the seat opposite. The train was just about to leave the station and there was a man just outside the window with a whistle in his mouth, holding a flag aloft and signalling to the driver that it was OK to depart. Julia dragged the jacket down, jumped to her feet and ran down the aisle, barging past an old woman who was standing up and rummaging in her bag still trying to find her purse. She dived through the sliding doors, and pulled down the window of the door of the train and shouted, 'Excuse me!' at the station man with the whistle, but it was too late. The train was already moving at a snail's pace along the platform. He had seen her, but didn't make any move towards her. With one massive effort she hurled the jacket back along the platform at him and it hit him in the face.

'Woman's jacket!' she cried. 'Passenger got off at Reading. Left this behind!'

The station apparatchik got her drift, and to signal that he understood, nodded and waved the jacket in a gesture of goodbye. Her last glimpse of him was when he plodded over to a small office next to the sandwich shop where, no doubt, the girl from the opposite seat would be almost weeping tears of joy in a few moments to discover that her lost property had been returned to her with such swiftness and efficiency.

Julia nipped to the buffet car, collected a coffee, and then got back to her seat. There was, by now, an old lady with a small Boston terrier sitting on her lap on the seat next to Julia's. The dog looked like it was distinctly unhappy with being on a train. It had, what her mother, a great dog lover, had once called, "travelling ears". The ears which should normally stand upright like little ping pong bats were poking out sideways in an attitude of submission and discomfort. Both the old lady and the dog looked a bit put out at having to stand up to let her back into her seat, but in a moment or two everything calmed down again. The dog gave a snort and a huge sigh of the sort common to all flat-nosed breeds, and wriggled its way into a sleeping position with its chin in the crook of the elderly lady's folded arm. Julia gave a quick grin at the man sitting opposite, picked up her book and commenced reading.

She must have read another page and a half when the sliding doors made their whooshing sound and Julia glanced up to see if it was the ticket inspector or just someone lurching along through the train to the buffet car. It was neither of these. It was the girl who had been sitting opposite, once again carrying her piece of hand luggage, but now with immaculate hair, makeup which transformed her face, and having changed into a very flattering skirt in exactly the same shade of blue as the jacket which Julia had thrown out of the train at Reading. The man opposite looked briefly up from his newspaper in Julia's direction as he stood to let the fashionable girl back to her seat. It was also at that moment that Julia took in the fact that she was wearing a little spray of freesias in her shirt...she was obviously on her way to a wedding. Julia knew at that moment what people mean when they say they aged by ten years. The colour drained from Julia's face and she tried to look back at her book, desperately computing all the possible responses. For a moment everything was quiet except for the Boston terrier who snorted, shuddered, and slightly changed his body position on the old woman's lap, and his toes started to open and close in concert with his jowls which also started to twitch as he entered the depths of a doggy dream.

The girl looked up briefly to the luggage rack, then back at Julia, and then at the man. Neither was looking in her direction.

'Where's my jacket?' she said, frantically looking back and forth between them.

'Where's my bloody jacket?' she asked a second time. The man looked at Julia but was obviously not going to say a word.

'I...er...I...er threw it out of the train.'

'You WHAT?!' screamed the girl.

'I thought you'd got out at Reading and left it behind. I was being kind. I told the guy who was in charge that you had left it on the train. They'll have it there for you. I'm so terribly sorry. It's just that you got up just before Reading and took your bag and...'

But of course she never got further.

'But I'm going to a wedding! I'll never get back in time! I've got to change at Didcot and catch another train! I really can't believe this is happening!' she was screaming almost hysterically by now.

'Look, I am so very, very sorry,' stammered Julia. 'If it's any help, please let me give you the train fare back to Reading. If you're lucky you may well find there's another train back straight away and it may not be too much of a disaster.' And Julia opened her wallet and started hunting for notes to hand over.

'Piss off!' replied the girl, and gathered all her bits of luggage and stormed out of the carriage in a rage.

Julia sat where she was, going hot and cold and feeling her heart pounding.

'It was a genuine mistake,' she said to her travelling companions but the man kept his eyes resolutely down and the old lady looked bewildered as she hadn't understood much of anything except the "Piss off!" at the grand finale. As for the dog, he just shuddered again.

'Oh God, oh please God, let me be in Cardiff, let me be off this train,' said Julia under her breath.

Chapter Ten

When the train arrived in Cardiff, Julia was deeply relieved to see Owen in the distance dressed in sports gear, and waving a copy of the *Western Mail.*

'Croeso! Welcome to the Principality!' he said, giving her a big hug and, to her slight embarrassment, a kiss on the lips rather than the cheek. He was a big, burly man with a beard and moustache and a bit of leer in his eyes. Sexual innuendo was never very far from his conversation and he was the kind of man who was unable to use normal everyday words such as "hard", "chest", "come" or "Roger", in any innocent context without implying there was an extra layer of meaning. Julia put it down to his schoolboy rugby days and pitied Miranda having to put up with it constantly.

'How's Miranda?' asked Julia straight away, wanting to get the conversation back to a point where she was establishing her main reason for the visit.

'Pretty good,' he replied. 'But a bit bovine. She can't wait to get it over with.' There was a slight pause and then he added, 'Neither can I; a chap's got to do what a chap's got to do.'

Too much information, thought Julia to herself, but simply gave a little insincere grin and put her bags into the back of the car, asking, 'And the kids?'

'Oh they're good,' Owen answered as he turned the ignition key and swivelled in his seat to make sure he wasn't mowing anyone down as he reversed out of the parking space.

'Ethan's into cowboys at the moment,' he said. 'You'll probably find him creeping into your bed wearing his holster and guns. That's my boy!'

God, is there nothing I can say? she thought to herself.

'Well I hope he likes my present,' she ventured. 'I've bought him a suit of armour; I was worrying that you and Miranda would think it was a bit too combative and aggressive.'

'No worries there; he'll love it.'

'Did you actually grow up in Cardiff?' asked Julia as they wove through the suburbs.

'Yep, see that tower block over there? That used to be an old brewery. I remember that they used to have big dray horses when I was a kid.'

Julia gazed across at the tower block trying to imagine how it must have looked in the forties and fifties.

'And that bus station used to be the old cattle market,' he added.

Julia now tried to show serious interest in his heritage.

'How fascinating,' she said.

A minute or two later he said, 'And that used to be a car park over there.'

Julia looked unsmilingly in the direction in which he was nodding as he drove.

It took a second or two for the penny to drop and for her to realise that it actually *was* a car park and that he was teasing her. She burst out laughing and realised that despite all the stupid sexy stuff he was a very droll bloke and no doubt kept Miranda amused. When she got out of the car about forty-five minutes later and saw the way the children flew into his arms, she realised that he was also a very good dad, too.

Miranda was in the doorway clapping her hands to shoo the chickens away from the front garden. Julia got out of the car and stood up trying to take in the entire panorama before her.

The setting was stunning. The farmhouse was on the south side of a huge rolling valley with a stream running through it. A cluster of sheep grazed in an upper field in the distance and cows were coming in a slow procession back through a gap in a hedge down near the stream. The air was sparkling and clear and the gentle warbling of woodpigeons was the only sound other than Poppy and Ethan screaming as Owen swung them round on the little lawn in front of the grey stone house.

'Blimey, sure you're not expecting quads!' exclaimed Julia as she saw Miranda in profile as she turned to open the gate and come to greet her.

'A lot of it's water, so my doctor says; Owen says it's all mashed potatoes and digestive biscuits but what would he know? At least it's not beer! But anyway, enough of me, how are you?'

'Well, don't even ask me about the journey,' laughed Julia. 'But in every other way, brilliant.'

'So what's his name?' asked Miranda.

And before Julia could tell her, Owen's voice shouted over, 'And has he got a big one?'

'Shut up, pervert,' Miranda chided him, and linked arms with Julia, taking her into the house. The house was like some kind of magical little folk museum with horse brasses, hunting horns, painted plates mounted on the walls and giant Welsh dressers laden with willow pattern china. A coal fire blazed behind an ornate fireguard and Julia spotted a toasting fork recently laid down in the hearth with a few crumbs beside it.

'I haven't toasted bread on an open fire since my grandma was alive!' exclaimed Julia.

'Oh this is toast city here,' said Miranda. 'But before we were so rudely interrupted, what's his name?'

'Robin...Robin Forester,' Julia complied.

'Mmm...Julia Forester...not bad,' said Miranda.

'Oh, for heaven's sake we haven't got that far yet!' said Julia in mock outrage, but couldn't deny that she had never run it past her own brain a few times and had even done the adolescent thing of trying a signature on a piece of paper, not to mention trying out children's names that went well with Forester. Beware of Maurice and Doris!

'Bring him down here and the old Welsh air will get him going,' said Owen. 'Look what it's done for Miranda!'

Miranda threw a Jeye cloth playfully at him while Ethan came into the room shyly and said, 'Julia, what's that sword thing in your bag?'

'That didn't take you long, did it?' she grinned. 'Come on, Eeth, come and help me find all the presents. There may just possibly be one for you...or was that the sword I bought for Pops?' But the sight of his little crumpled face made her immediately retract and say, 'Don't worry, the sword is yours, Mr Gladiator.'

They heard his little squeal of 'Oh wow!' as he scampered off in the direction of Julia's bag.

'I can't believe how they've both grown!' Julia said. 'But I suppose that's what all ancient great aunts say. Just listen to me! As if they were going to shrink or stay the same size!'

'Tea?' Miranda asked?

'Please,' answered Julia.

'I don't suppose there's any point offering you one, is there?' Miranda asked Owen.

'No, you bet there isn't. I'm off for a pint with Evan down at the Lamb and Flag. See you in about an hour, OK Randy?'

'Somehow I don't think that particular diminutive is exactly apposite right now!' his very pregnant wife replied and nudged him out through the door.

And with that, Owen was off and his estate car roared off down the bumpy track to the road where the rest of civilization travelled about half a mile in the distance.

'This is paradise, Miranda,' said Julia.

'Yeah, we've sort of achieved our dream location, even done the "good life" thing, but it scares me sometimes because it's so far from everything, like now, for example! Imagine how long it's going to take to get me to Cardiff Royal Infirmary!'

'Oh Lord, if it was me I'd already be camping down there in readiness,' said Julia, amazed that Miranda was being so cool about something that was quite scary. 'What'll you do about the twins?'

'Oh no worries. Owen's Mum's coming to stay next week and she'll just be here for the duration until about three weeks after this little monkey pops out. It's OK, Jules, don't look so worried. It's not for about five weeks yet, despite what I look like!'

At that moment Poppy and Ethan appeared in the doorway dragging Julia's bag along between them.

'OK! Let's pretend it's Christmas,' said Julia. 'Stand up straight! Eyes shut! Hands out in front!'

Miranda also obeyed and Julia gave her the chocolates but cautioned, 'I think Mummy had better open her eyes before I give her the wine, eh kids?'

'Well that'll be something for you and Owen to enjoy tonight,' said Miranda, opening one eye and peering at the label. 'My drinking days are over until I stop feeding Mini Griffiths number three.'

'Oh stop *talking,* Mummy!' said Ethan impatiently as he was jiggling up and down on the spot with excitement at the idea of his present.

'Right, Eeth, and promise not to kill your sister or chop the hens' heads off!' cautioned Julia as she handed over the large plastic mesh sack with its shiny grey plastic breastplate, sword, and helmet with visor.

'Brilliant!' he yelled, and plunged his head into the helmet.

'Eeth, careful!' shouted Miranda. 'You'll slice your ears off!'

But he was already struggling to put the breastplate over his head and realised that it wouldn't work unless he took the helmet off and started again. Meanwhile, Julia produced the gift-wrapped wand for Poppy who was waiting patiently, head thrown back and squinting out of little crinkled slits to get a stealthy peep at her present.

'Now listen to this, Pops,' she said. 'See if you can guess what it is.'

'Ooh, Poppy, let's see if we can work out what it is, shall we?' said Miranda.

Poppy was dancing up and down. Julia swung the wand down rapidly from its first position above her head down to knee-level. The magical 'bloop-bleep-bloop' sound came from within the package.

'What on earth can it be?' said Miranda, smiling at her daughter.

'A musical thing?' replied a somewhat baffled Poppy.

'What kind of noise is that? Shall we do it again?' asked Julia. She repeated the swishing motion, and reprised the sound.

'It's a spaceship sound,' suggested Poppy.

'Well, close…it's a magic sound,' said Julia. 'Now what kind of people use magic things?'

Poppy did that over-exaggerated facial expression thing that small children do so well, as if they are understudying Shirley Temple. But then the penny dropped.

'Magicians!' she screamed.

'No, but you're getting warm.'

'Wizards and witches?'

'Warmer…but think of something smaller.'

'Fairies!' yelled Poppy, and rushed over to take the wand from Julia.

'Well done, Poppy! And I think you'll find it's got some magic fairy lights too as well as magic sounds.'

'Isn't that wonderful, Pops?' said Miranda. 'Now what do you say to Julia?'

A little voice said a shy 'thank you' as she started to wave the wand around. However, no sound or magic lights appeared.

'We can wave that each time we want Daddy to come back from the Lamb and Flag, can't we?' Miranda said, and Julia noticed a fleeting sad and exasperated look pass over her friend's face.

'Come here, Poppy,' said Julia, trying to change Miranda's mood. 'Look, you need to do it a bit more violently otherwise it doesn't work. I'll hold your arm…one, two, three, whoosh! There you go! You did it!' And a burst of flashing lights and "bloop-bleep-bloop" noises filled the farmhouse kitchen.

'Congratulations! You're a fully qualified fairy now. You can go and cast some spells over your brother. You have to say, "Abracadabra" each time you do a spell.'

Poppy raced off down the corridor shouting, 'Abracadabra!' at the top of her voice, waving the big pink wand frantically up and down, attempting to turn her mini-gladiator twin brother into a bucket of horse poo.

'They're great, Miranda! You must be so proud of them,' said Julia.

'Great or not, they don't half exhaust me, and Owen is away at work such a lot of the time. And even when he's here, he finds the Lamb and Flag a bit more enticing than a game of the Incy Wincy Spider board game with the kids.'

'Are you worried about how much he drinks or just that he doesn't pull his weight at home?' asked Julia.

'A bit of both really…how much is too much? He says he's just a social drinker, but I think he would find it quite hard to live without it. And people, his mates that is, say he's such a laugh when he's had a drink that it makes him think it's kind of, I don't know, attractive I suppose.'

'At least his Mum is coming to stay and maybe she can instil a bit of sense into him,' said Julia reassuringly, but could see where Miranda was coming from, and, given the remote location of the farmhouse, it was not the perfect place for a woman with two small children, a baby and a good brain to be spending one hundred per cent of her life.

The two women prepared a pasta lunch for themselves and the children and Miranda proffered a glass of wine.

'OK, now about this Robert chap…'

'No, Robin,' Julia corrected her. 'Well, it's not all as plain sailing as it could be.'

'We've got at least an hour before Owen gets back, and the

kids will be happy with their presents for a while. Let's deconstruct it, Jules. First, how did you meet him?'

Julia proceeded to tell her the whole story, but, in detailing all
rather limited instances of physical intimacy considering that
these were two people who couldn't seemingly take their eyes off
one another, she felt a bit uncomfortable, as if, by telling it to
someone, she was having to admit a certain unease to herself.

'Maybe he's just a bit shy,' suggested Miranda. 'After all, he
had a long relationship with this Mark fellow, and it was
undoubtedly one of much rumpy-pumpy however you might
not wish to imagine it. Then maybe he's scared that he'll do it
wrong, that he won't measure up to what you are expecting.'

'Let's leave measuring out of it,' giggled Julia. 'Size doesn't
matter!'

'No, you know what I mean.' Miranda laughed. 'If he's feeling
anxious about a heterosexual display of bed games, then that
very anxiety may inhibit him and he may feel reluctant to do
anything physical that will lead you down the road to a mattress
and a feather pillow and a bit of striptease.'

'I sort of agree with you,' said Julia. 'That's just how I've ratio-
nalised it to myself. I keep telling myself that he actually does
fancy me, and that the whole man-on-man thing was a bit of an
aberration and that once we commit properly it will all slot into
place. He does, after all keep making references to all the things
we are going to do together as we ride off into the sunset. It's just
that when push comes to shove, he won't do any shoving.'

'There's only one thing for it then,' said Miranda. 'You'll have
to seduce him in a way that doesn't threaten him.'

'Oh shit,' said Julia, suddenly taking a massive gulp of the
Sauvignon, 'I'm really backward in coming forward and really
very shy and don't know if I could ever be brave enough. I'm too
scared of making a fool of myself.'

'You'd be brave enough if you were convinced it was going to
do the trick. Your problem is you are empathising far too much

with him and if both of you are dead scared it's all going to go horribly wrong. Then, even this beautiful marriage of minds and souls that you both have is going to be fucked and at present it seems like neither of you wants to risk that,' said Miranda, putting on her psychotherapist's cap for a moment. 'Let me just ask you this, Julia, and I hope you won't be offended, if he asked you to marry him but said that he didn't think he could cope with the physical stuff, would you still say yes?'

There was a long pause. Julia gazed into the flames of the log burner leaping away behind their little door. 'I hate myself for saying this, but yes. D'you know, at present, given the way I feel, yes, I would.'

'Well, I hope the beautiful union of souls is going to be enough. I kind of think that you are in serious danger of losing yourself, Jules. I really care about you, but you know what? You've got to stick up for yourself here. You're not some immigrant lesbian entering a marriage of convenience to stay in the country and get a British passport. You want to have kids; you want to have the kind of marriage that most other people have; just having him look lovingly at you simply isn't enough, and anyway, in the end he would fall for another bloke. The grass is always greener for people like him.'

'I know!' said Julia, in an ultra camp impersonation of Kenneth Williams, trying to diffuse this conversation. 'A girl's got her needs!'

'Kindness and humour will get you only so far, Jules, unless you take the bull by the horns and make the first move,' chided Miranda, and then, glancing out of the window, she yelled, 'Ethan Griffiths! Will you stop that IMMEDIATELY! You'll break Mummy's car if you go on whacking that sword around over there! Go and play on the other side of the garden!'

'Anyway,' said Julia, 'he's agreed to come to my birthday party that I'm organising for myself, and all the gang can give him the once-over.'

'I so wish I could be there.' Miranda sighed longingly. 'But I've got this little creature to prepare for,' and she cuddled her enormous tummy. 'I suppose Sarah and Nigel will be there. I'll have to ring Sarah to get the low-down.'

Owen came back so late from the Lamb and Flag that he didn't want any lunch. He said he'd had a sandwich with the boys and that he was off to watch a bit of rugby on TV and disappeared into the rather chilly sitting room on the north side of the house.

'Will you be warm enough in there? Why don't you light the fire?' suggested Miranda.

'No, I'll be fine, and Julia can always come and give me a hug to keep me warm,' Owen said.

Julia gave a weak smile that only involved her mouth but no other part of her face and looked down at the red tiles of the kitchen floor.

'Why don't you go and have a lie down yourself, Miranda?' she suggested. 'I can take the kids out for a walk over the fields. I'd love to go down and have a look at the stream over there. Can I borrow some wellies?'

'Fabulous!' said Miranda. 'I just can't get through the day without a rest; I've got terrible back ache with this one. Just half an hour and I'll be a new woman. You'll find some boots out there by the washing machine. What size are you? Five? Six? I think there are a couple of pairs of thick socks there as well if they're too loose.'

'Stay as long as you like,' advised Julia. 'I'm in heaven here; it makes me feel I'm crazy to be living in London.'

With that, Miranda dragged her heavy body up the ancient farmhouse stairs and Julia marshalled the children into their wellies, finding the appropriate pair for herself.

'Come on, kids,' she called as she strode off towards the gap in the hedge of the field opposite the house, 'let's see if we can find a four-leafed clover to bring Mummy some good luck shall we?'

The children scampered after her, shrieking with one false alarm after another that they had found the elusive four-leafed clover, but at least it gave them something to concentrate on as they did the first phase of the expedition to the stream. Julia stopped at one point to wait for them and as she looked down to see if she herself could find any clover, she saw a field mouse scuttling around in the grass. *That's just what I've become,* she thought, *scuttling, nervous, over-busy, needing this constant assurance from my pals…something's wrong and I don't know what it is.* However, at that point there was a shriek from Poppy. 'Julia! Help! Help! Ethan's sinking! He's disappearing!'

Oh my God! Julia said to herself and hurtled down the field not caring if there were whole nests of adders or craters of dead owls, headless torsos or any of the other nightmarish things her cousin used to tease her about and frighten her with when they had to walk home through farmland when she was younger.

'Where?! Where?!' she screamed back at the white-faced little girl who was scampering on ahead.

Then suddenly she saw him almost up to his waist in a very wet bog which had formed all around the edges of the stream. Here and there were large dark earthy puddles and the occasional very sloppy cow pat. Marsh marigolds bobbed about nearer to the brook and a couple of flag irises waved this way and that. Ethan's face was white. He was opening and shutting his mouth but no speech was coming out. His arms were outspread either side of him as if he was a bird about to flap and take off.

'Ethan! Stay still, sweetheart!' yelled Julia as she got nearer to him. 'Don't move, darling, just keep very still.'

The little boy was so terrified that he couldn't even cry. He just stared back at her with enormous eyes. As Julia plunged to within yards of him, she felt her own feet delve deep down into the muck, but didn't care what happened to her as long as she pulled Ethan out. As she lunged for him she shouted back over her shoulder, 'Pops, stay where you are! I don't want to have to pull two of you out!'

There was no fear of that. Poppy was transfixed, watching her Amazing Disappearing Brother. Ethan seemed to be rooted to the bog with semi-hardening superglue and it took all of Julia's effort to move him even a few centimetres, but then, with an almighty heave, she heard a loud slurp as his little legs, clad only in his socks, shot out of the ground. She hugged his wet, smelly, muddy body to her and cried with relief as she repeated over and over again, 'Oh Ethan, oh Ethan, oh Ethan!' But she didn't really want either of the children to see that she had been genuinely terrified, so, with great presence of mind, said, 'Just look at me, you two! All that effort made my eyes water! Gosh, you were heavy, Eeth, I thought you were the giant turnip and we would have to leave you there all night or else get a tractor to pull you out!'

But this wasn't the right thing to say and poor Ethan finally gave way to tears, beginning with a silent opening of his mouth to a giant rectangle, followed by an ear-piercing wail. Julia cuddled and hugged him in a desperate effort to calm him down, at the same time searching frantically for any sight of his wellingtons. Eventually, the wailing subsided and he was simply giving giant shudders and sighs and occasionally little shivers. Julia waded back, mud up to her own ankles, to a drier part of the field and sat him down and said to Poppy, 'Now, Pops, I want you to be very grown up and good and sit here with Eeth for a minute while I just try to find his wellies.'

'Yuk! They'll be all cow-poo-ey!' Poppy squealed, and both children shrieked with laughter, the kind of hysteria bred of relief that a drama had been averted. For some reason, Ethan found the word "cow-poo-ey" hilarious and repeated it over and over again. *I don't care if he's repeating "cunnilingus" a hundred times,* thought Julia, *just as long as I find his bloody boots,* and she returned to the scene of the crime and poked about with a stick which she found nearby. By digging her arms almost to the elbows in the gunk, she finally located the boots which, remarkably, didn't have too much squelchy stuff inside as there were two big impressions which had recently been filled by Ethan's legs.

She suddenly had an amazing sense of déja vu as she realised this was almost identical to a story that Robin had told her about his own childhood.

She picked Ethan up and got Poppy to carry the offending items which she held out at arms' length while Ethan cheerily chanted "Cow-poo-ey" over and over again and giggled all the way back to the house.

'What on earth's going on?' asked a bewildered Miranda as she waddled sleepily into the bathroom a while later. Ethan was standing naked in the bath, and Julia was busy showering him down. The bath was a swirling mess of black runny mud from the bog. Poppy by this time had lost interest and was playing a private game of her own with two plastic figures in the hand basin.

'Man overboard, I'm afraid,' said Julia. 'Well, not actually, but Eeth was re-enacting the Slough of Despond from *Pilgrim's Progress.*'

'That's why I love you, Jules,' said Miranda. 'Even when my silly little imp here has fallen in the bog, you've got a quote from John Bunyan. You should have gone on *University Challenge!*'

'I did,' said Julia. 'My team was rubbish and I only answered one question. Don't let's go there. I was so miserable and it was all so hot and stressful under the lights that I went out and threw up in the Granada car park while Bamber was back in the green room knocking back the hospitality Frascati and regaling the boffins from Newcastle about his latest oeuvre on the Mughal emperors.'

Miranda started giggling.

'What was the question? I hope you "well-interrupted"'

'Well that's the irony of it. As you know, I never did any

science subjects at school because I was always a language student. I picked up a "Quiz Time For the Family" book which had been on our shelf at home for donkey's years. I think I bought it in Woolworths when I was about thirteen. I read it on the train up to Manchester. To my utter astonishment, he started asking the very same question that I had read on the train, something about one of the planets being the hottest, and I buzzed and stammered out "Venus" and that was all I ever said.'

'Well just think what would have happened if John Bunyan had come up, you would have got into the finals! Look Ethan, you can put your Spiderman top on to show Julia if you like,' said Miranda, adding, sotto voce, 'He was so obsessed with it for a while that he wore it every day and wouldn't take it off to go to bed so I had to pull it off him to wash it after he was asleep each night and tumble it dry before morning.'

By the time she had finished, Ethan was already in his Spiderman top, and, in bare feet, climbing up the frame of the open bathroom door with his hands and legs spread-eagled.

'Oh no you don't,' said Miranda, scooping him up in her arms as he wriggled and protested at being dragged down when half way to the top, 'that's very dangerous. Just imagine what would have happened to your fingers and toes if someone had closed the door.' But he was already scampering off to his bedroom to look for another risky pursuit before she could add any further footnotes to her lecture on health and safety in the home.

'Come on, Mummy,' said Jules, grinning. 'Let's make you a cup of tea. I'll pop the kids' clothes into the washing machine as we go down. I'm not sure about the wellies. I think they just need to go near the boiler to dry out and then you'll just have to bang them up and down to shake out all the dried up mud and dust. On the other hand, they may end up a bit smelly. God knows how many cows plod about down there near that stream. I'm really, really sorry. I should have kept my eyes on them a bit more closely. I think I just drifted off in my head for a moment or two. It was such bliss to be out there in the fresh air.'

'Don't even give it another thought,' said Miranda, 'they're country kids. They've got to learn to deal with these things. Let's go and see if Sleeping Beauty wants a cup.' And she pushed open the door of the sitting room. 'Nope, solid gone,' she said, shutting the door gently behind her. 'He'll probably wake up in time to uncork a bottle for supper tonight.'

'Are you sure you'll be all right when the baby's born?' asked Julia, looking rather anxious at the idea of Miranda trying to look after three young children while her husband auditioned for Alcoholics Anonymous.

'Oh, don't worry, he'll rise to the occasion for a couple of months like he did with the twins,' said Miranda, and she flicked down the kettle switch and held the small of her back with her left hand as she bent down to pick up Poppy's discarded boots from in front of the stove.

'Is there anything I can do to help once we've had tea?' asked Julia, feeling that she wasn't really doing enough to help.

'How about if you just do beans on toast for the kids and then read them a story after their bath. That way I can get on with supper. It's almost all done anyway. I made a great big pot of spicy chicken casserole with heaps of coconut in it. I've just got to do some rice and we can probably make do with a bit of smoked salmon and brown bread to start. How does that grab you?'

'I don't know how you have time to wash your face once a day, let alone cook ahead of time with two little children and another on the way,' said Julia, shaking her head with disbelief.

'Well, you know what they say: If you need a job doing urgently, ask a busy person to do it.' Miranda smiled. 'I think I'd feel a bit different if we still lived in London, but it's so tranquil down here, at least when the kids are at playschool for an hour or two. I find it really therapeutic, except recently since I've developed a bit of back ache but it'll be OK. That's the trouble with being pregnant. You do the impression of someone balancing a sack of potatoes on their chest. You lean further and further back to compensate until you almost go over backwards.'

'I can't even begin to imagine being pregnant, let alone giving birth,' said Julia.

'When my waters broke with Poppy, Owen was so worried about me making a mess on the carpet he reached for the first thing he could find and asked me to jump into it. It was a big seed tray from the spare room that we'd used to stand all the geraniums in during the winter as we didn't have a greenhouse in those days. When I got to hospital and they told me to have bath, I stepped out of my shoes and all this earth and grit fell off my feet like I'd run over a bloody ploughed field to get there.'

'But did it hurt like hell?'

'Only sort of like having all your teeth pulled out without anaesthetic.' Miranda laughed as she saw Julia's stricken face. 'No, not really like that! Don't look so worried. To be honest I thought I'd really cracked it because I'd read about raspberry leaf tablets in some health food mag being very good for child-birth. I took loads of the little buggers every single day of the pregnancy and then when I got into the labour ward a big Jamaican midwife shoved her hand up inside me and said—' and here Miranda began to sound as if she was doing a Bob Marley impression '"—Your womb is very favourable, Mrs Griffiths." I was virtually punching the air and going "Yes! Yes! Thanks, raspberry leaves!" at that point as I thought I was going to drop Poppy out like a small poo.'

'And was it? Like a small poo, I mean?' asked Julia, now intrigued.

'I wish!' said Miranda. 'About eight hours later they were standing around saying if I didn't manage to push her out next time they would have to use forceps. I can remember saying back to them, "Use a bloody hammer and chisel or whatever it takes, just get it out!" I had really begun to panic by then.'

'And did they? Use forceps, that is?'

'Yep, they finally got her out and I burst into tears of relief and I have some vague recollection of an African doctor rummaging around with needle and thread somewhere between my legs while I sobbed like a baby and just stared at her. She was yelling too. God, what a pair we were.'

'Was Owen there? What was he doing?' asked Julia.

'Oh, yeah, he was there. I think if my memory serves me rightly he was pouring two large brandies – one for himself and one for the Tailor of Gloucester... Uh-oh, here comes the Master! Stand to attention.'

A tousled Owen wandered into the kitchen, rubbing his hand through his hair.

'One in the pot for the working man?' he asked sheepishly.

'Possibly, but only if you can walk in a straight line,' his wife said. 'I think I'll have to make a fresh one.'

Owen held his arms out as if walking an imaginary plank, pretended to wobble and threw his hands round Julia's neck. She squealed as he yelled,

'What shall we do with a drunken sailor?'

'Put his head down the loo and flush heartily would be the obvious response,' responded Miranda.

As Julia didn't react to his embrace, and could still smell the after-effects of the session at the Lamb and Flag, he disengaged and took the mug of tea from Miranda's outstretched arm.

'Mmm, great, I spy with my little eye something beginning with C.S.B.,' he said, and with that did an impression of a sailor holding a telescope. 'So I think it will have to be the Cabernet Sauvignon Blanc.'

The two women caught each other's glance and Miranda raised her eyes heavenwards in mock despair.

A couple of hours later Julia kissed both the children and quietly retreated from the bedroom. Poppy was lying back sucking her thumb, staring at the ceiling while her little cassette recorder was playing a tape of *The Wind in the Willows*. Just as

Julia reached the top of the stairs, Poppy called out, 'Quick, Julia! Come back!'

When Julia put her head round the door, Poppy said, 'Can you make the tape go past the scary bit? I don't like it when they're in the Wild Wood and they meet the weasel and ask for Badger's house.'

From the bottom bunk came Ethan's attempt at a sinister weasel voice saying, 'Go straight ahead; you can't miss it.' In fact he sounded more like a robot. Poppy hung over the edge of her bunk and hurled a teddy down by its ear but it missed and tumbled onto the floor. Julia duly picked it up again, fast-forwarded the tape while still on play mode so that it sounded like one of the Smurfs on helium, asked if Poppy now felt safe enough to be left alone with Ratty and Mole, and made her exit.

By the time she got downstairs, Miranda was already putting the supper out onto plates and Owen was slicing up a large solid-looking loaf of home-made bread.

'Wow, this really is just what the doctor ordered,' said Julia as she reached out to take the glass of wine that was being proffered.

'Nurse! The screens!' joked Owen, and put his arm around her shoulders as if to lead her into a dark corner of the kitchen.

'You never stop, do you?' joked Miranda, wagging her head and smiling at him as if he was a hopelessly mischievous child.

'As the actress said to the bishop,' replied Owen, and pulled out a chair for Julia. 'Come on, Jules, over here on my right, let's not forget the order of precedence. We may be humble Welsh peasants but don't half know how to behave when we've got company. My woman, here, will see that you've got everything you require.'

Supper proceeded in a pleasantly slow-paced way as they reminisced about people and places they all knew and Julia caught up with snippets of gossip from Miranda who had been a bit more assiduous in her letter-writing keeping up with their mutual friends. Julia had them falling about as she told them about her hideous gaffe on the train and, as ever, embellished it and added a few histrionic touches so that it became even better, or more excruciatingly cringe-making, in the telling than it had actually been in reality. As Miranda wasn't drinking, Julia and Owen polished off a bottle in no time, and although Julia had a glass from a second bottle, she was happy to leave the rest to Owen. Even so, the combination of the fresh air and the exhilaration at being away from the slightly suffocating atmosphere of London rather went to her head. It wasn't long before Miranda was taking her leave and waddling up the stairs, by now massaging her lower back with the palms of both hands.

'Sleep well, Jules,' she said. 'There's an extra blanket in the wardrobe, a towel on the chair, and I'll bring you a cup of tea in the morning. With this one inside playing basketball for most of the night I don't sleep brilliantly as you can imagine. And anyway, even without this great hump, the other two would wake us up. I used to think Poppy was an early riser, but compared to Ethan she's like Rip van Winkle. I don't know how he exists on so little sleep. Anyway, I'm going up now. Owen, love, can you put the stuff in the dishwasher?'

'Your wish is my command,' he replied, and while Julia busied herself covering up the remains of the food that could be put away into the fridge, Owen cleared the table.

'I think I'm finished, too,' said Julia, yawning and just walked back one more time across the kitchen to fill a glass with water for the night.

''Night Jules, go and get your beauty sleep,' he said, and leaned over towards her. She offered her cheek, but Owen planted a rather amorous kiss on her lips. She jumped away from him as if electrocuted, attributing his behaviour to the Cabernet Sauvignon, and immediately tried to laugh off any embarrassment by saying, 'Any minute now I'm going to turn into a frog and that's not a pretty sight, so I'll just hop off to bed.'

With that, she scampered off up the back stairs of the cottage, down the landing past the children's room and into her own little enclave. When she popped back out to the loo she could still hear the scraping of kitchen chairs on the flagstones as Owen tried to restore a bit of order to the house before another day started. A while later she could hear the faint babble of television voices as Owen was now directly below in the sitting room, probably with the remains of the wine bottle, flicking through the channels searching for something to amuse him before bed.

Because there had been so much to occupy her, especially Ethan's dramatic sinking adventure, she had spent fewer hours turning the whole Robin thing over and over in her head. Now, as she lay in the little guest bed in sheets that smelled of fresh air rather than fusty airing cupboards, she revisited each occasion they had been alone together, looking for hints and positive pull-quotes.

It was as if she was watching a series of theatre reviews which are taken out of context and blown up on posters advertising the production. Where the critic had said, 'This performance is the one brilliant piece of acting in an otherwise drab and uninspiring play' all that had been lifted had been 'Brilliant piece of acting!' And so it was with Julia and Robin. She could see the hoardings now: 'We're off on a trip to Venice!' when in fact Robin had said, while they sat in the little restaurant in South Kensington, 'Let's pretend we're off on a trip to Venice. What would you choose to eat on your first night?' or 'This is the first time I have ever felt like this about anyone' when in fact what he actually said was, 'This is the first time I have ever felt like this about anyone since I was in love with Marcus.'

There was a bit of a weak attempt at crying coming from the children's room and then a slight crescendo. Julia could detect Ethan's voice calling for Miranda. *It's not good if I go in there,* she thought. *At times like this they just need their mum.* After a few moments she heard the footfall of someone on the landing and the opening of the children's door followed by some muffled conversation, most of which was coming from Ethan, then silence, then the creak, creak of the floorboards and the soft closing of the door. *Good, crisis averted,* she thought, *let's hope this isn't going to be every hour on the hour. Bloody hell, it's hard work being a parent.*

Then there was a soft click and an ever-so-slight creak and Julia froze as she realised it was her own door that was being opened. There, in the deep gloom, helped only by the faint slit of moonlight coming in through a gap in the curtains, was the silhouette of Owen standing still in the doorway.

'Owen!' she said in a stage whisper. 'Shut the door! Go to bed; it's late!'

Silence.

He didn't move and at that moment her heart started beating just a little as this was a sinister new development. She was desperate not to wake Ethan and Poppy, and even more so not to wake Miranda.

'Owen, just bugger off!' she whispered again, trying to sound good-natured, and not panicking too much, but making it clear that his advances were not in the slightest bit welcome.

To her relief the door closed and she breathed a great sigh of relief, thinking to herself, *Poor sod, he's drunk, he's fed up, we've all gone to sleep and his wife is almost eight months pregnant.* She turned slightly and rearranged her body on the pillow and mattress and started to think Robin thoughts again. The next second there was a creak. Then another. Now, to her horror, she suddenly understood that Owen was still in the room and that he had closed the door behind him rather than exited. She turned over onto her stomach with her head turned away from where she knew he was now standing just from listening to the source of the noisy floorboards.

'Owen, just go, *please,*' she pleaded in a whisper, thinking to herself that at least if she lay on her stomach like this nothing could happen as it was so completely a sign that she wanted nothing of his testosterone-fuelled attentions. Why was it that men like Owen just assumed that all women found them irresistible? Was he really so unable to understand that she not only didn't find him and his creeping hands attractive but that she found the very idea of anything physical with him entirely repulsive, and, in the last moments, terrifying. Even worse, she couldn't cry to anyone for help since the only people who would hear would be his young children or his pregnant wife, one of her best friends, who was in danger of going into premature labour if deeply traumatised. Even if, at best, this didn't happen, how would they patch this marriage up in time for the arrival in just over a month of a new baby whilst already coping with the strains imposed by having two other children under five? She clamped her legs rigidly together and lay face down like a dead body on her bed, holding her breath.

The mattress creaked and she felt herself lean to one side as the weight of his body lowered itself slowly onto the edge of her little bed. Her brain was racing as she tried to think of ways to get him out of the room.

'Owen, this is crazy, get out! Go back to bed! Miranda's going to come looking for you! Don't be so stupid.'

Owen's hand slid under the sheets and started rubbing up and down the thigh nearest to him.

'Come on, you know you really want it, it's just a little bit of a cuddle between friends. You're not going to go all frigid on me are you?'

She was outraged, but at the same time hurt that he could use the word "frigid" to describe her. She had little confidence in her sexual powers, never having been someone who had found it easy to find boyfriends, and this made her want to cry and in some way refute it, but how could she say, 'I'm not frigid but you are just a big unpleasant dog with an erection looking for a bitch on heat'? She wanted him to think she was attractive but she didn't want him to demonstrate his admiration of her beauty by this outrageous assault. She wanted him to like her. She didn't want to be accused of being a non-compliant, unfeminine party pooper. This was the story of her life and it had got her into deeper shit than the bog that had almost swallowed up poor little Ethan that very morning.

Where did it come from? Was this hundreds of years of female conditioning where our great grandmothers told our grandmas and our grandmas told our mothers to respect the male of the species and do what they wanted as this way they would like us and look after us forever? What a pile of poo that was.

With that, Owen jerked away the quilt, the blanket and the top sheet and moved on top of her and she spun her head from one side to the other to avoid the wine-smelling breath and the scrubbing, rubbing sensation of his lightly stubbled face against hers. Now it was getting difficult to breathe properly as his whole body weight was on top of her, she could feel his massive erection like a branch of a tree wedged between them as he used one hand to drag her nightdress up out of the way and then lurched to the other side and did the same. She was wriggling, fighting, and whispering, 'Owen! Stop it! Stop it!' over and over again, but there was that awful, terrible moment when she knew she was going to be raped and she could do little about it except resign herself to her fate and pray fervently that it was not a fertile time of the month. There was a rational voice inside her going, *Just let him get on with it then he'll go. Show no indication that you are getting even the slightest pleasure from any of this and he will just do it and go. It will be two minutes of your life. Treat it like the time Dennis Charleston snogged you at a party when you were sixteen and you didn't fancy him. Lie back and think of England. Whatever you do, however unpleasant this is, it's not as awful as Miranda losing the baby and her whole family life being devastated. You can leave; you need never come back again.* As all this was playing through her head, he was forcing his huge penis into her from behind. She had thought it physically impossible with her lying so straight and rigid, but it was, nevertheless, happening. As she had suspected, it was only a moment before he suddenly withdrew sharpishly and his ragged breaths signified he was ejaculating onto the bed sheets. And the next moment he had left the room.

It was like some terrible, terrible nightmare. She felt like all her personal boundaries had been violated. The worst thing about it was that this was no balaclava'd stranger who had jumped out on her from a doorway and pulled her into a dark alley in Peckham. This was a man to whom, for years, she had been sending birthday cards, with whom she had shared so many laughs and good meals, a man who knew so many little tales of her past and her childhood, lovingly shared when the three of them had shared a bottle of wine of an evening.

Her mind raced; when did I last have my period? Can I leave this place tomorrow? No, impossible, my ticket's only valid for Monday morning. Anyway, how would I explain my sudden disappearance to Miranda and the kids? How would I get from here anyway? We're in the middle of nowhere. What if he tries to do it again tomorrow? Oh shit, the door! And she leapt out of bed to try to wedge the back of a chair under the door handle to stop him coming in again. It took a few moments to arrive at some passable means of barricading the door because she had to work in the gloom and avoid making a noise and waking anyone up. Finally, it seemed to be secure and she got back in the bed, lying in a tiny strip of bed right on the edge to avoid the offending wet patch which had been Owen's parting gift.

She lay there slightly shivering thinking back to the first time she had ever kissed anyone. She had been invited to a party by a school friend and was rather taken aback to discover that there were just five girls and five slightly older boys, two of whom she didn't know, all standing around drinking cider and looking a bit uncomfortable. At some point in the evening, and Julia didn't really remember how it had happened, as if by some private secret signal, all the boys sat down on armchairs and sofas and the lights were turned down low. Each girl sat on a boy's lap and one by one, while the others watched, each couple had to kiss. Julia had been petrified. How do I do it? Will they think I'm stupid? Will they know it's my first time? All these thoughts raced through her head as she watched her friend Brenda kissing Malcolm Norris. Their heads moved gently back and forth and their eyes were closed. Next it was Pat Guscott's turn with Ray Lavell. To Julia's astonishment Pat's hands were running hungrily through Ray's hair; they swerved and writhed together; his hands went up and down her back and their heads constantly gyrated as they seemed to be sucking the life force out of one another. And then it was her turn. Maurice Chambers put his arm round her and she felt his lips close upon hers. She felt nothing. She felt like a dead body. She was not remotely attracted to him and she hadn't a clue what to do. He seemed to suck a bit and move his head back and forth and finally stopped and the ordeal was over and it was someone else's turn. In the next round of the game the girls all had to move on and sit on the next lap. As Julia dutifully got up, straightened her dress and gazed down at her American tan stockings wrinkling at the knees she heard Maurice say, 'Bad luck, Ray' as she was about to move to Ray Lavell's lap. A little later, she began to get into the swing of it a bit more as she found herself with one of the boys who was a gentle but sensual kisser. He was not a boy from her school but she remembered seeing him at some of the dances in the British Legion hall in the next village. She felt his hand moving up the inside of her leg and fumbling at the tops of her stockings and reaching into her pants.

'Can I take you home?' he muttered in her ear as he fumbled.

And she had to speak the shaming words, 'Actually my father's coming to collect me in the car. He'll be here any minute.'

She was paradoxically relieved and disappointed when there was a knock at the door and she heard Brenda's father exchanging pleasantries with her dad. For a whole week afterwards, she burned with shame and embarrassment whenever she saw any of the boys in the corridor in school. Of course, none of them ever asked her out. She knew that she was not worth it, and they had probably spread the word that she was "hard work".

This wasn't how all the books said it would be. When was Captain von Trapp going to turn up? What about Mr Rochester? And where was Professor Higgins? Where was Mr Darcy? This was all she had been taught about romance: the gentle older man, the considerate teacher and lover. It had nothing to do with French-kissing boys with terrible acne who smelt of cigarettes and cider with their fingers jabbing away at the inside leg of your knickers. And that was precisely why she had developed that massive crush on Gethin Broadhurst the following term as he was the gatekeeper to the world of literature and fantasy where dreams really did come true – at least they did for Elizabeth Bennet, so surely it would be Julia's turn one day too?

After a while she began to hear the beginnings of the dawn chorus. She realised that Miranda had said that she would be bringing a cup of tea in first thing in the morning.

Oh God, she thought, *she mustn't find the barricaded door otherwise she will want to know why on earth I did it.* There would be nothing else for it but to lie awake and then get up and move the chair about six o'clock. He surely wouldn't return when it was already getting light. Between six and seven she managed to doze lightly and was just sinking into a deep REM sleep when she heard the door open. She turned in the bed with such speed to see who was coming through the door that she felt a small muscle twang in her back.

'Sleep well?' asked Miranda as she put the tea down beside Julia.

'Yeah, fine,' replied Julia. 'Thanks for the tea. Are the children already awake?'

'You bet,' Miranda said, then, looking at the bed added,

'Bloody hell, Jules, it's like the wreck of the Hesperus. Did you have a bad dream or were you just too hot in here? I thought you used to be able to get out of bed in the morning and it would look like it had never been slept in.'

'Ah well, it must be *The Deptford Trilogy* or the Caerphilly cheese you gave me last night,' responded Julia diplomatically.

'You should have had a camomile tea before bed. Owen's gone off to Cardiff to see a pal this morning so we've got most of the day to ourselves, not forgetting the terrible two of course. I thought we could drive up the mountain a bit further and see if there are any free slots at the riding stable for the children. I haven't booked but they both love it and it'll give us an hour of girl time.'

'Head 'em up! Move 'em out! Yee-ha!' she whooped. 'I'll be down in ten minutes. Just let me have a quick bath.'

Chapter Eleven

Once Miranda had left the room, the relief which Julia felt was so intense that, as she exhaled, she felt her body double its weight and sink deeply into the mattress. However, all she wanted to do was immerse herself in water as hot as her body could handle, to soak and soak and wash and wash until the memory of what had happened that night was gone.

'Yes, thank you, God!' she said under her breath as she tried to pull the bed back into some kind of decent shape for the next labour of Hercules: keeping the rampant Owen at bay for one more night. The door burst open and in ran the children, delighted to find that she was still in the house. Poppy was swinging the magic wand over her head.

'I just *knew* you were going to be here,' she said. 'And anyway, even if you weren't I had my wand and I would have magic'ed you back.'

'Oh Pops, what a lovely thing to say,' said Julia, restored by this vote of confidence in her from the little girl who was now in her arms, legs clamped firmly round her waist.

'Mummy said we're going up to Twisha's stable,' shouted Ethan.

'It's not Twisha, it's *Tricia*!' said Poppy imperiously from the great height of Julia's arms. "But Linnet and Conchie might already be booked out and we can't ride the others; they're too big.'

'Look, you two,' said Julia, 'I've got to have a bath and get ready otherwise we will get up there just as they are putting the horses back in the stable to go to bed. Give me a little while to sort myself out and I'll be down in a minute.'

If I've just saved those two little lovelinesses by enduring a miserable five minutes with that brute then it's been worth it, she thought to herself, but then, a second thought entered her head. *Why the fuck should I always be bloody Mother Teresa? Isn't it someone else's turn now?*

By the time she arrived in the kitchen, Ethan was sitting on the arm of the sofa, riding whip in hand, looking like a Mekon in his large riding hat. He was riding his imaginary horse and kicking his heels into the arm of the sofa to spur it on to greater speed. Poppy was looking like a bonsai version of an Olympic dressage champion, immaculately turned out, even down to a little hairnet into which she had inexpertly stuffed her hair.

'Pops, they might not even have a free slot, darling,' said Miranda, looking dubious about this great demonstration of enthusiastic preparation.

'Well, I'm taking my wand, so I know it will be all right,' she answered, totally confident in her own superior powers.

'Make sure you remember to swap the wand for the riding crop or you'll look a bit of a banana,' added Julia, smiling, and popped a piece of the seedy bread into the toaster.

Because the gods were being kind to them that day, as opposed to Black Saturday the evening before, there was, mercifully, an hour when both the ponies were available. The children were in a frenzy of delight as they bounded from the car and over to the loose box where one of the older girls who helped at the stable was sorting out some tack. Ethan, who had been so boisterous and voluble when mounted on the sofa arm, was now looking sheepish and shy once he was sitting up on the Welsh pony's sturdy back. Megan, the helper, was leading him along, while Poppy sat bolt upright on Linnet following behind, a wide grin on her face, unable to disguise her total pleasure and pride at doing something where she may, with just a little imagination, she thought, be taken for a twenty-five-year-old. She was, after all, not being led along like her brother. For one magic hour she could kid herself that she was riding her very own pony. If she did it convincingly enough, maybe people who passed slowly in cars might think the same. She was in heaven.

'Trish, you're fantastic,' said Miranda. 'Here's a tenner. You've made an old woman very happy. By the way, this is my friend Julia. She's just down for the weekend.'

Tricia stuffed the notes into her jodhpur pocket and grinned back.

'I'm sure Miranda and Owen are pulling all the stops out for you,' said Tricia.

Too bloody right, thought Julia to herself, but just smiled back and raised her hand in a farewell sign.

'Right, an hour of peace,' said Miranda. 'Let's drive up there to the forestry path. There's a little bench where we can sit and have a chat and if we're lucky we'll see the kids ride by without them seeing us, depending on which way Megan takes them. Don't they look sweet?'

'Sorry, what? I was miles away,' said Julia.

'Jules, you're hopeless! You were probably in a silky negligee luring poor innocent Robin into your sex den with your long scarlet talons!' she joked.

Nothing could be further from the truth. She had in fact been trying to calculate how many days from her last period.

'You're a mind reader, Miranda!' she lied, having just realised that there was an outside chance that her best friend's husband's sperm could quite possibly be rapping its knuckles on the front door of one of her eggs at this very minute. There was a long pause and then Julia asked, 'How d'you feel about being "Miranda Griffiths, mother of three"?'

'What, you mean when I'm arrested for a cruel axe murder or taken to a Bangkok jail on trumped up drugs charges?'

'Well, I can barely imagine being married, let alone being mother of three,' mused Julia.

'I suppose I've been lucky with Owen,' continued Miranda, with hideous candour and naivety. 'He's always been there for me in the end, even though he's a bit of a flirt when he's had a drop, but he adores the kids, and who else would put up with me and my moods?'

'What rubbish! You? Moody? You've got to be joking,' retorted Julia, shocked. She had never known such a calm, capable earth mother as Miranda. 'Blimey, having a bad mood for you consists as far as I can see of you walking around the kitchen frowning for a few moments murmuring, "Now where did I put top of the extra virgin oil?"'

'That doesn't mean I haven't been tempted to pour the whole bottle over Owen sometimes, or even over myself,' joked Miranda.

'Now we were talking bad moods, not x-rated sex games,' quipped Julia.

'Chance would be a fine thing with me looking like this!' added Miranda. 'You know once long ago when we were first married I decided to spice things up a bit and give him a bit of a surprise, so around the time he was due home from work, I took off all my clothes and draped myself across the piano stool. I waited and waited and then got fed up and wandered about looking out of the window and finally sat down on one of the wicker chairs by the French windows. I must have been there ages and I think I nodded off eventually through sheer boredom. When Owen finally arrived he just stared at me as if I'd gone mad and said, "What the bloody hell are you doing?" I got up to go and get a shawl or something and he started laughing hysterically. My whole bum looked like it had been the site of the elves' national noughts and crosses championships. I think I had the imprint of the wicker chair on my buttocks for the next three days.'

'Isn't it ridiculous what women do for men?' mused Julia.

'But Jules, that's precisely why I'm worried about you,' said Miranda, serious for a moment. 'Don't get trapped in something that forces you to be something you're not. It'll destroy you in the end. If I suspected that Owen was playing away, I don't know what I would do.'

As if sent by God at that moment, Poppy, trotting daintily, and then Megan, jogging along in wellies holding Conchie's rein, and finally Ethan, bouncing up and down as if he was being shaken to death loomed into view through the trees. Ethan was hanging on grimly but had none of the poise of his sister who was still showing off to an imaginary show ring of gymkhana spectators.

'Aren't you lonely at all down here?' whispered Julia.

'Not really,' said Miranda. 'We've got quite lot of friends; it's just a question of making the effort to get to see them. We used to go to the theatre and even the opera quite a bit in Cardiff but it's a different bunch from London. I remember once we went to see *Tosca* at the New Theatre and some old diva was playing the leading role. She was right at the end of quite a lengthy and successful career by this time and had looked a bit on the avoir-dupois side. When it got to the bit at the end where she had to throw herself off the battlements they were obviously dead worried she would hurt herself because of her serious bulk and so there were, I imagined, dozens of foam mattresses underneath so she had a soft landing. They had rather over-estimated and suddenly those of us sitting up in the gods saw her head bounce back up again like she was taking part in the Olympic trampolining event. Afterwards, as we were walking back to the car we had to pass the stage door and quite a few of the faithful were waiting there clutching their programmes waiting for the diva to sweep out. Suddenly there was a bit of a commotion and out she came in one of those old lady's beaver fur coats that were popular in the fifties, a hairnet on her head and probably a big bunch of flowers in her arms. I can't remember. As she settled herself into her chauffeur driven car, an old woman from up the Valleys rushed forward and started knocking frantically on the window squawking and flapping an LP at her. "Going 'ome now to hear yer rekkuds". We were doubled up laughing but that sort of sums up our cultural life down here. But it doesn't matter, because the kids are everything I want and more.'

'You'll let me know straight away when you have the baby,

won't you?' said Julia.

'Oh you must come down and see it as soon as you can. And bring Mr Wonderful with you.'

'I – er, well, I've used up most of my holiday and it'll maybe...' And here Julia was lost for words to explain that she would never, ever put herself in this nightmare situation again with Owen.

'That's OK, sweetheart, God, I'm sorry, I didn't mean to be presumptuous. I know you can't hurry things along and even if you have to come on your own, that'll be fine. Don't worry if it all goes tits up. That happens. I was just lucky with Owen. For every relationship that succeeds, a hundred go wrong. Just remember we are always here for you and I really do hope it all works out in a way that helps you to grow rather than feel diminished.'

Miranda just didn't get it. Julia quietly said a prayer, reached out her hand and touched the nearest bit of wood.

By constantly volunteering to amuse the children for the rest of the day, Julia managed to avoid any contact with Owen, but when she did occasionally pass him in a corridor or when he looked in the kids' playroom to see if Miranda was there, he acted as if there was absolutely nothing out of the ordinary, whereas for Julia, all she could think about was escaping from this torture chamber and never coming back. That evening, as she had anticipated, and as she had dreaded, Miranda casually mentioned that Owen would be able to drop her off at the station on his way to work. If she had said, 'No, it's fine, I'll get a taxi,' Miranda would have thought she was mad. And anyway, where out here in the middle of nowhere would she have got a cab, and, furthermore, how would she have paid for it? She was seriously to the limit with money after renewing her wardrobe so many times to impress Robin and couldn't afford to run up any more big debts. The journey to Cardiff was stilted and her replies to his attempts at banter were terse and monosyllabic. Owen tried to joke and chat as he had done on the first journey but in the end the events of Saturday evening stood there between them like a giant monolithic slab.

'Er, look, about Saturday, I – er,' he stammered.

'Owen, I don't want to talk about it. Miranda is one of my best friends, OK? You realise that I can never come back.'

At that point she expected him to promise that nothing of the sort would happen ever again, that he had been mad, that he was ashamed, that it was all because Miranda was pregnant, that they lived an isolated life, that Mercury was retrograde that week. Anything, just some kind of sorry. But nothing prepared her for his next speech.

'I – er, know a chap, a school mate of mine, who – er, well he works at the Royal Free but he does some private stuff now and if by any chance you – er, well, you know, you need a bit of help to get rid… I'm sure you won't be, but to be on the safe side, well, just give me a ring, eh?'

Julia just sat silent and hot, staring at the windscreen wipers bashing back and forth and wanting so badly to be away from this monster. As the car drew up outside the station she practically fell out of the door in an attempt to get away. On the three-hour journey back to London she managed to get from page 22 to page 24 of her novel. The rest of the time was a swirl of confusion where she went over and over the events of the weekend, and tried to focus on the more pressing practical task of arranging her birthday party which was now looming, as well as hoping dearly that Robin would have left some kind of message for her back at the flat to say that he had, at least, missed her.

She took a taxi from Paddington straight to the college and was grateful for the chance to have three quite intense teaching hours with two of her brighter groups that afternoon, thus leaving no time at all for speculation and reverie. The train journey had provided enough angst and unresolved issues to last a month. Robin was nowhere to be seen, sadly, and she really needed a ray of his particular brand of sunlight right now to bring her back from the dark place in which she found herself. She had been unable to shake off the feeling of dirtiness and cheapness which was hanging over her. In some ways she was quite relieved that he wasn't around since she knew that she would disappoint him by being glum and not full of Celtic travellers' tales as he had predicted. When she first had tried to explain to him where Owen and Miranda lived and what their lifestyle was like up there in the hills, his reaction made it seem as if she was going on a *Mabinogion*-themed weekend or was going to don a tall conical black hat and shawl and sit by a spinning-wheel for the duration. He had told her about his Welsh pal, Geraint, and they had agreed that at some point in the future they would try to get all of them round the same table. When she finally got back to her flat she felt she couldn't face the yawning emptiness of the evening or tackle the light grey dust film which was settling on everything. She was of the "you only do the housework when you've got people coming round" variety. She took a deep breath and dialled Robin's number. The minute he realised it was her, he started singing the chorus of *Cwm Rhondda* in a loud ostentatious voice and then, after the second "bread of heaven" stopped and asked in his best attempt at a Welsh accent, 'So how was Welsh Wales? See any dragons, isn't it? There's lovely!'

Julia laughed and felt a huge wave of relief rush over her to know that he still liked her, that he still wanted to hear her voice.

'Dragons? Tell me about it!' she joked. 'Talking of which, what are you doing? Can I pop over and touch base? I need to get all the Lego towers de-programmed out of my system, and as for the little toy animals, if I tuck another plastic squirrel up in a little blanket and put him in a scooped out log cot I'll go barmy.'

'Come straight over,' he enthused, 'a couple of duchesses are dropping in, but ignore them. It'll be lovely to see you.'

Oh. Duchesses. Yes, well... thought Julia. She realised that this meant that some of Robin's camp friends were going to show up, but then, he was with her now; he was being outed as "heterosexual after all". 'Sod 'em,' she muttered to herself. A split second later she chortled at the thought of what she had just said.

Julia was so eager to get to Robin's flat that she splashed out on a taxi. As it weaved in and out of the evening traffic she mused that Robin probably would never do this kind of thing to visit her. He adored her, yes, but was his degree of adoration so great and his love so helpless that he would be prepared to spend money that he really didn't have just to arrive twelve minutes earlier than he would have been able to do on the Tube? It was that kind of gesture she yearned for from him, but it still felt as if it was about four feet away from her arm and she was stretching out over a precipice with a 1,000-foot drop beneath. When she glanced up at the open window to where the raucous and slightly shrieking sounds of male laughter were coming from, she regretted having spent the money on getting there so swiftly.

I can't believe I've raced here to spend time with these people whom I suspect want to boil my kneecaps in hot oil and peel the skin slowly off my body with a scalpel, she thought to herself, but it was time to take a deep breath and go inside. To her surprise, the downstairs door was not properly closed so she just pushed it and tiptoed up the squeaky staircase and couldn't resist eavesdropping a little before she knocked the top door.

'And how's your intriguing new life?' she heard Jeremy's voice addressing Robin she guessed.

'Oh, flying out to Samarkand for a screen test with Robert Altman in the new movie that's set to take the lid off mirror-image identical twins in Moslem society in Uzbekhistan,' giggled Robin.

'But seriously, darling, what's going on? We're agog!' said a voice she didn't recognise.

'Nothing's going on; I'm just having a pleasant time,' he said non-committally and a little defensively. 'And by the way, how are you? You seemed to be having the usual screamy time. What's happened about Dennis?'

Robin was observing the golden rule when being interrogated which was to heave the spotlight around onto the interrogator's own life, or at least onto a person or an event that was even more compelling than whatever was preoccupying them about one's own situation.

Jeremy then launched into a blow-by-blow account of his trip to Brighton with Dennis and soon forgot to pursue his line of enquiry about Julia.

'So, you see,' continued Jeremy. 'I put these two tickets down on the table for a weekend in Amsterdam and he looked at them like I was offering him a bowl of warm human blood to drink. It's just his way, I know, but he seems to look at me sometimes like he's viewing me through a veil of thinly-disguised contempt. I don't know what I'm doing wrong. I love him but I seem to behave like a pitiful old dog dragging itself along behind its master, while he can just kick me aside with a flick of his boot.'

'Oh, alack, alas!' said Robin in mock sympathy. 'You seem to have endless bad luck in affairs of the heart!'

'Will you come with me instead?' entreated Jeremy. 'I just know we would have more fun than if I went with old misery-guts. Come on, we can go and see Adrian and Tom. It would be a scream!'

'You're on!' said Robin.

'Brilliant! You are the pig's earlobes and the fairy's tutu! Love you, Scrungebuttock! I'll let you have all the details and the times tomorrow. You've made an old queen very happy!'

Julia could stand no more and was almost about to turn and run down the stairs but something made her stay rooted to the spot and knock the door.

Robin hugged her and gave her one of his special smiles and then, not disentangling himself from her entirely, paraded her into the sitting room. Jeremy was lying back on the sofa chatting to someone she didn't recognise and there was an empty chair on the other side of the coffee table and a half-drunk glass of red wine where Robin had obviously been sitting.

'This is Felix, a friend of Jeremy's,' said Robin, indicating the stranger sitting next to Jeremy.

Felix inclined his head to her a little and went on listening to Jeremy who had been reading something from a newspaper when she entered the room.

'Oh, here it is, I've found the bit I've been looking for! Listen! "After stopping for drinks at an illegal bar, a Zimbabwean bus driver found that the twenty mental patients he was supposed to be transporting from Harare to Bulawayo had escaped. Not wanting to admit his incompetence, the driver went to a nearby bus stop and offered everyone waiting there a free ride. He then delivered the passengers to the mental hospital, telling the staff that the patients were very excitable and prone to bizarre fantasies. The deception wasn't discovered for three days!" How outrageous is that!? I can think of a few people *I'd* like to put in the bus. How about Jezebel for starters?'

'Oh, you'd never get him on a bus, dear,' said Robin. 'You know what he's like, he only travels by taxi!'

Julia squirmed at the 'dear' bit and could see that this conversation was going to consist mainly of laughing at mutual queenly acquaintances.

'Anyone seen Marcus lately?' asked Felix, picking his fingernails.

'Julia and I saw him a week or two back and he seemed fine,' answered Robin, a touch abashed.

Felix and Jeremy exchanged glances.

'And how was he? Is he directing at the National yet?' asked Felix.

'Well, I think he's just trying to pay off his mortgage,' Robin said, 'so he's doing a bit of acting at the moment. You know what it's like, the work is sporadic, and there are days, weeks, even months spent resting. On average, you get one out of every fifty ads you're seen for, and he's done it for long enough to read between the lines of the casting directors' relayed messages to his agent saying how the director absolutely adored him, how he couldn't possibly have done any better in the audition and that it had been a definitive portrayal of "the man in the second car", or "the man cleaning his teeth with Beam!", or "the man mowing his lawn with the new Greeno lawnmower". And for the life of him he can't work out how lawnmower man is going to transmogrify into sex god who's going to be the new James Bond or the director who will replace Sir Peter Hall.'

'To be honest I can't ever see him making it to the National now,' said Jeremy. 'But still with looks to die for—'he winked at Felix'—I think he will always find a way of funding his lifestyle if you know what I mean.'

Julia felt extremely uncomfortable on behalf of Mel, and just looked at the floor. This was a conversation she had no wish whatsoever to be part of.

'Julia's just been to Wales,' said Robin, changing the subject. 'How was it, Blossom? Did you yomp up mountains and do butch things like that?'

'No, it was just a simple weekend with chums who live in a farmhouse; they've got small children. It was good fun,' she said, realizing that Robin had been hoping for some witty performance from her, a comic set consisting of one side-splitting anecdote after another about the trials and tribulations of life in the Welsh valleys. He had constructed a persona for her in her absence and was acting as compère introducing her act. The others stared back like a matinee audience consisting entirely of old age pensioners. She smiled weakly but could think of nothing humorous to say except, 'My best friend's husband had a penis like a large wooden rolling pin and he jumped on my back and he shoved it into me and it was one of the worst experiences of my entire life.' But of course she didn't. She did the usual Julia thing. She racked her brains for something amusing to say because she didn't want to disappoint Robin. *As ever, the show must go on*, she thought to herself and she ended up regaling them with the tale of what had happened to her on the train. As she got into her stride, she began to actually enjoy herself, especially as she saw Robin lapping it up and looking on proudly. Even the miserable Felix was smiling towards the end.

'Oh my God!' exclaimed Jeremy, 'don't get throwing any garments out of the train when we go to Amsterdam on Friday!'

Julia thought in a wave of panic, *Amsterdam? Friday?!* What one earth was he talking about? Surely there was some mistake? She'd overheard the bit about Amsterdam while she was outside the door, but it was her birthday on Friday and she had invited eight friends to meet Robin. She felt as if she had just been shot.

'Uh, you didn't tell me you were going to Amsterdam on Friday,' Julia said to Robin, her face reddening.

'Oh you little minx, Mrs Forester,' said Jeremy. 'Fancy not telling the lovely Julia about your extra-curricular activity.'

'Actually, my dear, he's been an angel and jumped into the breach, haven't you?' Jeremy then said, turning to Robin. At the words 'jumped into the breach' Felix gave a snigger.

Julia knew that most people would, at that point, have stood up and said, 'You bastard, it's my birthday. You promised! How dare you!'

'Dennis pulled out,' Robin said to her, as if this was reason and excuse enough.

Felix once more sniggered unable to let even the vaguest double entendre go unnoticed.

Robin was looking at her with such innocent honesty that she realized that he had completely forgotten about her birthday and blamed herself for telling him at an inconvenient moment as he had nothing to write on when she told him hurriedly as she was about to get on her train home. Yes, it was her fault. It was her problem. She wouldn't make a fuss.

'I – er, I've got an early class tomorrow and I really think I'd better be running off home,' she said to Robin, and he jumped up to see her to the door.

'Please don't let me interrupt the fun,' she said to the other two. 'Lovely to have seen you both.'

As she left the room, she could hear the distant sound of Felix reading yet another improbable news item from some obscure American rag. 'When his 38-caliber revolver failed to fire at its intended victim during a hold-up in Long Beach, California, would-be robber James Elliot did something that can only inspire wonder: He peered down the barrel and tried the trigger again. This time it worked.' And once again, Jeremy and Felix were off into screams of laughter.

'I didn't realise you were going away,' she said, as Robin helped her on with her coat.

'But it's only for a weekend,' Robin said, hugging her reassuringly.

'Yes, but it's...but it's...' She couldn't finish her sentence. A huge tear was racing down her cheek.

'Sweet Pea, what is it? Whatever's the matter?' he asked. She was shaking her head vigorously.

'No, it's nothing, I'm sorry, I'm just being stupid. It's, it's, it was going to be my...it's my, it's my birthday.' And then she really did start to cry properly as the emotion of the whole past few days got to her.

Robin steered her into the bedroom and kicked the door shut with his foot.

'Oh shit, oh bum, oh God. I'm so sorry. I completely forgot!' he said.

'No, please, you can't cancel it all. It's air fares and you've said you'll go,' she said.

But Robin could see how upset she was, and said with great resolve, 'Don't worry about a thing. I'll tell Jeremy to find someone else.'

As she left the flat Julia knew one thing was for sure: the gay mafia would be out for her blood. How long would Robin last before they wore him down?

The next day in college she felt she could hardly face him as she had made such a fool of herself. However, he breezed into the Common Room and was his usual chirpy self with everyone. He was sitting with a pile of books on his lap on the sofa by the window chatting to Donna Kilpatrick about one of his students who had a pretty good chance of getting in to Oxbridge.

'I think I'd better talk to her,' said Robin. 'I really don't think Romily Saunders understands how bright and original she is. I think they'd take one look at her and realise that she is just the kind of person they want there the minute she opens her mouth. She's so self-possessed without being a show-off. She's bright as a button you know. She's so conscientious and so applied that she almost scares me! When I was the same age as her I was on a pretty routine pattern of French leave. I was always bunking off.'

'I've always wondered why they call it "French leave",' said Donna. 'It's one of those silly little bits of trivia that I should know. D'you know, Julia?'

'As far as I remember,' said Robin, looking quite serious and studious, 'it was some bizarre eighteenth-century custom where French dinner guests left without saying goodbye to the hostess. The English have always disliked the French or thought them to be rather sexually liberated so whenever it's something rather naughty they call it "French this" or "French that".'

'You mean like "French letter",' said Donna.

'Precisely,' said Robin. 'And there used to be references to "French postcards" in the twenties which were the acme of titillation, but the French do the same with us too, you know.'

'Oh yes, you're right...don't they call syphilis "the English disease"?' said Donna, really getting into the etymological discussion now.

'Yes,' said Robin. 'But going back to the French letter thing, do you know what they call them in French?'

'Well, it's an uninspired guess but how about English letters?' said Donna.

'No, the French also call condoms *"chapeaux anglais"*,' said Robin. 'A long time ago I heard this story of the not very worldly-wise Englishman who retired to France. A few years later his wife died and he arranged a formal family funeral in France. He realised that although he had a black suit, he didn't have a black top hat. He asked the outfitters for what he thought was the right translation: *"un chapeau anglais noir"*. 'The shopkeeper directed him to the *pharmacie* next door where, despite his surprise, he made the same inquiry.

'*"Nous avons un chapeau anglais normal, monsieur, mais pourquoi noir?"* the pharmacist said.

'*"Parce que ma femme est morte,"* the man replied.

'And the pharmacist answered, "Ah. *Quelle délicatesse!"*'

'Oh, brilliant! I love it!' said Donna.

The few others whose French was adequate to get the joke grinned silently and got on with their marking or preparation. Donna went over to her pigeon-hole and started rummaging through some papers. Robin sidled over to Julia and said casually, 'Jeremy's fine about Amsterdam. Bit miffed but there's plenty of time for him to field a substitute. What time do you want me on Friday?'

'Come at seven before the others. That way you can help me do the food.'

'Seven it is then. I'll bring my chef's hat.'

'You probably won't have any room for a chef's hat as you'll be staggering along with that big cake and all the presents I'm sure you intend buying for me,' she said.

'Funny you should say that,' joked Robin, 'but I thought of giving you my chef's hat as your birthday present as I'm a bit short of money this month. Oh, there goes the bell. Gotta dash.'

And with that he was gone, and Julia went off to take her Italian conversation class.

Later that afternoon when she got home, she sat looking through cookery books trying to plan the birthday meal and began to make a list. Although it was near the end of the month and she was in danger of becoming seriously overdrawn, she felt it was a case of "no expense spared" for this particular event. She decided that a Moroccan lamb tagine was quite a good idea and found a simple but impressive recipe using dried apricots and loads of coriander. Then of course there was the vegetarian problem. Maybe ditch the smoked salmon starter in favour of lentil soup and then make some sort of porcini risotto for Geoff. She wanted to impress Robin with her culinary skills and she wanted to impress her friends with Robin. As the list of stuff to buy grew to include a bottle of gin and a bottle of whisky as this signified that it wasn't just some sort of student Bolognese and red plonk event, plus her favourite expensive goat's cheese and some figs, she realised that, even without the alcohol, it was getting scarily expensive. However, the worry about money paled into insignificance compared with her anxiety about whether or not she could now be pregnant. Indeed, she felt sick at this very minute. Could you feel sick within days if you were pregnant? Surely not. What were the other symptoms? She abandoned the list and put on her coat and rushed out to the W. H. Smith in Putney High Street and went straight to the health section to see if they had any books on pregnancy. As she handed over the money she heard herself babbling, the guilt talking. 'My sister thinks she's pregnant. Just buying this as a present.' The girl at the till just smiled politely and gave her the change.

When she got back to the flat she got it out of the bag where she had been hiding it as if it were some kind of embarrassing pornography. She flipped at high speed through the first section with all the little diagrams of ovaries, fallopian tubes, sperm and models of what happens to the foetus in its first weeks of life.

There was a chart showing how to calculate the due date of your baby's birth based on the time of conception. The night with Owen had been just three days beyond the generally agreed unsafe period for sex if you were trying to avoid pregnancy. Now she flicked back and forth through pregnancy symptoms and saw that beside the regulation morning sickness and cravings for weird foods, pregnant women experience dizziness, painful breasts, and the need to go to the loo more often than usual. As with any form of hypochondria, she instantly felt that she needed a wee, felt faint, and needed to eat a jacket potato with a side order of jellied eels.

Well, I'll know soon enough if I miss my period, she thought to herself, threw the book on the bed and returned to the shopping list.

The phone rang and it was Robin.

'Just thought I'd check if I needed my serrated knife or my blender or my Parmesan grater…and where better to discuss these things than at the cinema? How d'you fancy coming to see *Nashville*?'

'Anything which doesn't involve marking essays on Dante or writing out unfeasibly long shopping lists sounds good to me,' she said jauntily. 'Where shall I meet you?'

'Come to the flat about eight thirty. Can you manage that?'

'I'll start out right away,' she said, and suddenly was in heaven again and all was right with the world. The gods were on her side and all the right connections happened as if by magic and she arrived early, unable to stop herself from hurrying to his front door half an hour ahead of time.

He buzzed her in and shouted down, 'Come right up! I'm on the phone.'

As she went through the inside door into the sitting room he blew her a kiss and indicated to her to go and sit down while he stood in the door of his bedroom talking on his bedside phone. The door was ajar and seemed to close a little more now that she was in the flat. She couldn't work out whether it was just swinging shut of its own accord or whether he was subtly closing it so that she didn't overhear him. He had a rather pretty antique ormolu clock on the mantelpiece and it was just striking eight very delicately. She wandered over to inspect the neat little row of gold-edged invitation cards. Most of them were from people with male names; only one was from a couple.

'Listen, Daisy Petal,' he said, addressing the person on the other end of the line, 'you've got to do what you've got to do; don't bring me into it. Of course I care about you but you've got to decide this one on your own.'

Julia wanted desperately to hear as much of what he was saying as was possible, but realised that unless she tiptoed over to the hall and stood right outside the door it would be impossible, and if she did this she would be caught red-handed at the dreadful crime of "ear-wigging" as they had called it at school. As she looked again at the invitations on the mantelpiece she saw a little note in Mark's unmistakeable handwriting which read: "Phone me at eight sharp on Monday night. I need your advice about something important. All my love. Hugs M. x x x" She glanced back at the clock and then at the closed bedroom door where she could hear Robin's voice still sporadically speaking. The words "Daisy Petal" sat heavily on her heart. She rehearsed her "happy face" for when he would emerge moments later having dispensed wisdom to his former lover. Robin bounded in and gave her the by now familiar swift and delicate peck on the lips, saying, 'The night is young! Come on, Sweet Pea, let's hit the town.'

Chapter Twelve

The film was like nothing she had seen before, and was so fast-moving and contained so many amazing vignettes and magic little cinematic moments that for its duration she was able to relax completely. It was like skiing, or driving down a fast-moving motorway. One could think about nothing else while it lasted, and this use of the pause button on one's otherwise overactive self-obsessed section of the imagination was forced to take an involuntary rest. Robin held her hand throughout the film, but hand-holding had become a habit which she suspected he did with other females, or with his mother or with old ladies. There was nothing suggestive or sexual about this form of touching, no hint that it may move into a more insistent physical gear, caressing or stroking.

As they came out of the darkened auditorium, Julia suddenly felt like she needed, uncharacteristically, to go to the Ladies. This, of course, set her alarm buttons jangling once again.

*I don't normally need to do thi*s, she thought to herself, *oh please God don't let me be pregnant!*

She was also aware that the phone call which she had overheard earlier in the evening had disturbed her. Was it right that he was calling a male ex-lover "Daisy Petal"? This in some ways seemed to downgrade all the little pet names he used on her. The name "Daisy Petal" also made her smile, albeit wanly, when she thought of Mark's very macho olive-skinned face, his rather chiselled features and deep, sonorous "actaw's" voice. She found it truly incredible that this man could have gone to bed with Robin.

When she emerged Robin was surprised to see her little face looking so pale and helpless, so much so that he was moved to ask, 'What's the matter, Sweet Pea? Is anything wrong? Are you all right?'

'Yeah, fine, fine, just a few too many late nights in Wales.

Nothing a few extra hours of beauty sleep won't put right.'

They sauntered along the wet night street and Robin began enthusiastically to deconstruct the film and give her twenty good reasons why he thought Robert Altman was a genius.

They had a late-night pasta and glass of wine in Soho and then parted company, as usual, at the Tube station.

'Now don't forget! Come early on Friday evening!' she said, as they hugged goodbye.

Julia went home and ran a bath, staring down at her middle to see if there was any visible sign of pregnancy. She laughed at herself as she did it realising that if she were indeed pregnant, the foetus would take about two months to grow to the size of a small prawn so how on earth did she expect to see a large pregnant stomach jutting out of her quite slight frame? She lay in the bath staring absent-mindedly at her pile of clothes lying on the bathroom floor, and wondered what to wear for her birthday. How different the world was now to that of her mother. She recalled how her mother had told her of her worryingly obsessive Auntie Doris who, back in the thirties when she had shared a B & B room with her mother and another friend, had astonished them by donning white gloves when she got down as far as her underclothes.

'Doris, whatever are you doing putting on gloves to go to bed?' her mum's friend Jessie had asked.

'Oh, I wasn't going to keep them on for bed; it's just that I put them on every night to stop the scratchy bits on my nails from laddering my stockings,' she had replied, much to the silent mirth of Julia's mother and Jessie.

No sooner had the stockings been peeled off by the white-gloved hands than they could see Doris standing anxiously in the moonlight looking back and forth at the bed and the bedroom door.

'Now, what is it?' Jessie had asked.

'Well, what about if you...if I, that is, if we need to – you know – if we need to spend a penny.'

'The toilet's down the corridor on the right,' Mum had answered.

'Oh, but I couldn't possibly walk around a strange house in the middle of the night...and what if they heard me – you know – doing it?'

More shaking of the mattress in the double bed which Jessie and Mum were sharing.

'I shouldn't worry, Doris,' Mum had replied. 'I'm sure there'll be a chamber pot under the bed. Just have a look. You can put the bedside light on, we're not asleep.'

Doris had crouched gingerly on the ground and ducked her head to one side.

'You're right,' she said. 'They've given us one. But...but...'

'Now what's the matter?' asked Jessie.

'But,' she had answered, 'you might hear me using it. I know I'll have to go; I always need to if I've had a late cup of tea. I know what I'll do. I'll tear a page out of the *Argus* and put it in the bottom of the potty and that way I won't disturb anyone.'

Mum and Jessie dined out on this story for years and it had passed into family lore. They had never been able to tell the story without screaming with laughter, especially when they got to the bit about Doris carrying her pot with pee-scented papier mâché out onto the corridor the following morning. Julia lay back in the bath and sighed. It was so good to be of a generation that wasn't riddled with the complexes and Victorian hang-ups of her mother's generation. But then again, what was freedom if she was now tortured by the idea of an unwanted pregnancy? Her only experience of this had been people with whom she had been at school who had gone off to stay with some distant aunt in another town, had had their babies in discreet nursing homes run by nuns, and had then given them up for adoption never to see them again. Either that, or they had struggled to bring the baby up alone, living with the eternal wrath of their father and the resigned pity and grudging and reluctant assistance of their mother. Abortion was a word she knew, but no one in her circle had ever had one. She knew you were supposed to do something with lots of gin and a bath but couldn't remember if the bath had to be boiling hot or stone cold.

That was a thought! Gin! With that she splashed out of the bath, semi-dried her feet and sploshed her way to the kitchen, returning with the gin bottle and a glass. She turned the hot tap on and let it run, almost filling the bath, adding to the water she had just left. Meanwhile she poured herself a tumbler of gin and downed it in three gulps. It was repulsive without the tonic in it, but although wimpish in some ways, Julia had the bit of determination between her teeth.

'Sod you, Owen Griffiths,' she said. ' Sod you!' and lowered herself into the searing hot water, screaming with agony as she did so. She gulped down a second tumbler and lay back feeling it immediately go to her head. When she finally got out, her bottom looked as if someone had taken a brush and a tub of scarlet paint to it. She slumped onto her bed and sank into a deep drunken sleep, the kind that comes to a brief halt about an hour and a half later when one has the uncontrollable urge to get up, drink eighteen pints of water and go to the loo, and then it is impossible to catch even a whoosh of fatigue. That's it for about an hour. This is precisely what happened to Julia, but she managed to go into a deep coma-like sleep at about 5 am. She dreamed that she was on an old-fashioned bus and that Robin was driving it. At one point he stopped the bus and she got out and found herself wandering along a dark lane, utterly lost and very frightened. A little later she discovered the crashed bus and Robin was nowhere to be seen. When she woke she was relieved to find herself in her own bed, safe, and not stumbling through gorse bushes and alien countryside. She felt vaguely pleased that she had dreamed about Robin, because, for Julia, even though her sub-conscious was banging on a large bucket with a metal spoon to get her attention, she was unable to heed the message.

She spent the next days with a cracking headache, lugging food home each time she came back from college, wondering how people managed to cater for large families every day of the week. It felt as if she had been asked to run a restaurant single-handedly for the night. All the money she had drawn out of the bank had gone, and she was now having to revisit. *But hell,* she thought, *for the first time in my life I am having a birthday with the man I love and I think loves me, and I want to share this with the world.* On Friday morning, amongst the boring cards from school friends, one from her grandmother, one from her parents, one from a now very ancient Auntie Doris, and a fabulous home-made one from Ethan and Poppy with a drawing of themselves on horses, she saw a small envelope in Robin's writing. It was an exquisite little Victorian Valentine card resplendent with embroidery, tiny seed pearls, minute glass beads, and antique silk. He had written on it, "Happy Birthday, little Sweet Pea! Love from your knight in rusty armour. Robin x x x".

Robin arrived as promised at seven, bearing a huge bunch of roses and a large gift-wrapped box. As she started undoing it, aglow with the idea that he had chosen something amazing for her, he confessed that he had been rushed off his feet all day and had actually almost forgotten about her birthday, so, instead had had to bring this present for which he apologised, although not overly. Out of the box came the familiar little ormolu clock that she had seen standing on his mantelpiece. She affected delight and hugged him, but inside it felt like when she had asked her mother to go through the pantry and find stuff she could give to the harvest festival at school and a couple of old tins of baked beans and Ambrosia creamed rice that were almost past their sell-by date were handed over, or when she looked for things for the summer fair in the village and would fill a bag with records no one wanted to play, books no one in the family really wanted to read and ornaments that had been not very welcome presents even in their brand-new state. This little clock she knew was valuable, and of course it was like owning a piece of Robin since she associated it very much with his flat. In fact, this made her feel rather guilty.

'God, what will you do without it? I mean, you can't possibly part with it; it's one of your treasures,' she said.

'Oh, don't worry, Jeremy's friend Felix has got a boyfriend who owns an antique shop. He's always getting me little pieces at discount. It will give me an excuse to go clock-hunting!'

She smiled weakly and went off to put the roses into water, thinking how much nicer it would have been if he had demonstrated the same enthusiasm about birthday present hunting for her rather than just reach out and lift something he already owned off a shelf. It was just that little bit too easy, and the fact that he so eagerly needed an excuse to get back to Felix, prince of the misogynists, irritated and hurt her.

She asked him to chop some fruit for a fruit salad while she put the finishing touches to the table out in the small patio area of her garden flat. She glanced up at the sky and it looked fine. The air was still and balmy and they would probably be able to sit out for the entire evening. Archangel Gladys may have induced Robin to bring a second-hand birthday gift, but at least the weather was going to be perfect for al fresco dining. About half an hour later the doorbell went and Celia came in blowing on a little tooter which uncurled as she blew into it, and she was waving a carrier bag in the air.

'Happy birthday, Queen Jules!' she shouted and handed over the large bag which contained the promised birthday cake with a dressing-up tiara from a party shop resting on top of the cake box. Julia giggled and put the tiara on and took her to meet Robin. He shrieked when he saw Julia's tiara, announced his name to Celia with great gusto, and asked where *his* tiara was.

'Now, this is a birthday, not a queens' confederation!' said Julia, laughing, but she couldn't help seeing Celia roll her eyes as she poured herself a glass of Pinot Grigio.

'Ooh, and you'll need these too,' said Celia, handing over a little box of candles. 'A bit DIY but they would have gone all wonky if I'd tried to transport it with them stuck in.'

Sarah and Nigel arrived next looking a bit frazzled.

'Where's Polly?' asked Julia, disappointed to see that they hadn't arrived with the travel cot and all the usual paraphernalia.

'Oh we decided to give ourselves a night off,' said Sarah. 'But we had a last-minute crisis with the babysitter. We managed to poach a neighbour's au pair for the evening. As a result we were convinced we were late. People must have thought that we were on the run from the law the way Nigel was driving. All we needed were black trilby hats and empty violin cases and we would have been mistaken for gangsters. We argued about which route to take for most of the way, and I'm surprised we aren't petitioning for a divorce after it. I can't believe that now we've actually arrived early.

Robin presented them with two glasses, saying, 'Alcohol is the only cure. My name's Robin. I've heard masses about you from Julia. You must be the Wonder Parents, but I'm sad not to be able to witness the living proof with my own eyes. Maybe some other time.'

Julia beamed with pleasure as she saw Sarah and Nigel's shoulders visibly drop with relief that they had arrived at a safe haven and were valued and cherished. She led them all out into the garden and was struck by how pretty it all looked. The hostas that she thought were dead had suddenly resurrected themselves as they did each summer, and were throwing out new leaves every day. The honeysuckle was just going over, but there were a few arum lilies out in the corner next to the eucalyptus tree. Despite the efforts by the slugs to decimate the hollyhocks, they were still making a bid for freedom, and it looked as if some of the plants would still flower even if the half-eaten leaves looked like lace handkerchiefs. There were about six magnificent

California poppies waggling about in a ridiculously too small flower pot. This was typical of Julia's attempts at gardening. She had had no idea of the size they would grow to and had innocently popped the seeds in a few years back. Now, each year that they flowered she promised herself she would take them out of the pots in a month or two and replant them in a bit of real earth, but then, as summer wore on, and there were other things to worry about, mainly the sweet peas, she usually forgot. There were geraniums of course, like one finds in every London garden, but they were the red of guards' uniforms and became almost luminous as the evening light faded. Even some delicate little weed with blue flowers that was invading every cranny and crack in the paving looked as if it had been planted there deliberately rather than just springing up by chance. The bell went again and it was Nat. He had come all the way from Acton by bike and they teased him about his Olympian stamina. He had actually once ridden his bike all the way from London to Dorchester where his parents lived.

'Nat's got to keep doing all this cycling otherwise we would have to sedate him,' said Julia by way of introduction to Robin. 'He's way too overactive. We think he was fed Coca-Cola intravenously as a child or something. He gets up at six to do some fencing practice three days a week, and plays squash before work on Fridays.'

'Well my only exercise is waving my arm back and forth to press the snooze button when the alarm goes off every ten minutes between six and seven,' added Robin.

The phone rang and Julia answered it. It was Francis saying that he and Angie were going to be a bit late. Despite how she felt about Robin, Julia was anxious about seeing Francis as she had spent a considerable amount of time convinced that he was the love of her life and all the others present except Robin had, at one time or another, listened to her tales of ecstasy or woe depending on how the rather imperious Francis had treated her.

It was even more strange that in the end he was now so pally with Angie. Geoff and Marie-Claire came next and gave her the most beautiful little watercolour of Porthcothan in north Cornwall where they had all once spent a holiday. Geoff himself had painted it and Marie-Claire had framed it. In thin brush strokes, down in the sand in the foreground she saw: "Painted for Julia, June 1975"

'You haven't forgotten about me, have you?' said Geoff.

For a moment she looked lost.

'Fatted calves and all that. *Verboten*, et cetera!' he added.

'Oh, God, no, don't worry. I've been up all night slaving over the veggie alternatives, done you some porcini risotto,' she said when the penny finally dropped. 'And Marie-Claire, you look great. I hope you can have a moratorium on the diet tonight. I've done my Moroccan lamb thing, you know, the one with the apricots.'

As everyone was replenishing their glasses, Francis and Angie finally arrived. Julia ran to the door, still in her tiara, and beamed broadly when she saw them.

'Bloody hell! You *shall* go to the ball!' said Francis. 'Happy birthday, Jules. Give us a big squeeze for old times' sake.' And then, sotto voce, added, 'Is he here? Prince Charming I mean?'

'Sshhh! Yes, of course, and no nonsense from you!' said Julia as she took them through to the garden. 'You know, no references to us getting caught by your brother when we were in your parents' bed!'

'As if I would be so indelicate!' he said. 'And by the way, Angie is only a good friend, so if you change your mind about Adonis, give me a call!'

Julia realised the irony of the situation. All those years she had so longed for what they had to be rather more than it was. Now that she seemed spoken for, she had suddenly developed some kind of magnetic power over all men, including her past boyfriend. It was ever thus.

The evening was such a success that she didn't waste one single minute worrying about if her waistband was getting tight or whether she needed to go out for a quick fix of marzipan-covered Brussels sprouts or some such craving. Robin nattered away and did his usual confident stand-up routine, earning his spurs as party animal, but she detected a certain nervousness in the speed at which he was speaking and the level of exaggeration in the stories since he knew she was on her familiar home ground and he was being vetted. She was very relieved that he hadn't referred once to his missed trip to Amsterdam and wondered shyly if he thought the evening was worth cancelling the trip for. As she was collecting up the last of the birthday cake plates, Celia announced that she had a fantastic game that she wanted them all to have a go at.

'You'll all need something to write with and it will only take a few minutes but it's brilliant, I promise you!'

'Twenty minutes to find enough pencils and three minutes for the game: it feels like some kind of deep comment on the human condition,' said Geoff as everyone scoured shelves and delved in pockets and bags for writing tools.

After much scuffling around searching for enough pens and pencils, and the tearing up of an exercise book, they settled down like eager school children awaiting their instructions.

'Now I want everyone to write the numbers one to eleven in a column,' said Celia.

'Now,' she continued, 'beside numbers one and two you can write any number you like.'

'Oh Lord,' said Robin. 'Is this going to be one of those where you magically end up with your own birthday by some spooky sorcery, or is it going to give us all the day the world's going to end?'

'None of those! Now pay attention!' said Celia in mock-headmistressy tones.

Julia wrote "100" in her space by number two.

'Next,' she added, 'write the names of members of the opposite sex next to numbers three and seven.'

Julia, of course wrote down Robin's name next to three, and, because he had been such a flirt earlier on, she put Francis next to number seven.

'Are there one or two Ns in Dunaway?' asked Robin. Then he quickly added, 'Oh shit, I've given it away. I was thinking of Faye Dunaway.'

'No, sorry, Robin,' said Celia. 'They have to be people you actually know. Go with your first instincts.'

Julia's heart sank. She had hoped that he would have written *her* name next to one of the numbers. Maybe she should change her own? Then she decided that it would be either bad luck, or that this was just some stupid game of consequences or some such and didn't matter anyway.

'Yes, miss,' said Robin, mock-deferentially.

'Has everyone done that?' asked Celia, tapping her fingers a little impatiently against her wine glass.

'Yes!' they all chorused.

'Now write anyone's name: friends or family by numbers four, five and six.'

This was easier. Julia wrote Mel's name next to number four, Celia's name by number five, and then, as a joke, wrote 'Fish', meaning old Martin Cox, the Principal from Haverstock College next to six. Everyone was feverishly scribbling, giggling nervously and covering up their papers with their arms as if they were eight years old and doing a school test and preventing their desk mates from copying.

'Now this is quite a hard bit,' said Celia. 'By numbers eight, nine, ten and eleven you have to write four song titles.'

'Corky-o-Rorky, Ceals,' said Nat. 'I thought you said this was going to take three minutes. You know what blokes are like with lists of stuff, especially songs. We could be here all night. Can it be any song at all?'

'Anything you like, even German lieder if you like,' said Celia.

There was quite a long silence while everyone concentrated and hummed little snatches of tunes. It was another exam hall moment. Julia racked her brain which suddenly seemed to blank out all tunes except advertising jingles. She could hardly put down "The Esso sign means happy motoring so call at the Esso sign!". She thought back to her youth and tried to remember the songs that had made a big impression on her. She'd adored Buddy Holly and still did, and quickly tried to choose a favourite. She had also had a serious folk music phase at university, and this led her on to all the stuff she had danced to at summer balls in the past or listened to incessantly as she was swotting for finals. She imagined that most of the group would be plundering the sixties for their song titles as it was the music of their teens.

'Bum! All I can think of are Eurovision tunes,' said Francis, chuckling at his own stupidity. 'I can't imagine "Boom-Bang-a-Bang" is going to be much use in this game, however daft it turns out to be!'

'Finally,' said Celia imperiously.

'Thank God for that!' interrupted Geoff.

'And finally,' said Celia, undeterred, you all have to make a wish.'

'Oh no!' they groaned in unison.

'I'm not making the same mistake as I did in Moscow!' Robin muttered to Julia who was sitting next to him.

'Well at least Ceals isn't going to make you eat the paper.' Then she looked up and said to Celia,

'You're not, are you, Ceals?'

Celia, baffled, replied, 'Not what?'

'Going to make us eat these pieces of paper?'

'Darling, I know it's your birthday, but how much have you had to drink?' said Celia, looking at Julia as if she was barking mad.

'No, it's just that Robin had to do this kind of thing once and they had to burn all their wishes and then swallow the ashes to make the wishes come true.'

'And what other voodoo practices are you into, Robin? Would you like to share them with the group?' teased Angie. 'What about eating lizards' blood or walking barefoot over glowing coals?'

'Nothing quite that bad,' laughed Robin, and looking knowingly at Julia, he added, 'But I have had to spend half an hour drinking Harvey's Bristol Cream with old Coxy, the Principal at our college. Does that count?'

Julia grinned, especially since she had already put old Fish's name on her own list.

'OK! All done?' asked Celia.

'No! Wait!' Julia said, and frantically tried to write something that was meaningful but not so personal that she would have to emigrate after her party, having revealed too much of her innermost desires to the group. In the end she scribbled, "Spend my life being loved by the person I love" and then she thought the better of it and crossed it out. In the end she settled for "Have babies before the menopause kicks in".

'Right! That's it! Pens down!' said Celia, still scarily sounding like a primary school teacher.

'Hands on heads, fingers on lips!' added Francis, grinning.

'George, don't do that!' said Robin, doing a perfect impersonation of Joyce Grenfell doing her nursery teacher monologue.

'Now, you each have to pass your paper to the person sitting on your left,' instructed Celia. Julia passed hers to Francis whilst Robin passed his to her. Julia looked fleetingly down the page to see if her own name was there, and, sure enough, next to number four, there she was. *Phew!* she thought. She smiled when she saw his choice of music.

'OK, who's going to start?' asked Celia.

'I don't mind going first, but what are we actually supposed to do?' volunteered Nigel.

'Well,' said Celia, 'this is a very spooky little piece of paper you each hold in your hands. The figure you all wrote beside number two is the number of people you each have to tell about this game. So, Nigel, how many people does Sarah have to tell about this?'

Nigel consulted Sarah's paper.

'Three,' he said.

'Lucky you!' said Celia. 'You'll realise why in a little while. So, to continue, Nigel, who has Sarah put next to number three?'

'With great imagination my darling wife has written my own name,' said Nigel.

'Perfect!' said Celia. 'Because number three is the one that you love, Sarah.'

Julia suddenly felt herself having a massive hot flush as she knew that Francis was holding a piece of paper on which she had put Robin's name next to number three. She glanced down to see who Robin had put in that space and after Faye Dunaway had been crossed out he had written, barely legibly, "Norah Forester".

'Oh, keep it coming, Ceals!' said Nigel. 'What does number four mean?'

'Number four is the person that you care about most.'

'Bloody hell, Sarah, ten out of ten!' said Nigel. 'You've got Polly down by number four so I've been relegated, eh?'

Sarah laughed and wagged her finger at him saying,

'Fact of life old sunshine. Any mother will tear her heart out for her own kids.'

'She is now turning into a pelican,' said Nigel. 'They actually do that, did you know? I suppose if you've run out of fish fingers it's a useful standby! Moving swiftly on, what about number five, Madame Arkady?'

'The person who knows you very well.'

'Wow! Spot on, Sarah, you've got your mum by this one. Hey,

this is fucking creepy! Now what? Six?'

'Six,' said Celia, 'is her lucky star.'

'Who the hell is Kaku Punjani?!'

'He's my dentist. How could you forget that name?' said Sarah.

'What the hell's *he* doing on your list?'

'Well, I remembered I've got to see him and the hygienist while we were doing this, and he just popped into my head,' replied Sarah as if this was a perfectly sensible explanation.

'I suppose if you need some expensive bridge work, who better than your lucky star? A brilliant choice, Sarah, if I may say so,' offered Robin. Nigel didn't look quite so enthusiastic, but was happy to read on.

'What about number seven, Celia?'

'Number seven is an interesting one. It's the one you like but you can't work out.'

Nigel grinned and looked at Julia.

'What's she written?' squealed Angie, unable to contain her curiosity.

'The person with this particular honour is Monsieur Robin Forester here,' said Nigel. And there was a chorus of saucy 'Ooh!s'.

'Now we come to the really good bit,' said Celia. 'The songs!' Everyone was absolutely silent and waiting for the explanation and analysis. 'The song next to number eight is the song that matches the person in number three. At this moment Sarah screamed with horror and hilarity. Nigel shouted, 'I don't believe it! Send for the divorce lawyers!' But he was roaring with laughter.

'Sarah, what did you write?!' begged Marie-Claire.

Sarah wiped small laughter tears away with her fingers and finally managed to tell them, 'I wrote "Help!"' whereupon everyone else joined in the hilarity.

'Fantastic!' Nat said. 'What's the next one? I can't wait!'

'The song by number nine is the song for the person you've put next to number seven,' Celia said. 'As far as I can remember that was you, Robin, wasn't it?'

Robin was holding his head in his hands, covering his ears, saying, 'Oh please don't let it be "You're So Vain" or "My Ding-a-ling".'

'No, it's a really good one,' said Nigel. She's put "Bridge Over Troubled Water".'

'We all know who to come to when we start fighting then,' said Angie.

'This is just like a horoscope,' said Robin. 'When it's nice you're convinced the whole thing is completely real and true; when it's not what you want to hear you say it's a load of bollocks. Talking of which, what's the next song supposed to be, Celia?'

'Song number ten is the one that tells you about your mind.'

'Oh, great!' Sarah said. 'I remember what I put for that one. I wrote "It's getting better all the time"; it's one of my favourite Beatles' songs.'

'I've got to say this, Celia, but this is amazing,' said Nigel, and what's so weird about Sarah's choices is that they all sort of fit the answers. I mean, she could have written "Delilah" or something and it would have just been nonsense.'

'We haven't finished yet,' said Celia. 'I haven't told you about song number eleven. This is the song that tells how you feel about life.'

As everyone tried to remember which song they had written as their last song, there was a mixture of groans and bursts of incredulous laughter. Julia felt sick, as she remembered all too well that this had been her Buddy Holly song. But whereas she could have written "I Guess it Doesn't Matter Any More", she had actually written, "It's Raining in my Heart". *Who had devised this bloody thing?* she thought to herself, *it's bloody witchcraft. How do they know this?!* However, she was interrupted in her reverie by Celia adding, 'You have to send this to the number of people that you wrote by number two and it will all come true. See what I meant when I said you were lucky, Sarah? You've only got to do it with three other people. I had to do it with nine others and *voilà!*' She gestured with her arms at the surrounding company, adding, 'So thanks, everyone, now my wish is going to come true! By the way, if you don't, it will become the opposite. Right, let's hear some others. What've you got there, Julia?' Julia had now to read out Robin's offering.

'Well, the person he loves is Norah Forester. That wouldn't be your mum by any chance, would it, Robin?' Robin nodded a bit shamefacedly.

'And the one he cares about most—' Julia blushed deeply '—is, ahem, moi.' And she blew him an ostentatious kiss to make light of the moment. 'The person who knows him really well is Jeremy; the person who is his lucky star is Mark.'

And here she affected as casual a voice as she could.

'The person you like but you can't work out is Donna, the music lecturer at college.'

'God, Jules,' said Celia. 'Hearing the name Mark, that reminds me, d'you remember that guy called Mark who used to be the director of our play group thingy when we went on the trip to Italy about five years ago? Wasn't he a tosser? He used to have his hands on everyone. And he was having that thing with Mel, too. D'you still see her, Jules? I thought you used to be really good mates.'

'Er, yes, I have once or twice,' said Julia, deeply uncomfortable, more for Robin than anything else. He had got up and was re-filling his wine glass with his back to her. 'I think she's still married though.'

'Thank God for that,' said Celia, completely oblivious of the situation. 'A year or two before that he made a huge pass at me, but he was so lecherous I couldn't bear him to touch me.'

Julia now thought she was going to faint, so immediately

swung the conversation back to the game.

'Hey, we haven't finished Robin's analysis, where was I, oh, here it is, the songs! How could we have forgotten those!'

Robin ostentatiously stuck his fingers in his ears and said, 'It wasn't me; I was possessed by a succubus or whatever they are. I'm not responsible for what I wrote! I pity Jules having to read these out!'

Julia now had the attention of the whole group once more.

'OK, here goes. The song that matches the person in number three…that was your mum if I remember rightly, was "Big Spender".'

'Absolutely correct in her case!' said Robin. 'That woman could spend for England. She thought she'd been a Pools winner in another life I think. That's why we were always poor. What did I put for the next song? I've forgotten.'

'The next song which is for Donna is "The Entertainer". Brilliant! That's quite right, and of course I would have expected you to put old Scott Joplin in amongst the songs.'

She looked at the others and said, 'Robin adores piano rags. Now song number ten. This is the one that tells you about your mind, that's right, isn't it, Ceals?' Celia nodded.

'That's—' She started laughing. 'Oh, nice one, Robin, "Puppet on a String".'

Robin did a mime of puppet arms at this point.

'Good gorilla impression, Robin,' said Francis, and Julia detected a little note of jealousy there.

'OK, sock it to me,' said Robin. 'What is the song telling me about life? It can't get much worse than what you've already read out.'

'"Satisfaction"!' said Julia, smiling, and immediately at least four of the others started singing along to the song in the spirit of the game. As Julia heard them all laughing and drunkenly singing "I can't get no-oh satisfaction" she thought to herself, *How right they are! Little do they know.*

'We didn't do his wish,' said Marie-Claire.

'Oh, this is worthy of Miss World,' said Julia. 'He wants universal peace and loads of money. Robin you naughty boy, I think I detect a bit of a piss-take here.'

'All right, Birthday Queen,' said Francis, 'it's payback time. Ready or not, I'm going to read yours.' Julia's brow furrowed, her shoulders came up, and she bared her bottom teeth in a look of mock-horror, as if anticipating being clubbed to death like a seal on a beach.

'The one she lurves is young Robin here. Congratulations my man! And the one she cares about most is Mel. That's twice Mel's name's come up in the last few minutes. By the way, why isn't she here, Jules?'

'Oh, she and Deke have gone away to Spain this week,' answered Julia, relieved indeed that they hadn't been there.

'OK,' continued Francis. 'The one that she knows very well is number five, Celia, that's you. Mmm when's my name coming up, Jules? And the one who is her lucky star is…Jules, I can't read it, it looks like Fish.'

'That's because it *is* Fish,' said Julia, grinning at Robin. 'That's Martin Cox's nickname. He's our boss.'

'I have to say,' said Robin, 'that the words "lucky" and "star" are the last two I would ever associate with old Cox, but I suppose he was a lucky star because that's where I had the pleasure of first encountering the Birthday Queen here.'

Marie-Claire gave Julia a sweet smile to show that she thought this was a moving little speech by Robin.

'Order! Order!' shouted Francis. 'This next bit's important. Silence in court! The one that she likes but can't work out is, ta-dah! Me!' Then, as Julia was shaking her head and laughing, he added, 'You had long enough, Jules.'

Julia was embarrassed but at the same time flattered to have Francis flirting mercilessly with her in front of Robin. It certainly made a change from the Billy No-Mates state of her love life up until recently.

'Now the juicy bits,' said Francis, and embarked on the songs. 'The one she chose for man of the match here, young Robin is, wait for it, "Dancing Queen".'

Sarah, Nigel, Geoff and Angie roared with laughter as they didn't know the story of Robin's past. Julia saw Celia tap Marie-Claire's leg with the outside of her foot. Francis wasn't laughing but he wasn't nudging anyone or giving Julia narrow-eyed "What's up?" looks. She wondered what Francis was thinking about her and Robin. She worried deeply about how Robin was taking this. Of course it had in no way been deliberate. How could it have been? She hadn't realised what the game was all about when she had started playing it.

'Oh Lord, my secret's out!' screamed Robin. 'I'll be starring with Danny La Rue at the Palladium next!' And he turned to Julia and said, kissing her, 'Thanks a billion, darling!' Of course this diffused the slightly scary moment and everyone applauded.

'And moving swiftly on,' said Francis. 'The song that is for ME is…oh, I think it's my lucky night, everyone; sorry Robin, it's "Plaisir d'Amour".'

Julia was eager to make a joke of this as it was becoming more and more uncomfortable.

'Oh, Francis, you pig! You *know* I picked that one because it was one of the only folk songs I could play properly on the guitar. It only had three chords and I played it endlessly. It's not my bloody fault it happens to be about love.'

'It could have been worse, Jules,' said Nat. 'You could have chosen another three-chord song such as "Blowing in the Wind". Oops, Geoff, sorry, forgot about you veggies. It was lentil soup, wasn't it?' and in that moment, all tension was gone and everyone was laughing.

'And the song that tells us about Julia's mind is – and this is a bit Ingmar Bergman – "Whiter Shade of Pale". Time to book in with the shrink, Jules.' There was silence.

'Well that shut you all up!' said Julia. 'If you think that's bad, just wait till he tells you what song tells you how I feel about life!' And she made a mock sad-face with an over-emphasised turned down mouth, lower lip pouting sadly.

'"It's Raining in my Heart",' announced Francis and there was a collective sympathetic 'Aaahh!' from everyone.

'That was a bit of a bummer, Jules,' said Francis. 'Next time we play, remember to put down "The Laughing Policeman"!'

'Don't worry, we haven't read yours yet, and who knows what we're going to get there. How about "The Carnival is Over" or "Please Release Me"?' she said teasingly.

'Oh damn!' said Robin. 'I wish I'd picked "Running Bear" and then you would have all thought I was a closet naturist if you'd been enjoying the pun.'

'Always wiser after the deed, as my old granny used to say,' said Geoff. 'And hey, Jules, we haven't heard your wish yet.'

'Oh it was just some tosh about having babies before the menopause gets me,' she said.

'Yes,' said Francis. 'But you have to play this game with a further one hundred people to make it work. That's the number you wrote at the beginning.'

'Well, see you in the convent then,' said Julia, winking at Angie and Marie-Claire.

Despite the few embarrassing glitches so far during the game, the evening was going well and Julia was happy that they seemed to be embracing Robin into their midst. In a perfect world he would be staying on after all the others left, helping her wash up and then taking her to bed. But she knew that this would not be on the agenda. Why on earth was she so diffident and nervous about tackling it with him? Possibly because she didn't want to hear the real reason which she all along suspected and could not acknowledge to herself.

Now it was Francis's turn to have his soul bared by Celia's bizarre game. Julia was a bit uneasy about what double entendres were in store, especially as all of them in the room, apart from Robin, had shared the tortuous years of her deeply dysfunctional relationship with Francis. She could tell that he had, what her grandmother would say, "a bit of the devil" in him that evening. He no longer really wanted her as his girlfriend, at least not in the sense of a partner with whom he would one day have babies, but he was desperate to prove that he could still win the flirting war and give a good old yank on her heart strings. Angie, who had arrived with Francis, was looking a bit bemused as she was not his new girlfriend, simply an old friend and was now in the role of honorary arm candy since Julia had asked Francis to "bring a girl". She, however, was not the one who was going to be reading Francis's paper. That duty was left to Nat who was sitting next to Francis.

'Are you sitting comfortably, or should I say uncomfortably, Francis? We are about to lay you bare to the world.'

Francis flung his arms and head back in an attempt to look like someone abandoning themselves to a ritual killing.

'You'll love this one, Jules! Number three, the person he loves, is you!'

There were whoops from the others and Julia felt a mixture of delight and embarrassment mainly on Robin's behalf. He had that kind of expression on his face which looked like he had just sat down in a wet cowpat but was trying to give the impression that he was fine and was hoping no one had noticed. She knew him well enough by now to read his face quite closely.

'The one you care about most is Georgie. Oh well, that's your sister so that figures. The one who knows you very well is Tim. Who's Tim?'

'We were at school together. He used to let me copy all his maths; I think I had the numerical bit surgically removed from my brain just after birth,' explained Francis.

'OK,' said Nat, 'and Geoff is your lucky star. Hey, something here I don't know about?' He winked at Francis.

'I've always wanted to be Jack Lemmon to his Tony Curtis,' said Geoff.

'I think you'll find, Sugar Puss,' said Francis, camping it up with gusto, 'that although Jack and Tony wore drag for *Some Like it Hot* they were not gay; how about me being Julian to your Sandy?'

'Ah, now you're talking!' said Geoff.

Julia began to feel uncomfortable again for Robin, as she realised that although he himself could make jokes about being camp, the conversation would be as upsetting for him as her sitting around a table with him, Jeremy and Felix all having a laugh at the expense of heterosexual couples. She intervened to change the subject.

'Who's number seven?'

'Er, let's see,' said Nat. 'Number seven is Vanessa. Over to you, Casanova!' He looked enquiringly down across at Francis.

'Just a little squeeze I see now and then,' said Francis, a trifle uneasily, and Julia could see that although this was a game he had inadvertently written the name of someone whom he had obviously marked down as a possible bed fellow. Maybe he was already seeing her, however he seemed to go no further with his revelations, saying, 'Oh God, I know what you're going to say next. It's the songs, isn't it?'

'Fraid so,' said Nat. 'And you will all be devastated, all of you except maybe Robin, to hear that the song which matches with number three, a.k.a. Julia, is the old Carpenters' hit – "I'll Say Goodbye to Love". There was a unanimous sigh and a lot of 'Aw!' noises.

'Well that's one rival out of the way!' said Robin brightly, once again throwing them all off the scent of the true complexity of his own sexuality and his relationship as far as it had gone with Julia.

'And I am sure the mysterious Vanessa will be thrilled to know that the song which is for her is "Good Vibrations"!' said Nat, followed by a la-la-lala rendition of the Wedding March tune.

The song which tells us about his unutterably complex mind is "Heartbreak Hotel". So maybe not such good news for Vanessa after all! And the song which tells us how he feels about life is "Those Were the Days". Well, we'll wait for your autobiography, Jules, to know what that was all about, and maybe Vanessa will be around to your house to take revenge so I'd get a few window locks fitted.'

'What was his wish?' Sarah asked.

'Oh, quite humble, really,' said Nat, grinning. He just wants "Fame, money and a title"! May I present to you, ladies and gentleman, Lord Francis Up-Yer-Bum, doyen of the Dempster column and owner of Moneybags Castle.'

'You'll see, you'll see. You'll be laughing on the other side of your face when I've got my Oscar and I live in a stately home!' laughed Francis.

'The only time I'll be laughing on the other side of my face is when I have my stroke in the Nursing Home aged eighty-five,' said Julia, and with that they took a break to open another bottle of wine. Robin muttered to Julia that he really had to be going since he had now promised an aunt who was unwell that he would travel down to the south coast the next day to visit her and had to catch a very early train. Despite her disappointment, Julia went to the door with him and hugged him and stayed frozen in the hug for a long while, saying as she did so, that it had been the perfect birthday.

'I loved meeting all your friends,' he said.

'And they loved you too,' she replied.

'I wonder what Celia really meant when she talked about Mark making a pass at her...before he started that thing with Mel he was with me,' said Robin.

'Robin, it's water under the bridge, and you know what Mark is, sorry, was like,' said Julia.

'Spose so,' said Robin. 'Ok, little Sweet Pea, and thanks again. I'll ring you tomorrow evening.' And with that he was gone.

Bugger it, she thought as she closed the door, *why was I so accommodating and comforting? He was talking about his ex-lover, his bloody ex-MALE lover, and there's me being sympathetic and soothing his ruffled feathers. I should have slapped his face and said, 'You're with me now, Buster' but I suppose that's just it...is he with me or are we just playing at "Boyfriend Girlfriend". I've got to push a bit more and find out, but I am so shit-scared of losing him altogether. I'd settle for anything I can get because I really don't feel I am worth any better or any more. I don't deserve it.*

With that, she opened the door into the sitting room where the rest of them were screaming with gales of laughter listening to Marie-Claire's choices being read out by Sarah.

She threw herself into the swim of things and in the hour or so after Robin left, Julia drank enough to make up for her earlier abstinence since she had been aware of her hostess duties and hadn't wanted to drop the entire tagine on the kitchen floor in a display of drunken laissez-faire. By one in the morning they had all left and Julia began the clear-up operation. It had all gone to plan and she was satisfied. However, as she gradually progressed to her third wet tea towel of the night, she began to revisit some of the earlier hairy moments such as her innocent choice of "Dancing Queen". It could have been any one of fifty Abba songs and yet she had chosen that one. Why hadn't she picked "Take a Chance On Me" for God's sake? Ah well, it was done, and now it was time to move on and look forward to the next event with Robin. She decided to leave the saucepans to soak, and drained her final glass of Merlot and went to bed, but was too high on the excitement of the dinner to fall asleep for a long while. 'Thank God tomorrow's Saturday,' she muttered to herself as she wheeled back along the corridor from the bathroom to the bedroom. Eventually sleep came.

Chapter Thirteen

On Saturday morning the phone woke Julia and she leapt up completely on automatic pilot and swung herself over the bedside table to answer it. Her mother now lived in a small village in Cornwall and owned a lurcher called Louis who needed a two-mile walk before breakfast each day, so for her, nine thirty was well on the way to lunch time.

'Hello, Mum? Anything the matter?' asked Julia.

'No, just ringing to see if you're OK,' the disembodied voice replied. 'And to wish you a belated happy birthday. I've just come back with Louis from the field. He chased a rabbit and I had the devil of a job getting him to come back. He always does that sort of thing when I'm in a hurry to get back. It's as if he knows and he's just trying to be awkward.'

'Mum, I think you're projecting a bit too much,' said Julia. 'You'll be choosing TV programmes because you think he'll like them rather than watching what you're interested in if you're not too careful. He's a dog, Mum, and you need to teach him you're the dominant one. I saw a programme on TV last week about this very thing. Apparently you should never let your dog go through the door in front of you; you should make him wait so he can see that you're the 'dominant dog', and you know how you always give Louis his dinner when you get home, well, you should feed yourself first and make him wait.'

'Oh that would be a nightmare,' said Julia's mother. 'The thought of him sitting beside the table looking at me with those big watery dark eyes is too dreadful to contemplate. Dad and I wouldn't be able to eat.'

'You'd have to wear one of those aeroplane eye masks that you get when you fly across the Atlantic,' joked Julia. 'But if you make him wait, it's another sign that you are the leader of the pack. And, Mum?'

'Yes, what, dear?'

'He's not on the bed is he?'

As she was talking, Julia was aware that she was feeling a bit queasy.

Silence.

'Mum? You bad, bad girl!' He's running the house! He'll be telling you when to pay the gas bill next!' said Julia, but she was laughing as she said it.

'But he feels so comfy up against our feet,' said her mother, guiltily.

'Mum, you're incurable!'

'Well, enough of me and my fixation with being inferior dog in the pack. What are you up to? Have you seen the new boyfriend again? What's his name? Robert, isn't it?

'Robin actually, Mum. Yes, he came round to dinner last night with a load of people. You know: Sarah, Nigel, Nat, Geoff and few others. It was great. We had a real laugh with a game that Celia had cooked up. I'll try it out with you and Auntie Muriel when I come down. You'll love it. Uh, Mum, can you excuse me? I think I need the loo a bit urgently.'

'Of course, dear, phone me next week and let me know how things are going.'

'Yep. Promise. Got to dash. Thanks for ringing.'

Julia slammed the phone down and ran to the bathroom and retched.

'Oh God! Oh God! Oh God! Please don't let me be pregnant!' she said aloud, and burst into tears. She brushed her teeth and went back to the bedroom to consult her calendar. She should have a period in the first few days of the following week if she wasn't pregnant. The stress was already showing on her face. She felt that the combination of worrying about the relationship with Robin and the possibility of this devastating unwanted pregnancy had aged her by about ten years. She began making silent pacts with God. 'I'll say a psalm every day if you promise to let me have a period. I'll join a Good Neighbour scheme and visit an old lady three times a week if you let me have a period. I'll give ten percent of my earnings to the poor in Africa if you let me have a period. I'll volunteer to have my bone marrow taken away and given to someone in need.' And so on... She stopped short of promising to join an enclosed silent order of Carmelite nuns but it was almost going that way.

She had a bath, got herself ready for the day and completed the washing up and putting away of everything and the shifting back of furniture. While she was throwing the empty bottles in the bin she heard the phone go again. It was Celia.

'Jules, thanks so much for that night. I hope you enjoyed your own birthday party. Great to meet the famous Mr Forester at last!'

'What d'you think?' asked Julia anxiously.

'Funny, good-looking, obviously very fond of you and I thought a bit nervous...and I have to say this and I hope you won't be offended, if you hadn't already told me about his previous relationship I think I might have sussed out that his sexuality was a bit in question, but, as you say, it's not cut and dried. It's not as if he's gay...I honestly don't know enough about bisexuality to give you any advice. You've just got to go with your own gut instincts. Just be careful and don't get hurt.'

'Thanks, Ceals,' said Julia. 'It's just that...how can I explain it? When people say in those awful Barbara Cartland books that the heroine "gave herself to him" when she finally succumbed and slept with the hero, well, we've never slept with each other but that's exactly how I feel. I've sort of given him my heart for safe-keeping but I'm terrified he's going to put it up on some dusty shelf and forget all about it. I don't think he realises how totally and irrevocably I've fallen for him. Or maybe he has and he's scared shitless by it and is backing off. I just don't know any more. Anyway, let's change the subject. I don't want to sound like some everlasting agony column letter writer. Thanks for the cake. It was wonderful. God, all that cream and chocolate!'

'Actually, I was going to apologise for it, Jules. I think it was a bit OTT on the cream and chocolate front. In fact I have to confess I yakked up a bit when I got home. I think the combination of the cake and that last bottle of red wine just took my stomach a bridge too far. I was already a bit pissed and I hadn't even undressed. I found myself bending over the loo, trying to be sick when suddenly one of the strings of pearls on the choker I was wearing burst and pearls started bouncing all over the bathroom floor. It sounded like a hailstorm and it put me off my stroke. I stopped wanting to be sick and then spent about ten minutes on my hands and knees picking up pearls. I was actually sick later when I got up for a glass of water, and I have to say I felt better afterwards. Sorry to be so graphic. And God, I hope no one else was sick; if so it's all my fault and that bloody cream.'

'Everything's fine. Don't worry! I love you, Ceals,' said Julia, laughing.

'Eh?! What? Jules, have you gone completely barking?' said Celia.

'No, it's a long story, but I was sick too and I thought I was pregnant.'

'But I thought you hadn't slept together,' said Celia, quizzically.

And Julia then began to tell an outraged Celia about her ordeal in Wales.

'Good God, I would have kicked him in the balls,' said Celia.

'Well, there are lots of "would haves" and "should haves" here, Ceals, but what about poor Miranda? What would I have done if she had heard me and had come in? I felt so awful for her.'

'Jules,' said Celia, 'what about feeling awful for *you*?! You need to value yourself more, you know, and you are in danger of doing the exact opposite in this particular little set-up with Robin. Does he realise what he is doing to you? You really shouldn't keep beating yourself up all the time. You deserve better than this. I know I'm not a great one to talk, but I want the old Jules back. The one that had us pissing ourselves laughing every night at the dinner table at college.'

'I know,' was all Julia could say. She felt she had wandered off alone down a long tunnel in an underground cave complex and that the battery was about to give out in her torch. *Oh how could this have felt so right and yet be turning out to be so wrong?* was her constant thought.

Sarah phoned later and so did Marie-Claire but Julia didn't have the heart to ask them if they too had been upset by the food. Robin phoned that evening and told her that an old school friend and his wife had invited him to dinner the following weekend. They lived in a magical old rectory in Hertfordshire and when he had mentioned that he had a girlfriend that he wanted them to meet, they had instantly included her in the invitation. Julia was over the moon and deeply relieved that this time she was going to meet heterosexual friends of his. And he'd called her "his girlfriend". Phew!

'It's completely informal,' he said. 'I'm not teaching on Friday afternoon but I'll meet you at Liverpool Street at six o'clock. I'll be by platform six.'

'Terrific!' she said. 'See you there.'

Throughout the following week she tried to concentrate on her lesson plans and banished thoughts of pregnancy since she was under such a mountain of work. Every day she expected to get the warning signs of the hormonal headache but there wasn't even the faintest ache or tension in the shoulders or the vague distant throbbing in the nape of her neck which was so often the precursor.

God, if only you could do a pregnancy test yourself in private, she thought, *maybe it'll happen one day. I'd give a Nobel Prize for science to the person who invented that!* Julia had an appointment to see the doctor which she had booked a few weeks previously as she had needed a medical for an insurance form. While there, and certainly divulging none of the details, she mentioned that there was the slight possibility that she might be pregnant although it was, at this stage, probably too early to know one way or the other. The doctor, who was a rather no-nonsense Scottish female, asked her, as they always do, to 'Just pop up on the bed for me'. Julia duly obeyed, thinking that really the doctor would dismiss her concerns as fantasy borne of fear. Dr McCormick pressed firmly down in several places on her abdomen with the palm of her hand, and then said in quite a casual way,

'Well yes, your womb does seem a wee bit distended.'

It was as if Julia had been hit in the chest with a jack hammer and she said very quietly, 'What can I do?'

She was expecting the doctor to come up with some instant simple solution such as 'Just take this course of tablets and avoid alcohol for five days and you'll be fine' but she retorted, even a little tetchily, 'There's nothing I can do except help you to have the baby safely if, indeed, you are pregnant. You had better give it a few more weeks and then come back if you haven't had your period.'

Julia swallowed hard, thanked her, and then left the surgery forgetting, in her confusion, to take her insurance form with her. She blundered back, murmured 'Thanks again, Doctor,' and rushed out.

All the way to the bus stop she cried very quietly and had to fumble for her sunglasses so that people didn't think that she was either mad or had just had tragic news. She had really asked the doctor about the possible pregnancy because she thought she was being stupid and letting her imagination run away with her. The idea was that the doctor would look at her and pooh-pooh the idea and tell her she was being a silly-billy, not add to her terror.

When she got home she rang Marie-Claire who convinced her that it was surely a phantom pregnancy as she knew all about this sort of thing as her Golden Retriever, Chloe, had once suffered with the same problem, and had exhibited every symptom in the textbook apart from actually giving birth to puppies. She added, in her slight French accent, 'Don't be nervous, Julia, you probably don't 'ave a puppy either, it is just air, no?'

Julia smiled weakly, nodded and thanked her and decided that alcohol was the only medicine worth bothering with. What she resented most about this whole situation she was now in was that she was turning into a bit of a drama queen, someone who seemed to lurch from one crisis to another and never seemed to have interest in or time for anyone else's lives and problems. Instead of enriching her and freeing her up to live her life in a normal way, it was obsessing her. After a couple of glasses of wine, she felt slightly more mellow and opted for an early night.

Just as she was drifting off to sleep, the phone went. Rather insanely cheerfully, as it was the alcohol talking, she announced her number and was jolted back to consciousness when she heard Robin's voice on the other end of the line.

'Hi! I thought you were busy all week,' she said, frantically rubbing her face to simultaneously wake and sober herself up.

'Yes, I am absolutely deluged with college stuff, but I just wanted to sound you out on something. Richard and Helen have suggested that it would be more sensible to stay Friday night rather than dash back on the last train. I said I'd check it out with you? Is that OK or do you have to be in town at the crack of dawn for anything?'

'No, no, wonderful, great, toothbrushes at midnight it is then!'

'It seemed like a good idea,' he said. 'Especially as they've got some pretty stunning countryside around where they live. We might even manage a bit of a walk on Saturday morning.'

This was getting better with every sentence.

'And wellies at dawn as well,' she added.

'Yep, I don't think we are expected to go completely native and milk goats or anything like that, but we may get to remind ourselves what sky looks like, and trees. Don't see much of that in central London. So still OK for six o'clock?'

'Absolutely,' she said. 'Thanks again. Night night.'

'Night, Sweet Pea!' he said and there was the click of the line going dead.

The next day Julia took a look at her three rather sad pairs of pyjamas and the one nightdress she had had for about six years and realised that drastic measures were called for. In her long lunch break the next day she went out hunting for some rather more alluring nightwear, and realised that she had somehow to find a compromise between looking like hooker or a middle-aged suburban housewife. As well as Robin, there were his friends to think of. They may be outraged if she wore something too sexy. But the fact remained: her existing nightwear was far too cosy and comfortable. As ever, the nightdress that she liked best because it was made of expensive silk, cost the most, and she took a deep breath and presented her credit card, telling herself, "Speculate to accumulate". What she also realised was this whole exercise was making her feel deeply uncomfortable as it was so much out of character. Francis had always taken the initiative with her and they had fallen into a pattern of her smiling coyly and him reading the signals and, caveman like, carrying her off to his lair.

Just before she went back to college, she realised that she also needed to buy a present for Robin's friends, and bought some chocolates and a rather beautiful pot pourri.

Finally, she had the small bag packed and she watched the clock most of Friday afternoon while she was invigilating for the students' exams, longing for the moment to come when she could race off to Liverpool Street.

Robin, as ever, looked like an eager and happy schoolboy when he spotted her scuttling along the station concourse towards him. He looked into her eyes and gave her a twinkly smile saying, 'Isn't this exciting! Our big adventure out of town!'

Helen met them at the station and drove them to the village

where the house was like a film set for a Jane Austen novel. The first thing Julia noticed when she got out of the car was the amazing and overpowering scent of wisteria. They crunched across the gravel from the car and trooped past the pond with the giant plastic heron designed to keep the real thing at bay.

'Hideous, isn't it?' said Helen, as she noticed Julia looking at it. 'A few months ago we had a visit from a heron and he took almost all the fish. I couldn't believe it when I looked out of the window and saw him. It was like a turkey on stilts and he was standing gazing at the water choosing which ones he was going to eat like he was in some kind of specialist fish restaurant choosing his meal from the tank. I galloped out there waving my arms and when he took off it was like watching some great ptero-dactyl. They fly in such slow motion and they've got these giant wings. When you see them by a river they sort of look in proportion but in the garden it's like something from a horror film.'

'But it's such a wonderful garden,' said Julia. 'You're so lucky to live here.'

'Well, Richard has this big commute each day,' Helen said, 'but we think it's worth it.'

Julia imagined what it would be like living somewhere like this with Robin, thinking how perfect it would be.

'I could never live in the country,' said Robin, to her surprise. 'I'd go bonkers. I need the art galleries and the cinema and the theatre...and the people. Even in the Bible they talk about the celestial city. See, paradise is a city, not a place where you need a car to do everything.'

Helen smiled and said, 'We've got about eighteen hours to convert you. We'll do what we can even if it takes a whole case of Shiraz!'

'As long as I don't have to go rounding up geese or anything,' said Robin.

'I think snipping a few chives from the herb garden will be as much as we may ask of you,' answered Helen. 'And how about a drink? Richard's already here. He's having a shower and he should be down in a moment.'

Soon all four of them were sitting round a bottle of white wine at a little circular wooden garden table in the corner of the rose garden with the scent of lavender drifting up into the evening air.

'So how are you both?' said Robin. 'It's been absolutely ages since I was last here. Been up to anything I should know about?'

'I've been back and forth to the States more times than I've had hot dinners, and that's about all I can remember about work for the past six months. The more I go to America, the less I understand it. Most people are so insular and inward looking; they've got very little concept of Europe apart from a small minority who've done whistle-stop tours and an even smaller minority who have worked or studied abroad for a while. A work colleague of mine summed it up brilliantly with this slightly apocryphal story. He said that in a worldwide survey conducted by the UN, the only question asked was: "Would you please give your honest opinion about solutions to the food shortage in the rest of the world?" The survey was a huge failure because in much of Africa they didn't know what "food" meant. In much of Eastern Europe they didn't know what "honest" meant. In Western Europe they didn't know what "shortage" meant. In China they didn't know what "opinion" meant. In the Middle East they didn't know what "solution" meant. And in the US they didn't know what "the rest of the world" meant.'

'I love that,' said Julia. 'Clever! Anything I can do to help with the dinner, Helen?'

'No, it's all under control, but thanks anyway,' answered Helen.

'It's OK to have a laugh at the expense of America,' said Robin. 'But really, Richard, this country's just as bad and as stupid in its own way. We're soon getting to the point where a pizza will get to your house faster than an ambulance, and I read some stupid statistic about the number of people who crack their skulls each year while being sick in the toilet!'

'Trust you to bring that one up...pardon the pun! You can hardly talk, Robin. D'you remember the little incident at our wedding?'

'I'm always ready for a bit of Forester scandal,' said Julia.

'I would never have come if I knew you were going to taunt me with that one!' Robin said.

'Well, Julia,' said Richard, 'let's just say that Robin didn't seem to know that one has to raise the toilet seat before one throws up.'

Julia and Helen screamed in mock disgust and mirth and made a chorus of 'Yuk!' noises.

'Richard, if I ever get to be prime minister I will have to bribe you never to tell that story,' said Robin. He turned to Julia and said, 'I promise never to misbehave like that in front of you. I'm a reformed character.'

'Reformed in lots of ways,' said Richard, raising an eyebrow and sending an ironic non-verbal message to Robin, obviously relating to the fact that he had turned up with a real female partner at last. Robin was embarrassed and immediately swung the conversation back to less personal things.

'Did you ever come across anyone who owned a gun when you were on your many trips to the States? If we read the papers we're led to believe that in the USA every home should have one. I just don't get it.'

'I knew a family in Atlanta who definitely had a gun in the house, and also some people up in Maine, but that was mainly because he did a lot of hunting. But there's a great story about some interview on NPR.'

Robin interrupted to ask, 'What's NPR?'

'National Public Radio. OK? Some female broadcaster was interviewing a chap called General Something or other, who was about to sponsor a Boy Scout Troop visiting his military installation. She asked him what things he was going to teach the young boys when they visited the base. He told her they were going to be taught climbing, canoeing, archery and shooting. When she heard the word 'shooting' she was outraged and suggested that it was a bit irresponsible. He couldn't see her point because he assured her that they would be properly supervised on the rifle range. I think her next words were something like: "Don't you admit that this is a terribly dangerous activity to be teaching children?" To which General Reinwald replied, "Don't see how. We will be teaching them proper rifle discipline before they even touch a fire-arm."

'She was still really going for the jugular and said, "But you're equipping them to become violent killers!" And apparently he came out with the classic riposte: "Well, you're equipped to be a prostitute, but you're not one, are you?"'

'Then what happened?' asked Helen.

'Apparently the radio went silent and the interview ended.'

'Well I'm with the interviewer on that one,' said Julia.

'Me too,' said Helen. 'God, I would have slapped him. I'm just popping in to the house to bring the food out. Oh, Richard, you ought to try out that test you did with me last week on Robin.'

Robin groaned.

'Not another dissection of my innermost soul, please!' he said, grinning at Julia as he said it. 'I was at Julia's birthday party a few days ago and we had to do this hideous thing with songs that summed up our personalities. I failed miserably and ended up as the "Dancing Queen"!'

'Plenty of opportunity to prove the theory wrong this weekend, then,' said Richard slightly leering, and Robin gave a very quick, slightly frantic smile. Julia looked down at her feet and tried to count how many periwinkles she could see flowering between the cracks in the paving stones where they were sitting. She wondered whether Robin was regretting accepting the offer to stay the night. Totally oblivious of what was going on in both their minds, Richard ploughed on with his test.

'This is going to tell me how professional you are, Robin.'

Robin laughed and said, 'Ask old Cox or the ghastly Cosgrave and they'll tell you I score nought out of ten.'

'I don't believe you're that bad,' said Richard. 'Let's find out...question one: How do you put a giraffe into a refrigerator?'

'This is obviously a trick question,' Robin said. 'Is the answer "You can't" or is it a bit like that elephants in the mini car joke in which case the answer is two in the front and two in back.'

'Well, apart from the fact that a fridge doesn't have front and back seats,' said Richard 'the correct answer is: Open the fridge, put in the giraffe and close the door. This tests whether you do simple things in an overly complicated way.'

'Failed from the start,' said Robin.

'Hang on a minute,' said Richard. 'You still have a chance to redeem yourself on your ability to think through the repercussions of your actions. How do you put an elephant in a fridge?'

'Open the door, put him in and close it?' asked Robin gingerly.

'No, Robin, it's about repercussions,' offered Julia. 'Isn't he supposed to take the giraffe out before he puts the elephant in?'

'That almost qualifies you for MENSA,' Richard said to Julia. 'Now try the next bit, Robin. The Lion is hosting an animal conference. All the animals attend except one. Which animal does not attend?'

'I'll guess – monkey,' said Robin.

'Nope,' said Richard, 'wrong again, it's the elephant because the elephant is in the refrigerator. This tests your memory. OK, you still have one more chance to show your abilities.'

Robin sighed. 'I'm sorry, Richard, but I'm a completely hopeless case, but ask me anyway.'

'There is a river you must cross. But it is inhabited by crocodiles. How do you manage it?'

'I can work this out surely. Give me a moment,' said Robin. 'How about throwing some fish in further down the river so that the crocodiles leave me alone...or maybe go in a boat?'

'Sorry,' said Richard. 'The correct answer is you swim across. All the crocodiles are attending the Animal Conference. This tests whether you learn quickly from your mistakes. According to Andersen Consulting Worldwide, around ninety per cent of the professionals they tested got all questions wrong, but many primary school children got several correct answers. Anderson Consulting says this conclusively disproves the theory that most professionals have the brains of a four-year-old.'

At this moment Helen appeared with a big tray so that Robin didn't have to dwell too much on his humiliation and anyway, he was, as usual, taking it in good spirit, saying, 'I hope I do a bit better in the swimwear and national costume section!'

'Ah, my favourite Helen recipe,' said Richard, lifting the lid of a large pot that she had left on the table while nipping back into the house for the salad. 'You're very honoured, Julia!' It was a wonderful seafood paella and it looked completely authentic.

Once they had all started eating and Richard had poured the wine, Richard said, 'Big bowls of rice like this always make me a bit nervous. It all started when I went on a business trip for the bank to Samarkand. It sounds such a romantic, exotic name but it's the pits. It's muddy, dusty, kind of Soviet and miserable too but still weird because it's kind of eastern as well. Everyone looks like they're an agricultural worker and all the blokes wear these funny little skull caps that sound something like "Chubby Checkers"?'

'What?' they all shrieked. 'They can't be!'

'Well I can't speak Uzbek so I haven't a clue, but that's sort of what my interpreter said. Anyway, they have all these bazaars and the men seem to sit around drinking green tea, but the main thing about Samarkand is plov.'

'What on earth is plov?' said Robin.

'The weird thing is,' said Richard, 'there's no recipe so I can't tell you, but basically it's rice and lamb, a kind of pilaff really, plus loads of onions and peppers and someone told me the reason it's so fatty is that it's got sheep's tails in it.'

There was, understandably, a chorus of 'Ew' at this point.

'But the main thing about plov is that you eat it with your fingers from a communal dish,' he added.

'Bloody hell, hope the guys you were eating it with had clean fingernails,' said Helen.

Julia just looked nauseous and said, 'Thank God for some things, then, at least we've got a serving spoon and we're eating with forks!'

Supper continued with the usual mix of gossip, banter, jokes and the occasional reference to world politics or mutual friends from Richard's and Robin's past. Julia liked them both a lot and felt that they were giving her the once over and that she was passing the test. She hoped so.

'Has he stopped talking in his sleep yet?' said Richard suddenly changing the subject and turning to Julia.

Robin, sensing that she would be floored as to how to answer, jumped in and said,

'What an indelicate question to ask a lady and what an indelicate slur on a gentleman's honour! You've got a nerve after the display of Olympic-standard snoring you subjected me to three years ago when we went on that walking weekend in the Lake District!'

And Robin jabbered on, taking his cue from the weather, the garden or whatever was on their plates. Helen had removed the paella bowl and was bringing out some delicious crêpes suzettes for pudding. Robin prattled on relentlessly, eager not to have any more references to double beds, babies, or engagements.

'Did you hear about the Englishman, the Scotsman and the Irish man who sat down in a bar talking?' he raced on, unstoppable now. 'The Englishman said, "I'm proud to say that my son was born on April twenty-third, St George's day, and, in honour of the patron saint, I have named him George." "That's funny," said the Scot, "I've got a son too. He was born on St Andrew's day and I have called him Andrew." "Well, would you ever guess it?" said the Irishman. "The very same thing happened with my son, Pancake."'

Genuinely tickled they all gave little snorts of laughter.

'I can never remember a joke for more than about thirty minutes after hearing it,' said Helen. 'So it's no use asking me to tell you one. Look, there's a second pudding here if you don't want the crêpes. It's poached apricots. You can have these as well if you like.'

'That looks fantastic,' said Robin. 'I thought they were poached eggs before you told us. What are those little bird-droppingy bits on top?'

'Pistachios,' Helen replied. 'But talking of bird-droppings, well, actually, talking of birds, I want to tell you something really spooky that's been happening this last few days. I was in the little front sitting room reading the morning paper a couple of days ago and I thought I heard someone rapping on a door or a window with their knuckles. I got up and went to the front door and looked out and there was no one there. Then I looked out of all the front windows and realised that there was no sign of anyone. After a while I got a bit worried because I thought there might be some weirdo lurking at the back of the house and this is pretty isolated and I was all on my own. I tiptoed upstairs and peered out from the side of the window frame, a bit like an old curtain-twitcher, to try to see if there was a mad axe man in the garden but everything looked completely calm and normal. There were a couple of squirrels in the garden and some blue tits and a goldfinch on the bird feeders in front of the kitchen window.'

'So did you carry a baseball bat around with you for the rest of the day?' asked Julia.

'Well, I thought about having something to hand, but then decided I was just being jumpy and stupid so I went back down to the paper again, and then I heard it a second time. I sat very still and tried to work out exactly where it was coming from. It stopped and started and stopped and started and I crept out of the sitting room door into the hall and then stopped and stood stock-still, waiting. When it started up again I realised it was coming from the kitchen. When I got in the kitchen I couldn't believe my eyes. I've got some big terracotta pots outside the kitchen window and most of them have got geraniums in them, but a few have got sweet peas and I had stuck some tall bamboo canes in the pots to help train the plants up. One of the canes was just outside the kitchen window itself, probably about three inches above the bottom of the frame and about two inches away from the glass. Sitting on top of this tiny thin bamboo cane there was a chaffinch. It was staring straight at me, exactly as if it knew me. Usually the little birds that come to the bird feeders are all a bit nervous and they whizz away if I open the back door or get too close to the window. I walked in slow motion towards the chaffinch and it seemed transfixed.'

'Darling we're all transfixed when you do that funny walk,' said Richard, teasing her.

'Shut up, this is really fascinating,' she continued undeterred. 'You won't believe what it did next.'

'It said, "Boo!"' said Robin.

'Robin, you're as bad as Richard. Will you please shut up and listen. This is a free nature programme you're getting. Now listen! I got almost to the window and then the chaffinch started fluttering its wings and kind of ascended all the way up the window pane, fluttering and knocking on the window with its beak as it did it, then it flapped back down in slow motion and landed on the cane again. After a while, it seemed to get its breath back.'

'Hang on, do birds breathe or what?' said Robin.

'I don't care,' said Julia. 'I'm listening. Carry on, Helen. Then what happened.'

'Thanks, Jules. It did it again, and again. In fact it had done it so much that there were loads of little mucky beak and claw marks all over the window. I watched it for a bit and then tiptoed away. I could hear this spooky knocking for ages afterwards. In the end I opened the French windows and went out and watched it from the garden. Poor thing. It must have been quite exhausted. Anyway, because it had freaked me out so much, I was in a bit of a psychic superstitious moment, and you know my mum died a year or two back and my dad is really miserable in his old folks' home because he misses her so much, well – and I know you are going to think I'm stark staring mad here – I thought that maybe it was the spirit of my mum coming back for Dad. You read sometimes how, when people are dying, members of their family appear to them to take them out of this life and into the next. Well, I was so convinced that this was Mum that I actually spoke to the chaffinch out loud and said, "Mum, is it you? If it is, then give me a sign and fly across onto the garden chair." And I waited.'

'Medication time!' shouted Richard, and they all laughed, even Helen.

Julia said, 'And did it do anything?'

'Nope, nothing,' said Helen, smiling at her own gullibility. 'So then I thought that maybe it had been trying to kill little insects which were buzzing about and maybe creeping about on the glass, but I couldn't really see any. So in the end I had to come to the rather sad conclusion that this poor old chaffinch was just seeing the reflection of the bird feeders in the window, and also seeing its own reflection and thinking it was another chaffinch.'

'Oh bless!' said Julia. 'But all it had to do was turn round and there was a three-course meal waiting, except of course there wasn't because all the other birds would have been tucking in while your chaffinch was beating itself up on the kitchen window.'

'It's obviously a special needs chaffinch,' said Robin.

They all roared with laughter at this concept, but Julia still felt sorry for this poor disillusioned bird.

'Maybe if you moved the cane it wouldn't be tempted to do it so much,' she suggested.

'I've tried that already,' said Helen, but it's launching itself from a tree now. I really have that awful sense of foreboding that sooner or later I will go outside and find it dead on the ground.'

'You could put up a little signpost,' said Robin, 'saying "CHAFFINCH FOOD – THIS WAY!"'

Julia raised her wine glass and said, 'Well here's to the "special needs" chaffinch! I think that's a really poignant little story. Is it still here? D'you think we may be treated to a demonstration of it tomorrow morning?'

'Oh, most likely,' said Helen.

'Well, I'm going to find out if it's got insurance. If it goes on much longer we'll have to have a new pane of glass. I think I'll get the airgun out," said Richard.

'Oh God, I can't believe you actually said that,' said Helen. 'Just you leave it alone.'

'Ooh look, there's a daddy-long-legs up in the corner. Auntie Ethel, is that you?' shouted Richard as he ducked out of the way of Helen's elbow nudging him firmly in the ribs.

'Julia, Robin, coffee or herb tea?' said Helen.

'I'd better not have any,' said Richard, jokingly. 'I may stay awake having nightmares.'

'Coffee for me,' said Robin.

'And for me too,' said Julia. 'And we can have some of the truffles I brought if you like. I think we need to cheer ourselves up after that pitiful story. You know I really feel sad for that little bird. I shall probably dream about it tonight.'

'Oh yes, and talking of tonight,' said Helen. 'You're in the room to the left at the top of the stairs, and you're on the futon in Richard's study, Robin. Plenty of books in case you can't sleep!'

Julia blushed slightly, and wondered what would actually

happen now that they were being given an opportunity on a plate, albeit a discreet plate at that, to share a bed, if one of them was brave enough to tiptoe down the corridor. It was quite delicate of Helen not to have assumed that they would automatically be in the same bed and in the same room. All Richard's little asides seemed to assume that they would, of course, have been sleeping together for ages. Maybe Helen *had* asked Robin and maybe he had requested separate rooms. At this thought, she felt sad, anxious and confused. Haunting her were Miranda's words to her that she should take the bull by the horns.

'You're looking pre-occupied, Julia,' said Richard. 'Everything OK?'

Startled, she said the first thing that came into her head. 'Oh, sorry, just thinking about my second-year A-level Italian students…lot of stress at work at the moment with exams and all that. The Principal is leaning on us all heavily to get the results up and improve on last year's grades.'

'Well, I have the perfect stress management technique,' replied Richard. 'And it really works.'

'Oh great, I can do with some good advice.'

'Now Julia, I want you to close your eyes and picture yourself near a stream.'

'Done it,' Julia replied with eyes tightly shut.

'Birds are softly chirping in the crisp, cool, mountain air,' continued Richard. 'And no one but you knows your secret place.'

Julia smiled as she thought about the magical scene that Richard was guiding her through.

'You are in total seclusion from that hectic place called "the world",' he said.

'It's already working,' said Julia with a beatific look on her face.

'The soothing sound of a gentle waterfall fills the air with a cascade of serenity… The water is crystal clear.'

'Mmm,' said Julia.

'You can easily make out the face of the person you're holding under the water...'

'Oh you pig!' screamed Julia, poking her tongue out at him.

'Sanctuary!' he shouted, running towards Helen who was in the doorway with the sugar bowl in her hand.

Eventually, they all made their way upstairs and disappeared for a while in the various bathrooms getting ready for the night. Julia unpacked her little bag and put on her new nightdress, cleaned her teeth, brushed her hair, and squirted a little Mitsouku behind her ears. *In for a penny, in for a pound*, she thought to herself as she turned back the sheets on her bed and waited for the house to go silent so that she could embark on her nocturnal mission as instructed by Special Agent Miranda Griffiths.

She tried once or twice to open the door of her room in total silence, but, because it was such an old house, every floorboard creaked mercilessly. In the end she decided to go confidently to the loo and then metamorphose into some kind of Tai Chi practitioner, taking large slow motion steps, putting her heels down first and then lowering the rest of the foot one millimeter at a time. She finally arrived at Richard's study, her heart pumping and opened it so that she could just peep in through the chink.

'Fancy some company?' she whispered.

Robin, propped up on the futon with his book looked startled, and said, 'You naughty, naughty girl!' which she took to be a flirtatious invitation.

She tiptoed over to the futon, and turned out the bedside lamp while he moved over to make a space for her.

For a moment they were both silent.

'It's taken a lot of courage for me to do this,' she said, just desperate to break the yawning silence which had sprung up like an inflated airbag between them. He took her hand in the dark and, like a Regency gentleman, brought it to his lips and kissed it, then leaned across and started to kiss her properly at last. However, after all the stress, tension and effort of getting to this point, the emotion of the past weeks and the terror that she might, even now, be pregnant, suddenly washed over her, and she burst into tears.

'Oh, my precious petal, what is it?' he asked, now taking control as it suddenly gave him a role other than reluctant seducer. She was unable to speak and just clung to him and shook. He seemed happy and patient enough to just hold her and stroke her hair. After a minute or two, he sighed, extricated himself from this comforting embrace and reached out behind her for the light switch.

'Shall we talk?' he asked, mega-serious, and she knew that the 'S' word was now going to need attention.

'I'm so sorry, I'm so sorry,' she gulped. 'This was supposed to be me doing my siren act; God, I even bought this bloody night-dress because I wanted you to want me, but the thing is…the thing is…I think I might be pregnant.'

Chapter Fourteen

Nothing could possibly have prepared Robin for this particular bombshell. For a moment he was totally speechless.

'What?!' he said, incredulously.

And she proceeded to tell him the whole gruesome story of what had happened in Wales. He was, rightly, indignant and furious with Owen, but also keen to placate her and comfort her. In fact, at that moment, he could not have been more of a rock to which she could tether her bobbing, unstable little raft. His arms enveloped her and he stroked her hair while she recounted the events of that dreadful night and the subsequent hours spent at the farm. He periodically gently wiped her tears away with his hand, and gave her soft little kisses on her head just as one would do to a child who had fallen over and gashed its knee or lost a favourite toy. It was, of course, exactly what the doctor ordered. Julia had never loved him more than this moment when he became her masterful, but gentle, protector. It was all she wanted from the man in her life. Robin, too, although appalled by what he was hearing, suddenly had his role as the good and faithful saviour of the damsel in distress. He threw himself into the role of master of ceremonies and completely took charge.

'Now look,' he said. 'First of all, you are sleeping right here and you are not to worry for one more second. I'll look after you and we'll sort it out. In the first place, you may not be pregnant at all, but obviously, all this anxiety has burrowed into your psyche and you are not my little uncomplicated Sweet Pea at the moment so we are going to concentrate on getting you to open your petals again and enjoy the sunshine. And this isn't some kind of sexual athletics race. This is reality and the reality is that you are in no state to be taken advantage of by me.'

Despite her terrible distress, Julia realised that she had just given him the perfect alibi. He even seemed almost grateful that this crisis had arisen and that they had been overtaken by events and had this joint new project to concentrate on. Tonight at least she was not about to find out if he had led her down a path where he was not able to follow. And there were other more urgent problems to solve right now.

'If we look at the worst case scenario, and you are actually pregnant,' he said, turning her head to look her straight in the eye, 'you are I are going to deal with this together. You are not on your own. Do you understand?'

She nodded, and more tears ran silently down her face.

'It's just, it's just...' she began but had to wait until the lump in her throat the size of a mandarin orange reduced its size. 'It's just that I was keeping it all to myself and I feel so stupid now. I want you to see me as a self-possessed, self-assured, competent, sensuous, funny woman, and I've lumbered you with this pitiful child.'

'Don't talk such rot,' he said. 'Who on earth is going to be sensuous and self-assured if they've been raped? It's hardly a life-affirming activity, is it? Come on, snuggle down, dry those tears and let's go to sleep. We'll get a proper pregnancy test when we go back to London and we can take it from there.'

'Sod it,' she said, beginning to laugh a little. 'I imagined we'd be exploring erogenous zones, and I feel like all I need is for you to read aloud to me from *The Tale of the Flopsy Bunnies* right now.'

'Well, I could always root around Richard's bookshelves and see if he's got the adult version: *The Flopsy Bunnies go to a Sex Show in Amsterdam*.' She laughed, but the mention of Amsterdam reminded her of the trip Robin had almost made, and the company in which he would have made it. She sighed deeply, snuggled into his armpit, closed her eyes, and very quickly fell into an exhausted sleep.

Next morning, Richard and Helen naturally assumed that they had done what any full-blooded couple would have done, and, judging by their physical intimacy and the protective way Robin behaved, they both assumed that it must be love. After breakfast they went a long walk over the fields and into a small wood where they tried to outdo one another identifying wild flowers.

'That's a campion,' said Helen.

'No, it's not, it's a ragged robin, look, you can see the raggedy petals,' retorted Richard. With a sly smile he said, 'And talking of ragged robins, did you sleep well, Robin?'

'Couldn't have been better,' said Robin, giving Julia's hand a conspiratorial squeeze. 'And while we are on the other subject, what's willow herb?'

'Oh, you townies,' said Helen. 'Now listen, a willow herb looks a bit like a campion. I give you that; they're both magenta coloured, but a campion has five petals and a willow herb has four petals. And see this little pink thing here?' and she pointed with her toe into the undergrowth. 'That's herb Robert.'

'Blimey, it's like going on a nature walk with Capability Brown,' said Robin, now putting his arm cosily round Julia. If it hadn't been the thought of what she must do in the coming week, this would have been the most blissful morning for Julia. Never had Robin been so physically close to her, so affectionate and so caring. She felt entirely protected by him and was aware that he was putting her interests first all the time.'

'Listen!' Richard said. They all stood still and in the distance there was the unmistakeable sound of a cuckoo.

'Now is that a blackbird or a lark?' said Robin, in mock serious mode.

'No, it's a bloody cockerel,' said Richard. 'Come on, we've got time to walk over there to the village before I have to take you back to the station. Sure you'll be all right? Don't need me to walk ahead with a machete and cut a path or anything?'

'My mum would love it here,' said Julia. 'She's got a lurcher and has to take him out on huge walks each day. He'd adore this too. I think even my dad would too, but he's not so potty about the countryside as she is. She doesn't mind though, all she requires of him is that he wears matching socks, remembers her name on occasions and doesn't retell the same story too often.'

Robin could see that Julia was recovering her old form now that he had rode in on his charger to take care of her, and was pleased that his friends liked her so much.

'Well that's great for people of advancing years,' said Richard. 'All *my* mum wants from my dad is that he doesn't scare small children and he doesn't forget why he's laughing.'

A little later Richard dropped them off at the station. There was a small, drab bus station outside the railway station and it was one of the bleakly depressing depersonalised urban areas that make one lose the will to live. *Fingal's Cave* and an assortment of easy listenin' classical hits blared uncharacteristically out of some hidden PA system; pigeons pecked at bits of detritus under the metal seats, and Julia felt that any minute she would see tumbleweed drifting across the empty bus stands.

'Come on, let's go inside the station,' said Robin, 'it's too depressing here and after such an idyllic walk in the woods it'll spoil the mood.'

'Talking of spoiling the mood,' said Julia, 'I'm so, so sorry about last night. I feel like such a drama queen; you must feel you've taken on some kind of nutter.'

'Look,' said Robin, putting his arm round her and squeezing her tightly, 'we're in this together. It's going to be fine, just you see.'

As he said these words, Julia was thinking of Felix, Jeremy, and the other "duchesses". This would confirm every prejudice and horror they had about women – manipulative, messy, proprietorial. But Robin seemed to her to be almost more comfortable now in this role of protector, the one who would sort things out, than he did last night when she had first blundered into his room like some kind of threatening Mata Hari. But what would they do if she was indeed pregnant? He was doing a good job of hiding his thoughts even if he might be panicking inwardly.

'You look sad again,' he said. 'I'll tell you a story to cheer you up. How about this one? A husband and wife were having dinner at a very fine restaurant when this absolutely stunning young woman comes over to their table, gives the husband a big open-mouthed kiss and says she'll see him later and walks away. His wife glares at him and says, "Who the hell was that?!"

'"Oh," replies the husband, "she's my mistress."

'"Well, that's the last straw," says the wife. "I've had enough, I want a divorce."

'"I can understand that," replies her husband. "But remember, if we get a divorce it will mean no more shopping trips to Paris, no more wintering in Barbados, no more summers in Tuscany, no more Mercedes in the garage and no more yacht club. But the decision is yours." Just then, a mutual friend enters the restaurant with a gorgeous young woman on his arm.

'"Who's that woman with Jim?" asks the wife. "That's his mistress," says her husband.

'"Ours is prettier," she replies.'

'Oh nice one, Robin, you should do stand-up!' Julia said, clapping her hands, 'And look, here's our train coming.'

'I know, why don't you come back to my flat as soon as we get back to town,' he said. 'You can go to sleep, read a book or we can just play Scrabble...whatever you want. Maybe we can go to a film.'

'That's great,' said Julia. 'I don't think I'm quite in the mood to be sitting alone in a basement in Putney, and I dare say the geraniums will survive without water for a day; we're not exactly experiencing a heat wave.'

The centre of town seemed hot, dirty and smelly after the rural idyll they had just experienced but once in the safe little enclave of Robin's flat with a cup of Earl Grey in front of her, she realised that this was the only place she wanted to be. Robin said he had to make a few phone calls and so she dozed off on the sofa while he disappeared into his bedroom. When she woke she had no idea how long she had been asleep. It seemed like hours but it could have been just twenty minutes.

'Awake. Good,' he said. 'Now, if you're up to it, we're going to Acton but we have to hurry. It closes at five o'clock.'

'What does? I mean, what closes? I don't know any museums in Acton,' she said, looking somewhat dazed.

'Well, I've made a few phone calls and there's a private lab that does pregnancy tests on the spot. I think it's better that we find out sooner rather than later, don't you? At least then we can take some action. I'm all for pre-emptive strikes.'

'I – uh, what – er, I don't…well, yes, I suppose so, you're right of course. What time is it now?'

'It's half past two. If we go straight away we should be there by three thirty,' he replied.

And with that they were out on the streets once more and dashing off to Tottenham Court Road. The train rattled off westwards in what was, for them both, alien territory, but Robin was treating this like a military mission and was armed with his A-Z, and holding her hand constantly to reassure her that it would be OK. Almost as if they had time-travelled to get there, as she had no awareness of time passing, they were walking into a nondescript low-rise building on a trading estate which would have been busier on a weekday and where small boys kicked balls against garage doors and lone men seemed to emerge here and there from 'units', get into white vans and drive off.

'Come on, Sweet Pea, deep breath,' said Robin as they went through the door.

It was all ridiculously swift and simple and then they sat down to await the result. That, of course seemed to take eternity. Neither of them had anything to read, and the selection of magazines was the usual drab pile of out-of-date women's mags, a copy of *What Car?* and a couple of gardening magazines plus one three-year-old copy of *Country Life* open on a large black and white formal photo of a girl wearing a string of single pearls, her face set in an attitude of pseudo-relaxation, gazing into the middle distance. After about twenty minutes, a lab assistant came through to the reception area and called her name. As she stood to go to collect the tiny slip of paper she felt her knees almost buckle. It looked remarkably like the little slip of paper that had come through her front door to tell her what her A-level grades were. She carried it back to where she and Robin were sitting, glanced at him and then opened it out.

It said one word: "negative".

Robin threw his arms round her and said, 'I knew it, I just knew it, you silly sausage. Come on! This calls for a celebration! We're going out for the meal of a lifetime and it's on me!'

Julia could not match his extraordinary euphoria because all she felt was a gigantic tsunami of relief sweep over her. They raced out of the lab, desperate to be away from this no-man's land of chain-link fencing and Portakabins.

'First things first!' he said. 'We can stop off at the off-licence on the way to my flat for some champagne, and then, I think it has to be Simpsons in the Strand. I'll ring immediately we get back. I'm sure we'll be able to get a table.'

Julia wasn't able to think clearly. She just felt as if a concrete slab which had been pinning her to the ground had just been lifted off with a winch. They were holding hands and almost skipping along the pavement with delight. Once they were on the east-bound Central Line train once more, he looked at her and said, 'Now that we've been through this together we're like blood-brother and blood-sister. We joined at the hip.'

She realised that he was trying to say something charming and touching and yet she realised it was making her smile back at him with only the lower half of her face. A little voice inside her was saying, 'I don't want him to be my brother or my Siamese twin; I want him to be my lover and my husband.'

Brilliant, competent and amazing as he had been, there was a large part of her which wished he had never had to see her like this: upset, pitiful, helpless. What had attracted him to her in the first place was completely the opposite – someone who was clever, funny, well-travelled and confident. What on earth was she going to do to reclaim her ground again and become a person who evoked desire rather than compassion, lust rather than concern?

They were both already high on the emotion of the trip to Acton when they arrived back at Robin's flat with the champagne which, as they had taken it from the fridge in the off-licence across the road, was still chilled and ready for consumption. It felt like having a winning premium bond. They giggled, clinked glasses and grinned insanely at one another. It was as if a whole new chapter of life was beginning. He began talking about making plans for the summer and wanted them both to have a holiday somewhere. He had a friend with a small house in a village in Malta, he said, so how about it?

'Oh, I'm not so sure,' she said, and watched his face fall a little.

'Have you got other things planned?'

'Well, it's just that I've always preferred Cadbury's flakes to Maltesers,' she replied, grinning, waiting to be punched in the shoulder for teasing him. She would have gone with him to a corrugated-roof shed in a shanty town in a black township in South Africa if he had asked, not to mention a slum in Tiger Bay, but she needed him not to think that. She felt that she was actually levitating she was so thrilled at the idea of going away with him. The effort of concealment of her adoration was exhausting, and she wondered if there would ever come a time when she could stop pretending and just love him and be loved back without worrying she loved too much. At the same time as she was thinking these thoughts she felt the vaguest suspicion of an impending headache beginning across her shoulder blades. She hoped she had some painkillers with her, since once a headache took hold of her, unless she could go away and lie in a pitch dark room, she would be wiped out for days.

'Come on,' he said. 'We can talk about it over dinner. Finish what you've got in your glass and I'll put the magic stopper in the rest and we can walk down to the Strand. We'll be there in fifteen minutes and it's a great evening for a pre-dinner stroll. Damn, we should have booked somewhere out of doors to eat. Never mind, it's too late now! I'm starving! I've only just realised we never ate lunch after that obscenely big breakfast with Richard and Helen. Now, Miss McCallum, no doing "Knees Up Mother Brown" on the tables in Simpsons. I know you're a bit euphoric but take a grip.' As he said it he stumbled over a little metal strip across the floor in the doorway and did a kind of inadvertent music hall tumble.

She exploded with laughter shouting, 'Enjoy the trip!' as they clattered down the stairs and out onto the street.

As they were walking hand in hand down Drury Lane, she started to feel a gnawing, heavy feeling in the pit of her stomach. She realised the tell-tale symptoms of the onset of a period at last. But although it was two weeks late, now at last it was here; she wasn't pregnant and she was celebrating. What the hell? She'd take some painkillers when they got to the restaurant.

The combination of the champagne, the anxiety of the past few weeks, and the warmth of the restaurant had a completely soporific effect on her. All around were ultra-formal waiters lifting the monstrous silver cloche lids off the joints of meat on offer, then approaching, giant, scary knives in hand, as if to perform a serious surgical operation as they carved the vast slabs of flesh for the diners.

'Good job you're not a vegetarian!' said Robin as they slumped back finally on the velvet chairs and waited for the coffee. 'Hey, I know what we should do! We ought to go to one of the open air plays in Regent's Park later on in the summer. I think it's "the Dream" this season. What d'you think? I'm assuming you like Shakespeare.'

All Julia could think of now was the cramp in her

stomach…happy cramp because she was still not over the elation of the good news from Acton, but nevertheless, agonising. She felt as if her entrails were being extracted with a suction pump. However, she rose to the challenge, saying, 'Oh I've sought out that many dewdrops and hung that many pearls in cowslips ears I can hardly think to tell the truth… Act two, scene one; we did it for O-level, but I still love the play despite that, so the answer is an unqualified yes.'

He beamed approvingly.

'We'll have to go after we come back from Malta. My weekends are a bit tight at the moment. Obviously if the weather's a washout we'll have to think of something else. I won't get the tickets until a bit nearer the time.'

'All I can think of right now is how all the boys in my class laughed at the line "then slip I from her bum, down topples she" as they thought it was so hysterical to be saying the word "bum" in front of the teacher, or, even better, to hear Miss Heythrop saying it. Things are a bit different now. Blimey, my second-year A-level lot are pretty X-rated I have to say.'

She looked around behind her at this point, 'I don't know about you but I think I'm in need of a strong black coffee to make sure I get home without finding myself slumped on a Tube station bench in the early hours of tomorrow. I don't even possess a dog on a string so no one is going to give me any money.'

'I was thinking the same, and I'll get the bill too. This one is completely on me. No arguments.'

'Robin, I can't thank you enough for what you did for me today,' she said, suddenly serious. 'I was slowly disintegrating and you helped scoop me back up off the ground and stand me on my feet again. I was such a chump,'

'That's what I'm here for, dummy,' he said. He made no offer to her of staying with him that night, but actually, since she had already spent one night away from home and only had her small bag with her, she thought that it was probably a very good idea if she returned to her own place. Besides, her begonias needed her. The terracotta pots would be in crisis. There had been no rain since Tuesday.

It was past midnight when she finally staggered in through the door of her flat. By now the headache completely occupied one side of her cranium and she felt as if major archaeological excavations were going on there. How come when you had a headache your teeth suddenly felt as they all needed pulling out too? Julia remembered how her grandmother had suffered with headaches and used to put vinegar and brown paper round her head. What was that about? And the Asian girl in the local paper shop sometimes sat glumly behind the counter with a wide elastic band around her head, saying it seemed to ease the pain. Right now, Julia was ready to tie a pound of chipolata sausages and a toilet chain round her head if it was going to alleviate this headache, but all she really had to hand was a packet of white tablets that may just take the edge off it for a few hours.

The next day Julia began to regain some semblance of normality to her life. When the phone rang she hoped it would be Robin, but in fact it was Mel, now back from Spain.

'Mel! Great to hear your voice,' said Julia. 'How was Spain?'

'A bit like the curate's egg. You know, good in parts,' said the voice at the other end. 'Deke's given me an ultimatum and I don't know what to do. Mark is just like a powerful drug. I've tried so often to give him up, but it's still such a force, I can't help myself, but at the same time Deke is like a part of my own body. We met when we were still at school and I can't imagine my life without him in it.'

'Did you actually feel you were having any good times at all with Deke when you were in Spain?' asked Julia.

'Yes, of course, we know each other backwards and we share the same values, the same sense of humour; it's just that the raw lust bit isn't there.'

'But, Mel, look at it realistically. How long have you two been married? Eight years? Nine years? Do you want kids? I have a feeling you're never going to get Mark to commit to living together let alone fathering babies and he might always revert to— 'But here she stopped herself abruptly.

'Revert to what?' asked Mel.

'Revert to, uh, fancying other people, going out with the lads rather than you. God, I don't know. It's just that he seems to love the idea of an affair with all its spice and secrecy but he's got a real problem with commitment. Don't you feel cheap just being his mistress all the time? What does it do to your self-esteem, Mel, and what does it do knowing that you're cheating on Deke all the time? In some ways I think the honourable thing for you to do would be to leave Deke, but I can bet my last shilling if you did that you would lose Deke and you would look round and Mark wouldn't be there either. He's got too much of a roving eye and I don't see him sitting on the sofa every night watching the news and then padding up the stairs in his bedroom slippers. He's far too much of a lounge lizard for that.'

'That was a pretty devastating character assassination, Jules,' said Mel. 'So how is your "perfect" love life?'

'Far from perfect, Mel, but at least I'm not knowingly betraying someone else. I know this isn't what you want to hear, but it's reality.'

'Jules, you haven't changed one bit since we were in Italy and what I hate most about you is I know you're right. The trouble is, I actually think I am so addicted to Mark that reason doesn't come into it. I'm going to leave Deke and that's it. Mark and I have been an item for so long, albeit in secret, that I know the thing between us is indestructible.'

'For God's sake tell me when you're about to jump ship, Mel, because I can well imagine Deke will be on my doorstep with a loaded pistol. He's either going to go to pieces completely or just get so angry that he will be in danger of committing some criminal act. In some ways I wish you hadn't told me all this.

Does anyone know what you are planning?' Julia was hating this conversation.

'No one, not even Mark.'

'All I can say is good luck then,' said Julia. 'I suppose you ought to do it sooner rather than later. This situation you've got at the moment is intolerable for all three of you.'

'OK, Jules, thanks for listening,' said Mel, and the phone clicked then went silent.

The next morning Julia had recovered from the nightmare of the weekend and went into college. There was a general feeling of "school's out for summer" even though the term technically still hadn't finished. Julia was mostly giving feedback on her first-year A-level group's end-of-year exams, and reading them the riot act for their poor performance. This was a pretty routine practice to galvanise them into action for the coming academic year. She saw little of Robin as he was helping some of his own students with an end-of-term drama production. They were trying to put together a satirical review and Robin was throwing himself into helping with the writing as this was what he adored doing.

On the Wednesday evening, Julia had taken a watering can out to the small flowerbed next to the stair well in front of her basement flat. There were just a few small shrubs grimly hanging onto life in what was deep shadow, coupled with the fact that this pocket handkerchief of soil seemed to have become the public lavatory for most of the cats within 100 yards. She was bending over, watering can in one hand and small trowel in the other, trying to flick the cat turds over the wall into the neighbour's equally unsightly patch when she heard someone gasp her name. She looked up and it was Mel, standing there with puffy eyes and streaming wet cheeks.

'Good God, Mel, whatever's happened? Come in!'

Julia abandoned the trowel and led Mel into the cool flat. Mel sat heavily down on the bed and cried again before she was able to speak coherently.

'It's Mark,' she gulped, 'he dumped me.'

'What?' Julia asked in amazement. 'But he adored you! He's always loved you! What happened?'

It slowly emerged that Mel had gone to Mark's flat with the intention of telling him that she was going to leave Deke. Before she could begin he had said, 'Mel, we've got to talk,' and proceeded to tell her that he didn't feel the same about her as he had done for many years. The spark had died. He was just going through the motions with her.

'How did you react? What did you say?'

'I was dumbstruck,' Mel said. 'All I could think of was how I had planned and rehearsed this evening over and over, about how delighted I thought he would be. I don't know if he sensed that things were coming to a head and he would at last have to make some sort of commitment to me or what. It was hard for him, too, Julia, he was crying when he was speaking. He kept telling me he was sorry.'

'So he bloody well should have been!' said Julia, enraged on her friend's behalf. 'I suppose he wanted some kind of absolution for shitting on you like this.'

'I thought maybe he wanted me to fight for him, to try to negotiate, but I could see that it was useless. He just kept looking down at the floor and then he just said, "Go now, Mel," and that was it, not even a hug, nothing.'

'Oh, Mel, I'm so, so sorry,' said Julia, putting her arms round her pal, 'but you know, this is maybe a God-sent thing that's happened. Now at least you can try and work out if staying with Deke is what is really your destiny. Who knows, maybe you will end up with someone else entirely, but at least this way a decision has been made for you and you won't beat yourself up about destroying Deke. I have to say, the man is a saint, considering he has known about this thing for a while.'

'He realised, bless him, that it was just "more powerful than both of us" as the cliché goes, and he always hoped that if he was patient and loving enough the storm would blow over. And I guess now it has.'

'Come on,' said Julia, 'let's open a bottle of wine and salute the good times; the sooner you make your peace with all this the better. It was good fun while it lasted, but it's time to move on, Mel. I'm sure Mark is really miserable too at this moment, but if it's not to be, it's not to be.'

Mel nodded resignedly and followed Julia to the kitchen.

Later that evening, after Julia had dispatched Mel back to her husband, she rang Robin.

'Hi, Sweet Pea!' he said, excitedly. 'I've rung William and he says three weeks from now would be fine for him. If we can get cheap flights it would be perfect timing, especially as it's before the school holidays begin. Is that OK? Can I go ahead and book the plane tickets?'

'Er – yes, lovely! Do that. I – er, sorry, you caught me off guard for a moment; I'd rung about something else.'

'Oh, stupid me, I'm always charging in like a bull in china shop. Oh, and you'll never guess what! This is really an unbelievable bit of news! Mark is engaged! And you'll never guess what! She's only eighteen. She's still at drama school and he met her when he was casting that play for the Edinburgh Festival. Can you believe it? He's like a dog with two tails. Tell you the truth, I think part of the attraction is that she has a twin brother who looks like a male version of her. Jeremy said he'll probably end up screwing the brother. Mark's *such* a tart!'

At this point Julia didn't feel she had the energy to go into Mel's despair and misery, so she just let it go and tried to sound interested in the Knights of St John, lace tablecloths and the Siege of Malta.

Barely two days after term ended, Julia and Robin were boarding a plane at Gatwick. Julia was now on the Pill, convinced that she had put all her bedtime anxieties behind her and confident that now, since the whole holiday had been Robin's suggestion, everything would be fine. All they needed was good wine, sun and time together. Six blissful days. She couldn't believe her luck. Robin immediately opened his book even while they were waiting on the tarmac for take-off clearance and seemed totally unaware that she had been expecting him to talk to her. He was obviously just doing what he always did, being a great bookworm, and he was totally oblivious to her, assuming that she, just like him, would have something riveting to read in her hand luggage. For a minute or two she flicked through the in-flight shopping magazine, wondering how she had ever managed to get through life without a Hermès scarf, a £45 tube of skin cream and a small model of Concorde. Why was it that once one arrived at an airport or even opened these stupid magazines, one turned into an instant shopaholic? For about fifteen minutes she just allowed herself to drift along in her own thoughts, imagining how, exactly, Robin would initiate the evening's romantic adventures. This was, after all, like a kind of honeymoon for them, although he hadn't said so in so many words. Eventually she, too, got out her book. She had now progressed from the *The Deptford Trilogy* to another weighty Robertson Davies. *Good Lord*, she thought to herself, *I don't think I could ever manage to write anything longer than one hundred pages. How did this guy come to write two whole trilogies?!* and she opened up *The Salterton Trilogy* on page one, testing the weight of the book as it was resting in her left hand, and then peeped ahead to see exactly how many pages lay ahead of her.

Hours later, the thick, heavy heat of Malta swept over them like warm treacle as they made their way to the airport building. Before too long, they had their bags and as she shyly stood there smiling in the Arrivals hall, Robin embraced William with gusto.

The car journey to the tiny village of Mqabba was barely ten minutes, yet William insisted that he wasn't bothered by aircraft noise since they arrived and took off in a different direction and also his house was so old that the stone walls were like those of a fortress. The house itself was right on the narrow street and once inside it was cool, smelling of roses, and dark, although as soon as her eyes became accustomed to it, Julia could make out some exquisite small pieces of antique furniture and a lot of photos in little silver frames on a occasional table. Over in the corner was a piano, and, against the wall, an elegant inlay writing desk with a statuette on it. There was a rattling as William undid the shutters and then opened the large French windows to reveal a stunning white-walled courtyard. The walls went up and up on three sides, and the house itself formed the fourth side. There was a balcony above them and this, Julia assumed, was William's own bedroom. In one corner was a massive banana tree; on the other walls there was a tumble of jasmine, bougainvillea, and stephanotis. A gentle trickling came from a small spout of water gushing from the mouth of a lion poking his head out of the courtyard wall and trickling into a little dish under his chin. The whole mood of Tuscany came back to her and she sat back with a contented sigh.

'Now, first things first, alcohol! Gin and tonics?' said William, and he trotted inside to prepare the drinks. Robin leaned across to Julia and took her hand in his.

'Paradise!' he said. 'I think this was an inspired decision. You'll love the island.'

'Now make yourselves completely at home,' William said. 'While you're here, this is your house too. Trouble with this house is it's a bit of a pixie palace; all the rooms are tiny. And of course I hope you've brought the mosquito spray. They eat you alive. Come on, bring your drinks. I'll show you round.'

They started up on the roof, an amazing large flat space where they not only could see the dome of the large village church but also the churches in all the surrounding villages.

'The bells will wake you tomorrow morning, they're mad on their church bells here,' said William. 'But after a few days you'll get used to them, and then it will be time to go home! And this is the best, best place to watch the fireworks. All the villages have their own festivals during the summer and they have the most amazing firework displays. We'll be able to bring our drinks up and enjoy the show. Now let's go down to the next floor and I'll show you where the sleeping quarters are.'

They ducked as they went under the low lintel and back into the house. William went ahead of them into the guest room. The area just outside was just like a little ante-chamber with its own circular table, statuettes, delicate gilded chairs and a rather beautiful chaise longue. Julia was disappointed to see that the room itself was miniscule with a really tiny single bed, a vast dark walnut wardrobe and a large linen chest.

'The bed's a bit on the Lilliputian side, I'm afraid, but two can squeeze in! George and Mario had no trouble when they were here a few weeks ago!' He winked at Robin. Julia felt slightly nauseous that once again she, poor little simple heterosexual Julia, was being dragged into this gay cabal, and everyone assumed that she was easy with it, that she understood its rules and its language, its nuances and innuendoes. Suddenly, as if someone had bumped into her heavily in the street, her head was jolted with Robin's casual reply, 'Oh, it doesn't matter; that's for Julia and I'll be fine over here on the chaise longue.' He gestured to the little sofa outside the door.

'No, look, you can't possibly,' said William, 'you'll look like her royal protection officer or a servant. Look, one here' —he bounced down full-length on the bed and lay, like a pencil, down one side—'and one here.' He rolled over and did an exact replica of his first pose but on the other side of the bed which was no wider than a child's cot.

'No, no, William, don't be stupid, the chaise longue's fine. And I need my beauty sleep. Now when are we off to Valetta?'

Julia's heart sank once more; she knew Robin well enough to understand that he was not bluffing. This was what he really wanted. Just as her tears and her phantom pregnancy had come like a gift from the gods at a moment of truth for them in Hoddesden, now he had the perfect gentlemanly excuse; he wanted her to be comfortable, he would suffer on the chaise longue while milady had the luxury of the bed. She knew if she tried to set him on fire she herself would be badly burned in the process. Now that she had him here all to herself for a week, she would make the best of it, and just enjoy being with him. The idea of having a conversation about the sleeping arrangements was about as attractive to her as doing a tightrope walk across the Niagara Falls. With feigned nonchalance, Robin said, 'I'll just leave you to put your stuff in the wardrobe, Sweet Pea, and I'll pop down and catch up on some gossip with William. He's working in the museum all the time we're here so we won't have that much time for a long chat. You OK?'

'Fine,' and she smiled. 'He's so lucky to live here, and we're lucky to be his guests. Thanks so much for bringing me.'

Ever polite. Ever accommodating. Never able to shriek at him that he had brought her here on false pretences and that she was already beginning to hate the place that she thought she would love.

That evening William drove them to Valletta to show them the museum where he worked and to give them a bit of an orientation lesson. Much of the area that he wanted to show them was closed to cars and so they parked on a steep hill and walked to the historic old town. On the way they passed a large villa in a gated compound. Everything was overgrown and the building had fallen into semi-ruin. As she stared at the tangle of grasses and stone statuary, she noticed a skinny cat, then another, then another, and realised that the entire place was alive with these stick-thin feral felines. As they walked past the final bars of the railings, a scruffy man who looked like some kind of down-and-out sat, head bent, next to a pathetic pile of tins of Kitekat. There was a saucer containing a few coins and a small square of cardboard was propped up next to the tins, and on it, in thick black crayon, was an exhortation to '"Make happy the cats".

William was a veritable walking encyclopaedia on the history of Malta. He had lived there for years and clearly adored the island. They sat at a small out-door restaurant near the Upper Barracca Gardens and listened to William while he told them about everything from the Turkish invasion to Malta's role in the Second World War with a sub-plot involving Dom Mintoff. Every now and again he interrupted his story to hold his palm up in friendly salute to passers by that he knew, murmuring 'Bongu' to each of them. Julia noted that most of the people he said 'Bongu' to were men of a certain age, immaculately dressed and occasionally accompanied by wives and babies. She said nothing. She was thinking about the evening ahead. They arrived back at the little house when the sky was inky black and the air was balmy and went straight through to the courtyard where William turned on the cunningly concealed lighting system illuminating a single plant here, a trickle of water there, and in general giving the little enclosure an enchanted feel. Somewhere a too-loud TV blared out the news and not far away a mother and male child were arguing about something trivial, although the boy was whinging loudly about some injustice in the family arrangements. The two men had a whisky and Julia had a small glass of Cointreau with ice. She knew she didn't have the courage to make the first move on Robin, having already attempted it in Hertfordshire with dismal consequences. Her only hope now was that he would repay the compliment.

Half an hour later she realised that despite his attentiveness, affectionate concern about whether or not she would be OK and comfortable, his gentle kiss on the lips, and enquiries whether she needed the shutters closed, the mosquito machine turned on, and so forth, he was going to take his leave and sleep like a monk on the unyielding piece of furniture just yards away.

Their days were spent visiting the old towns of Mdina and Rabat, going on little boat trips, absorbing an obscene amount of history and visiting fish markets and beaches. Their mutual pleasure in each other's company, their shared jokes and their delight in having the sun on their bare skin again after a long London winter was evident, but the volume of stuff unsaid was piling up like a heavy Victorian wardrobe between them. On the final afternoon, while they were sauntering along the harbour in Sliema, Robin said, 'We need to talk.'

It was the conversation she had been dreading. However, Robin made up for his lack of seductive physical initiative with his forthrightness. They sat on a bench.

'Look, Sweet Pea, this trip maybe isn't turning out as you would have wanted it – correction, as *we* would have wanted it, but we are so, so lucky to have one another and to share so much. I always want you in my life. You don't have a clue how much you mean to me, but it isn't as if we were engaged or anything and it was all going wrong. We never got ourselves up that cul-de-sac in the first place thank God, although it won't have been for lack of pressure from our friends such as Helen and Richard on my side and Lord knows how many on yours, but maybe this is where we start from, here and now, rather than see this as an ending of anything. You are always, always going to be in a special place in my heart.'

Strangely, although he was smashing all her hopes and dreams on the floor, he was saying it in such as way as she almost felt she ought to feel grateful and happy, and was guilty about being disappointed.

'It must have been so hard for you to say all this, Robin,' she said, almost as if she was sorry for him, and needed to boost his morale even now.

'Listen, Sweet Pea, I have no intention whatsoever of abandoning you. Just you see. All those silly old queens have got it completely wrong. When we get back we are going along straight away to book up the Shakespeare in the park. How about Saturday night?'

She smiled through her tears and as he put his arms on her shoulders and turned her round to face him, she nodded silently, swallowing very hard, but unable to stop one stray tear from racing very fast down her face and plopping on the back of her hand. The proposed "date" to Regents Park had gone over her head somewhat as all she was latching on to was the bit about "those old queens have got it completely wrong". What the fuck did they know? How dare they! What had they been saying to him? Why did he assume that she knew they had been cynical and critical of this relationship? She was so, so angry inside but it would only come out as tears. He hugged and cuddled her and kissed her on the cheek, and anyone passing them at the time would have been touched by their obvious love for one another. Still, still, she couldn't bring herself to elaborate more on what was going wrong exactly. What was it about her that had not been attractive enough, sexy enough, forward enough, funny enough or clever enough?

'Come on, let's go and drink to our future,' said Robin, taking her by the hand.

All she could think of was "what future?" but she followed him like a shell-shocked lamb.

William of course seemed oblivious to all the Iris Murdoch-style goings on. He was too busy with his museum duties, his antique collection and his slightly dubious social life of which they had had a sniff now and again in encounters witnessed in the street or in half overheard telephone conversations. As their plane home the next day was very early, they said their goodnights and thank yous that night and crept out like cat burglars to get into the waiting taxi.

Chapter Fifteen

Immediately on her return from Malta, Julia went to visit her parents in Cornwall. She needed to return symbolically to her childhood situation to re-group, think about her place in the scheme of things, and escape from the emotional running machine on which she had been pounding along for far too long. She just wanted to be the child again.

For Cornwall, the weather was baking hot. Compared with Malta it was chilly and breezy, but it was just what she needed to help her take deep breaths and think deep thoughts. She took Louis down to the beach and plotted a long walk up over the springy turf onto the cliffs leading over towards Padstow. Louis bounded back and forth with a manic doggy grin on his face, chasing imaginary rabbits, and exhibiting that usual skittishness which affects all dogs when the weather is windy. The poppies were out in the fields to the right and the north Cornish sea swirled remorselessly around the rocks way below her. In one small inlet she could see a seal appearing to be standing on its tail and just poking its head out of the water, looking for all the world like an old man in a bathing hat. Fulmars and shags screeched in competition with the roar of the waves and the cliff faces were positively alive with sea birds. Swifts and corn buntings darted about over the fields and in the distance, ironi-cally out of Louis' field of vision, she saw a hare leap through the wheat field.

It was only now that Julia was able to take stock of her life. It was as if someone had asked the man who operated the funfair roller coaster to stop as the lady with the messy hair wanted to get off. Back here she seriously felt as if maybe she had got life entirely wrong; maybe she belonged in the countryside and not holed up in a smelly city. She remembered some old eastern European proverb which said, "If you run with the pack you must wag your tail" and she realised that she had been wagging her tail manically for far too long. So what was she going to do about Robin? She was still completely confused as to what should happen next. She knew of course that it was going, ultimately, nowhere, and she had lived long enough to know that only a subsequent love affair – and a powerful one at that – was going to erase some of the pain that she was going through now. She was so thrilled that Robin still wanted her in his life that she was prepared to pay the price, however high. She was trying so hard to pretend to him that she could handle the relationship on his terms that she had almost convinced herself. Now, staring out at the immense skyscape (the one thing she missed so badly in London) she began to see this was damaging and stupid. But doing anything proactive herself amounted to smothering a handicapped child with a pillow. However much one's head knew it was right, the old heart wouldn't let go. She sat down on a stile and fumbled in her pocket for the flapjack that she'd squirreled away for a moment just like this. She also threw a dog biscuit down for Louis.

'See, I'm as considerate with you as I am with Robin,' she said to the lurcher as he wolfed down the biscuit almost whole in his eagerness. The wind went quiet for a moment and she pulled her sweater up over her head. Not very far away she heard the most exquisite birdsong.

Now if I was a real child of the countryside, she thought to herself, *I would know what that is…is that the one they say sounds like "a little bit of bread and no cheese?" No. Bollocks. How on earth can a bird's whistle sound like that? You may as well say that a snatch of birdsong sounds just like "Now where did I put my reading glasses?" or "I must remember to buy some margarine when I go to the supermarket on Friday".* She twisted around on her perch to see if she could see any small bird that could be the producer of such an exquisite song. There, just on top of the gorse bush, she saw a chaffinch opening and closing its little beak, cocking its head from side to side as it sang.

How can it make that amazing range of sounds from that tiny body and that rigid little beak? she thought to herself. She stared at it, and also decided that it was one of the prettiest of all the common small birds because of the beautiful shades of blue and pink in its plumage. As she gazed at it, it seemed to be singing just for her, and she suddenly remembered Helen's story of the chaffinch that kept throwing itself against her kitchen window. What did they call it? Ah yes, the "special needs" chaffinch. She identified completely with that poor little creature: an almost kamikaze determination to get to the object of its desire, but going completely in the opposite direction from where the true prize was. And yet it didn't learn from its repeated collisions with the window pane; it merely came back again the following day and began afresh to beat its head on the glass. Like the chaffinch, she needed someone to hang a curtain over the window so she couldn't see a false treasure that would only damage her in trying to attain it. But who was going to do it? Louis suddenly barked at her, impatient to be moving on, or at least to be given another biscuit. The chaffinch was startled and flew off at great speed to a hedge in the large wheat field and the moment was over. Further along the coast path a family with small children were walking briskly towards the Round Hole. This was a vast hole in the cliff where the rock beneath had been eroded into a cave over millions of years, and then the strata above it had simply fallen in and been washed away. There was no protective rope around the rim of the hole, which looked like the inside of a volcano, except that the sea was swirling around deep down at the base of the cliffs and splashing upwards as it collided with the rock face, giving off great plumes of spray. It was a dangerous place for small children and dogs. It also had a weird effect on some adults and instilled vertigo. She jumped down from the stile and turned towards home.

The village had once been a tiny hamlet with a few large houses and a lot of sheep farmers. Now it had turned into a second-home enclave, with its discreet little bungalows containing marine-chic knick knacks: a driftwood mirror here, a shabby linen chest there, large sculptures of ammonites nestling among small palms and ornamental grasses; a farm shop selling artisan bread and retirees playing canasta or croquet in the afternoons. It suited her parents perfectly and they couldn't understand why they had not quit their semi urban lives before and come to this wind-beaten paradise. On the small beach the tiny Arthurs and Isadoras were scampering about in rock pools and making sand castles. The state schools had not yet broken up and so the Paiges and Bradleys had not yet arrived at the caravan site. Surfers were way out at sea waiting patiently to catch the next set of good waves, and the Padstow lifeboat was chugging across the bay, no doubt returning from a minor emergency somewhere further up the coast. Handmade signs attached to telegraph poles invited Julia to any number of craft fairs, ceidlihs, fund-raising events, tapestry groups, quiz nights in the pub, and the ubiquitous W.I. meetings. In fact, on her way up the hill she bumped into Miss Bolton, bastion of the W.I. and gave a weak wave and a smile. *I wonder if Mum has ever been along to listen to Miss Bolton talk about her favourite spoon or to share some marmalade-making tips,* mused Julia with a grin as she plodded along at the end of Louis' lead past the Old Farmhouse and Dave's Field.

'Oh, can't you stay a few more days?' her mother begged her, but Julia was restless and needed to get back to her flat. She also needed to see how Mel was coping. She hadn't told her what Robin had said about Mark's new liaison since she thought Mel was in enough of a pit of sadness already, but maybe it would help her harden her heart and lay the past to rest somewhat. Also, she was well aware that the following weekend was the one she and Robin had earmarked long ago as their Shakespeare in the park outing.

'I'm not going to ask, but I can see from your face that all's not well,' said her mother, perceptively as they stood on Bodmin

Parkway station waiting for the train, 'but I don't want to pry.'

'Thanks, Mum, I love you for that. I hope I'm better company when I come down next.'

'Well don't leave it too long. Louis misses you too much.'

And with that, she was gone. The train back to London seemed to take forever and Julia drifted in and out of sleep. She careened down the aisle in search of the buffet car in the end just to see if buying an egg sandwich and a gin and tonic would cheer her up. When she got back eventually to her place clutching her small paper carrier bag, she thought she would try writing her thoughts down for Robin. As the train trundled through Reading and on to Paddington she scribbled little snatches of thoughts as they fluttered across her brain, but it made her very melancholic and she stuffed all the pieces of paper into her bag before the train pulled in, thinking that she was still too much in the maelstrom of the relationship to be in any way articulate about it.

Once she got back into the flat, as ever a huge greyness crept over her. What could possess any sane person to swap a Cornish cliff in summer time for a dingy basement in London with a dubious geyser trickling out a dribble of hot water into a bath in a drafty add-on bathroom? The flat felt alien, not belonging to her. She was seeing it with the eyes of a stranger. She needed urgently to put on the radio in one room, the TV in another, boil a kettle, make loads of phone calls to pals to assuage the misery she experienced on being back here, alone. After ringing Nat and then Celia she felt a lot better, and decided to see if Robin was home. He was thrilled to hear from her, and massively enthusiastic about his own plans to leave London the following week to visit friends in Suffolk. He bombarded her with questions about her own trip to the coast, convinced that she had had a simply wonderful time just because it was an adventure out of town. Little could he imagine the bleakness in her heart as she had sat there on that lichen-covered rock, watching the chaffinch. There was no mention of her going with him to Suffolk and he didn't specify whom exactly he was going to see. But of course, he brought up the subject of Regent's Park which was the main reason for her return to London.

'It looks like the weather's going to be fine this weekend, so are you still on for it or would you rather do something else?'

'No, great, I'd love to. D'you want to eat first or what?'

'I've got a brilliant idea,' he said. 'Why don't I make us a picnic and we can go early and just enjoy the park at the time when most people are leaving. If I bring some chilled white wine we must make sure we don't get too pissed otherwise we'll fall asleep! Imagine that! After planning it for so long to have some bloke nudge me for snoring and making a noise.'

'Can I do anything?' she asked.

'No, just bring your lovely self. Can you make it over here by five?'

'No problem. See you then. Take care.'

And that was it.

Sure enough, Saturday was warm and still. Julia spent a long time getting ready for the evening. She viewed it as a kind of ritual akin to a Chinese tea ceremony...the afternoon bath, the washing of the hair, the careful choosing of the clothes and perfume. And finally off she went, much too early, but deciding to take a book and sit upstairs on a bus rather than plunge into the foetid atmosphere of the Tube. She resolved that if she was early she would just take a stroll around the British Museum. In fact, the traffic was slow and the last quarter of the journey took an age, so much so that she almost thought she may need to get off and run. At about ten past five she rang Robin's doorbell. He came clattering down the stairs, opened the door and kissed her and deposited one large hamper with her and then scampered back up to collect a rug. When he returned he suggested a taxi for which she was grateful, having spent more than enough time on public transport for one day.

They found the perfect spot quite near to the stage area and spread the rug and the contents of the hamper as if laying out a royal banquet.

They started with crab paté, followed by slices of tortilla filled with chorizo which Robin had got from the Spanish deli in Portobello, olives stuffed with garlic and parsley, barbecued chicken drumsticks, a small lentil and blush tomato salad and a wonderful soft ripe goat's cheese and a crusty granary loaf with a mountain of seeds on top. Finally there were raspberries, blueberries, strawberries and tiny meringues glued together with dollops of whipped cream. Robin had also provided a magnificent very dry rosé to accompany it, with proper long-stem crystal glasses of course. Robin would never have been one to use plastic. People strolling by looked at them in their little bower and smiled to see two people taking such delight in their gastronomic feast.

'To us!' Robin said, as they chinked glasses. Even as it was happening, Julia was storing this particular event away under "Romantic evenings, sub-section – al fresco meals". They eventually threw all the debris in a bin, packed away the crockery, cutlery and glasses and made their way to their seats. In the distance there was the occasional cry of a bird or animal over at the zoo on the other side of the park. They lay back in their deck chairs and Robin, as ever, took her hand, and they settled down for the performance. It was made all the more magical by the slow approach of twilight, so that the fairy characters somehow merged with the rocks and plants and everything became illusory and enchanted. When the interval arrived, Julia remarked to Robin how amazing the twilight was and how it had enhanced the atmosphere of enchantment.

'The French call twilight *"crépuscule"*,' he said. 'But I'm sure with your omniscient brain you knew that anyway. It's such a beautiful word.'

'Well in fact,' she replied, 'did you hear how the Frenchman, the Englishman, the Italian and the German were discussing the merits of their various languages and the Frenchman said—' she put on her best French accent '"—I seenk ze word *"papillon"* is so wonderfool; eet convey perfectly the delicate wings of zee creature. *Papillon...papillon"* Then the Italian said, "But we 'ave also a fantastic word: *farfalle*. Leesten to eem: *farfalle"*. Of course the Englishman joined in and flapped his hands as he repeated "butterfly" over and over. Not to be outdone, the German sat there stern-faced and finally said—' Julia barked out the German's contribution as if he were directing a platoon '"—Vot is wrong vith "schmetterling?!"'

Robin giggled and clapped his hands.

'I hope we'll always make each other laugh like this?' he said. 'It's just as well you didn't do science at university. If you were telling me a physics joke I would be staring back at you like someone in a trance.'

After the interval, as the air got chilly, they pulled the picnic blanket over themselves. Now and then Julia's attention wandered off and she of course dwelt on her predicament. Here she was with the one person she needed to be with, but he was living for the joy of the moment and she would be re-living it over and over again, trying to read things into this phrase, that phrase, this compliment, they way he momentarily squeezed her hand, the way he glanced fleetingly at her during a poignant moment in the play. This was her schoolgirl crush on Mr Broadhurst all over again. But how could it possibly not be right?

Finally, the play was over and they made their way back to the perimeter of the park. There was the occasional alarm cry as a bird zoomed from the top of one tree to another, possibly spotting some predator. The traffic was still a distant hum, and they were still sufficiently within the radius of the park to be able to smell the evening scent of stocks and nemesias.

'Wasn't that superb?' she said. 'What a wonderful production. It must be such a nightmare for them when the weather's wet. I wonder how wet it has to be before they cancel.'

'And even worse, what happens if they start in the dry and then it starts to rain halfway through?' Robin said. 'But wasn't Lysander marvellous?'

'Yes,' she said. 'And the guy who played Puck too, and I know I've seen the actor who played Bottom before. Isn't he on the TV? Or have I seen him at the National?'

'I'm not sure...' replied Robin, lost in thought.

'Penny for your thoughts,' said Julia.

'Get you gone, you dwarf,
You minimus of wandering knotgrass made,
You bead, you acorn.'

At this he pretended to push her theatrically away.

Julia giggled and played along with the mime, adding, *'Nothing but low and little!'*

Delighted with themselves at remembering these snatches of the play, they continued playing the game of "I can remember more than you can" for a while. Then, after a while, Robin said, 'But he *was* extraordinary, wasn't he?'

'Who? Bottom?'

'No, you acorn, Lysander. And did you notice his legs? Oh my Lord they were legs to die for! In that rather skimpy costume he was like some total Greek god. Wasn't he wonderful?'

Julia's blood ran cold. Robin had suddenly taken the conversation to a place she couldn't possibly go. This was some purely lascivious response to another man's body. She was female, and if anyone should be drooling over male thighs it should be her, but that wasn't what the evening had been about. It had been about enjoying a Shakespeare play together, having a picnic together, spending an evening in each other's company. Bugger it, they had even toasted one another over their meal and now he was slavering at the memory of Lysander's bloody legs. At that moment some imaginary finger clicked an "off" switch in her head. She suddenly saw with immense clarity that this wasn't the direction she wanted to go for the rest of her life, that the whole business was tearing her heart from her, and taking away the very core of her sense of self. She was ashamed for allowing herself to be so emotionally plundered. Now, all she wanted was to return to her centre, re-group, and heal. What lay ahead for her in one direction was a life with someone who would always be fancying other men, and probably would leave her altogether in the pursuit of this aim, or else would be bitterly resigned to being trapped in a way of life that was at odds with his own soul. She realised in an almighty flash that the only way to save herself, and him, was to cut him right out of her life. There could be no friendship, no companionship. In fact, there could be no possibility of seeing him every day at work. She would have to resign. All of this happened in her head over the course of about three minutes. All she wanted now was to be away, not masochistically prolonging this feeling one moment longer. As they came out of the gates of the park she said, 'I'm absolutely dropping with fatigue. I think I'm going to treat myself to a taxi. I'm not actually feeling too brilliant.' With that, her arm had gone up as she saw an orange light in the distance.

Robin didn't really realise for a moment what was happening, and genuinely believed that she was tired and needed to get to bed urgently.

'OK, you can drop me off on your way, are you sure you've got enough to pay for this?' he said.

'No problem, Mum gave me some money. I think I'm going to treat myself to a return journey which befits the grandeur of the picnic and the play.'

They both jumped in, kicking the hamper into a corner of the taxi and settling back together on the seat. They were both quiet for a few minutes and, as it was late, the taxi made it to Robin's flat in just ten minutes.

'Night, Sweet Pea, I'll give you a ring in the week, thanks for a sensational evening! It was pure midsummer magic,' he said as he hugged her before getting out.

'Goodbye you,' she responded, 'I'll never forget this evening. It was really, really special. Thank for everything, and I mean it from the bottom of my heart.' She kissed him and he got out. And with that the taxi pulled away. She turned to look through the back window at the cheerful waving figure clutching a basket with a rug draped over his arm about to unlock his front door. He had even taken a handkerchief out of his pocket and was waving it histrionically. And that was it.

She fell into a deep, deep sleep when she got home, and when she woke at dawn she got out a large block of writing paper and started to pen her farewell and to let him know that she finally understood. She would have so loved to have written a short, pithy note summing up all she needed to say in one side of A5, but that was not her way, and the letter became a kind of therapy for her. When she finally signed her name at the bottom of the sixth and final page and drew the last of the three kisses, she had a sense of closure and of release.

The following weeks went in a kind of daze. Julia went through the motions of living, joining a group of friends in a villa in Portugal and then back down again to Cornwall. There were days when she just sat in her flat and howled or just went over and over the whole past year again and again, analysing and dissecting what could have been done differently to save it. How could it have begun so spectacularly, and ended in such pain? She tried to tell herself that it was because, in some weird way, Robin still loved her too, but whereas she was merely coping with the plain and simple sad ending (is it ever plain and simple?) of a love affair, he was having to come to terms with some pretty hard truths about himself. This, however, was no comfort to someone whose world had just turned bleak and featureless. What she couldn't get out of her mind was how magical and romantic this had all been. She supposed if he had just been some rugger bugger who had only been interested in eating curries and meeting up with the lads, she would not have been so enchanted. And enchantment it had truly been. Maybe Puck had stepped out of the play and into her basement and put the potion on *her* eyes too.

She decided that the only way to combine earning money (other than teaching in Haverstock which was now out of the question) and trying to exorcise Robin from her psyche was to go abroad. She scanned the educational journals and found an advertisement for teachers of English in Sweden. Miraculously, because of a cancellation by one of the candidates who had already been accepted, she was seen and chosen to replace him at very short notice. Six weeks later she was on a plane to Stockholm. The little town to which she had been assigned was quaint and had the charm of a large Cornish village. The children that she had to teach in the small town's two primary schools made her feel she was in an adaptation of John Wyndham's *Midwich Cuckoos* because they all had the same straight blond hair and stared back at her with huge blue-grey eyes. She discovered that she loved teaching young children, only ever having taught Italian to older and more academic teenagers bound for the linguistics departments of universities. She bumped along the cobbled main street each day on her old bicycle and smiled to think how liberating it was to be away from the hustle and bustle of London. Because she was a foreigner, people found her interesting and special.

According to an old tradition stretching back to the twelve hundreds, the tower in the main square was a look-out point for fire or invading enemies. Now, upholding the custom, every quarter of an hour through the night, a man would sound a long horn through the window of the tower. Some nights when she was unable to sleep, Julia would hear the familiar mournful blast on the horn and know that at least one other person except her was awake in the little town. It was on a night like this about five months after she had first come to the town that she woke up suddenly in the middle of a dream. As she eased herself onto one elbow to peer through the darkness at her clock she heard the slow motion trumpeting that sounded like a distant elephant calling to its fellows. Three fifteen…plenty of time to go back to sleep again before the alarm would wake her for her first class of the day. As she lay back on the pillows and pulled the duvet up over her shoulders, she realised that she had just had an extraordinarily vivid dream. The whole dream came back again as she gave herself time to meditate on it. She had never lost the habit of trying to write down her dreams. She knew that the fact it was still with her meant that her psyche was trying to tell her something.

She had dreamed that she returned to her Putney flat one day to find that the door was unlocked. As she gingerly pushed it open not knowing quite what to expect, she was greeted by silence. No one was there. She walked slowly down the corridor to the kitchen and found to her surprise that both the taps had been turned on and water was racing into the sink and pouring away, giving off billows of steam since the boiler was roaring too. The first thought that struck her was that she had been burgled. She spun around to see that on the stove all four gas taps had been turned on and ignited and were blazing vertically in big fingers of blue flame. The oven door was open and heat was coming from it in thick waves. The fridge door was open and water from the melting ice was spilling over the floor. All the energy sources in the room were blasting out in full, and yet being wasted. She fell to her knees in a panic and looked inside the kitchen cupboards and then had a huge shock. Instead of the usual plates, spoons, washing powder, boxes of cornflakes, bags of sugar, and pots, there were piles of fruit: pineapples, strawberries, mangoes, pomegranates and grapes, boxes of expensive biscuits and Florentines, jars of chutney and marmalade, exotic vegetables, extra virgin olive oil, sauces, smoked fish, crusty French bread, cheeses, jars of paté and other preserves, olives, pistachio nuts, jars of caviar, pink champagne, chocolate and Arabica coffee.

As she recalled each small detail, she realised that her subconscious was gently telling her that a scab had healed over the wound, and that far from being almost destroyed by her relationship with Robin, she had received incalculable gifts, but the price had been high. It was time now to turn off the water, turn off the gas taps, to stop wasting all the energy deconstructing the whole sad period, and just enjoy the things that the burglar had brought.

Next morning she got up and made her breakfast with a new sense of optimism. She lit a candle, sat quietly drinking a cup of coffee and munching a slice of toast and honey. She left a little earlier than she needed to get to the small department store in the centre of town where she was teaching English once a week to the sales assistants and rode off down the hill to Svensson's bookshop. She always smiled in a slightly puerile way when she remembered that the Danish word for bookshop was "bog handel". The bicycle had been given to her by one of her adult pupils, and whereas English bikes had brakes on the handlebars, you stopped this one by back-pedalling. She felt that she was developing calf muscles like cricket balls with all this strain to pull the bike to a halt on inclines. She popped into the shop, selected a postcard with a rather delicate botanical watercolour of birdsfoot trefoil and fool's parsley (how right!) and wrote simply on the back,

I'm absolutely fine, loving life, and wish you lots of love.
I hope you find your holy grail.
Thank you for everything you gave me.
Julia x x x

and sent it to Robin's flat.

Once the class at the department store was over, she rode down to the sea. The Baltic looked gun-metal grey and chilly. She propped the bike up in the sand dunes and walked for about a mile along a deserted silver beach and tried to fathom out what it was she wanted from life. For all its beauty and security, this little Swedish town with its half-timbered houses, shops selling gingerbread men, smoked eel, mulled wine and meatballs was not her home, although it had been her sanctuary for a while. She loved her work and she loved her pupils, even the feisty old age pensioners whom she taught in the little library in the village twenty miles away who were never ever going to be able to speak good English even if she spent eight hours a day with them until they died. She was fed up with old ladies telling her that 'Prince Philip is the most "impotent" man in England' When would they ever learn to pronounce "important" correctly?! What she missed more than anything was her friends. London was exasperating and filthy but it was where everyone either lived or passed through, so it was where she had to be. It was time to move on. Sweden had been an effective convalescent home for her very mangled heart. As she cycled home there were light snowflakes in the air and it was already getting dark even though it was not long after lunch time. She got her contract out of a folder and saw that her final day was the 28th May. After that she was free to go back to England.

That night she wrote in her diary:

This has been overwhelmingly a year of love, life, death, heightened senses, extraordinary happiness, exquisite lovingness, union with nature, suicidal sadness, great depths, expanding limits. It made me feel like a blind person who had their sight restored. It is like having mirrors all around me but being able, in a dreamlike way, to walk through them. In a way, a year of finding my childhood then of losing my innocence, partaking of the tree of knowledge; a year of so much feeling that it was too much feeling; a year of longing to explore more but quickly desiring numbness; a year of giving so much; a year of receiving so much; a year of dreams, both beautiful and nightmarish; a year in emotional top gear; a year more than any other to thank God for; a year of wallowing, self-indulgence, beauty, growth.

I have known depression as never before; I have known loss as never before; I have known happiness as never before; I have known trees and flowers as never before; I have known childhood as never before; I have known sadness as never before; I have known love as never before; I have known myself as never before.

Shit, Jules, she thought to herself as she read it, *you should be the fucking poet laureate!* and she actually laughed out loud. What had it all been about? Even now it felt as if she had been offered, for a short time, a mirror in which, for the first time, she was able to see her own face and understand the very depth of her being with a clarity so total that it was excruciatingly painful. And then the mirror was not only taken away, it was dropped on the ground and broken into hundreds of sharp shards of glass just to be swept aside by a municipal broom and scooped up and thrown into a skip. It was as if she had at some point been able to make an incision in her own chest, delve in and take out, very gently, her own heart and hand it over, as if it was the most precious gift she could give. The recipient had taken it for a moment, looked at it and then said, 'Yes, now where was I?', put it down absent-mindedly, and continued with a former conversation, while all she wanted to do was scream, 'But that's my HEART!' But it hadn't been wanted on board for that particular voyage.

In the true spirit of kissing a lot of frogs before you find a prince, Julia subsequently spent quite a few more years in search of her own holy grail.

Chapter Sixteen

1988

Just as she was about to she set off to pick up the children from school, the phone rang.

'Hi, Julia Cavendish speaking,' she announced and waited for a voice at the other end to announce itself, suspecting it was probably her mother wanting to make school holiday arrangements for Cornwall.

'Jules! We're back!' screamed a female voice. 'Leo, will you be quiet! Mummy's talking to her friend, no, you *can't* put that on the table. Deke! Just a minute, Jules. Deke? Where are you? Can you take Leo out of the room for a moment, I'm on the phone to Jules.'

Julia broke into a broad grin.

'Mel, how fantastic! I didn't know you were back yet. I thought you wouldn't be coming home till September,'

'You'll never believe this, Jules, but I'm pregnant again…and I'm nearly forty-two! Can you believe it? How crazy is that? Because I'm so ancient we decided that it would be best to come home to get all the antenatal stuff done here. If my body can survive the onslaught it'll be worth it. It will be good for Leo to learn that he's not the pampered prince. I mean, he's almost seven now and God knows it took enough medical intervention for him to be born, and I just didn't think I could have any more after that. It's bizarre. I can't believe that after that ectopic pregnancy back when we first moved to Spain for good I ever managed to have him. I suppose that's rubbed off on him and so he sort of knows he's a bit special. This new baby will really teach him a few life lessons. I pity him because it will put his nose out of joint a bit but I think he'll be grateful in the end. Deke was an only child himself and he said he spent a lot of his youth trying to persuade his parents to adopt a Vietnamese orphan because he wanted brothers and sisters so badly! They would probably all have turned out to be mathematical geniuses getting into Mensa before they were eleven and he would have hated it.'

'And how *is* Deke?' asked Julia.

'Oh, like a dog with two tails; he adores Leo, but the idea of a second one has sent him into a total tail spin. He's more like a granny than a dad; he's so emotional about it you just won't believe it, and he's treating me like a bit of precious porcelain.'

'But, Mel, that's sweet! Make the most of it!' Julia said. 'I can't tell you how pleased I am for all of you. Just think, twelve years ago and we were all at sea and now here's me with my three, and you and Deke and Leo getting all excited about a new baby. What is it? Boy or girl? D'you know yet?'

'It's a girl, but don't tell Leo; we want it to be a surprise.'

'Maddy'll be delighted,' said Julia 'when I had the boys she was so miserable; I think she just wanted a little princess doll she could boss around. She went through the Mothercare catalogue choosing her new sister from all the pictures of babies modelling stuff. That's what she imagines a sister would be. She tries hard with the boys, but it won't be long before they'll beat the shit out of her when they get fed up with being organised. Have you been in touch with any of the others yet? Have you heard from Celia? You know she's divorcing Carl, don't you?'

'Oh no!' said Mel. 'The last time I heard was a Christmas card and everything seemed fine. What happened?'

'I don't think things had been very good for quite a while, and they tried counselling but the spark had sort of gone out and it was on the cards that sooner or later one of them would meet someone else, and Carl did just that. In fact I think it had been going on for quite a while. Apparently they were both at a party in the New Year and he disappeared for while, to the loo as Celia thought, and this girl he was having a bit of a fling with came out of the bathroom, so someone else said, with her dress on back to front! And he slunk out a bit later. Can you believe it!?'

'How shame-making! And poor, poor Ceals. We had Geoff and Marie-Claire out to stay a month or two ago and they filled us in on quite a few bits of gossip. By the way, hasn't Francis done well for himself? I saw his picture in *The Times* not long ago and a really fascinating interview that he'd given. I must say, we all used to tease him about his ambition, but good for him, he's followed his dream and he deserves it.'

'Yeah, we're all a bit pleased to know him these days.'

'Now look, Jules, any chance of you coming over? It'd be lovely to see you all. I can't wait to see Felix. He was just a baby in the last picture you sent. He must be talking by now.'

'Oh he's talking all right. He's at nursery school now. Get this: he plays the violin! It's a teeny weeny little thing and he looks so sweet. Oh, heavens! I've just seen the time! Mel, I'll have to go.'

'I'll ring you in a day or two when we've got our diaries. Oh, and by the way, wasn't it awful about poor Robin? I'm so very sorry. We had no idea until we saw it in the paper. Obviously when it said "Donations to the London Lighthouse" we realised what had been the matter. Did you go to the funeral?'

Julia sat down slowly on the nearest available seat which happened to be the children's toy box.

'No, I – er, I didn't know he'd been ill. I mean, I consciously didn't keep in touch, and I think maybe anyone who knows me kind of never brought up his name. When did it – er, I mean, how, was it—?'

Julia had become completely inarticulate. Her working-mother-of-three composure dropped away. 'Mel, I had no idea. I can't…I can't…er…'

'Oh shit, Jules, I thought you knew,' said Mel, 'and how awful of me to just drop it into the conversation when you've got to rush off and collect the kids. Listen, go now, and I'll fill you in a bit more later on. Just give me a call, OK?'

'Yep, I'll do that. 'Bye. Oh, and Mel, it's great to have you back!'

'Mum, who're you phoning?' asked Maddy.

'Oh, just someone I used to work with a long time ago,' said Julia, and took the phone into the bedroom and closed the door.

First of all she rang Mel's number again.

'Jules, I feel dreadful,' said Mel. 'I went to find Deke and tell him what had happened. I had assumed someone else would have told you, but I suppose it's a bit like me and "you-know-who". I don't even know where he lives now. Deke reminded me that there was quite a conspiracy of silence around the whole thing after you left the country, and anyway we were out of the loop really because we were out of the country ourselves.'

'So you don't know any details then?' enquired Julia.

'No, sorry, Jules, I suppose it was AIDS as he was at the London Lighthouse,' replied Mel. 'I'm not really sure where you could start. What about his parents?'

'No,' said Julia, 'I'll leave that as a last resort. I think I'll try the College first.'

'Fine,' added Mel, 'and good luck, Jules. Bye!'

'Hi,' she said when the phone was answered at the other end, 'I wonder if it's possible to have a quick chat with Donna Kilpatrick? She does still work at the College, doesn't she? Oh, sorry, yes, Donna Henderson, I forgot she was married. I know that lessons have finished for the day but I thought maybe she might still be in the staffroom. Thanks, yes of course I can hold.'

Silence. Then she could hear the receptionist saying, with her hand cupped over the phone,

'She didn't give her name, Mrs Henderson, but she asked for "Donna Kilpatrick".'

'Hello?'

'Hello, Donna? Hi, it's Julia – Julia McCallum as I was then. It's Julia Cavendish now.'

'Julia! How wonderful to hear your voice! Goodness me, what a blast from the past! How are you?'

'I'm fine. I do a bit of private teaching these days but with three children, you know how it is. And I'm trying to write a novel as well. And you, you're still hanging in there at Haverstock. What about Martin Cox? He must have retired by now.'

Julia could hear her own voice getting a bit silly, and jabbering on too fast.

'Actually he went on to Sheffield. I think he's vice principal or something. And of course he's on this quango and that. He always did love that kind of thing, meetings, feeling important, committees. Look, Julia, why don't you drop in and see us one day?'

Donna sounded seriously keen to get Julia up to Haverstock.

'I'd love that, but I'm not often up in that part of town, but maybe I should make an effort. Er, by the way, someone mentioned to me a while ago that Robin, Robin Forester, that is, had tragically died. You don't happen to know anything about it, I suppose? I don't even know how long he went on working at the College after I left.'

'Robin hadn't been well for quite some time, but I think he soldiered on bravely for a long time. A few of us knew that he would have to stop work at some point, but to be honest I didn't think it would all happen so quickly. We still have some of his stuff here in a cupboard. A friend of his rang the College quite soon after and said that he would be in London to deal with some of Robin's business arrangements. Apparently he lives in Rome and he and his partner run a restaurant near the Piazza Navona...I think that's what he said. Yes, that's it. It's coming back to me now. I think Stella took that call and then passed the phone on to me because Robin and I go back quite a long way here.'

'You don't know any more details, then?' Julia asked tentatively.

'No, not much really, this chap...I think he said his partner was called...oh hell, now what was it? Oh, here it is! I wrote it down. How stupid am I? The restaurant is called *Da Giacomo*. Yes, that's right, it's named after his partner. Apparently this friend of Robin's is the business manager but this partner used to be a waiter somewhere in Tuscany and he's very hands-on. I've got a number here. You can ring it if you like.'

Julia's hand shook a little as she copied down the number.

'Have you got a name as well?' she asked. 'I speak Italian, obviously, but it would be good to know who to ask for.'

'The man's name is Belmont, Mark Belmont,' said Donna.

'Donna, that's really useful, thanks so much. I was really fond of Robin; he was such good fun. I probably will try to contact this, er, this Belmont man. How fortunate that you had the details. Is he coming over to clear out Robin's things?'

'He wasn't specific, but we'll hold on to them for as long as we can. It would be sort of indecent not to, but I hope he comes before the end of term.'

'Quite. Well, lovely talking to you, Donna, and do give my love to anyone who still remembers me, won't you?'

'Will do,' said Donna, 'Bye! Take care.'

It was a good few days before Julia felt able to dial the Rome number. Several times she got as far as dialling the country code for Italy, and then put the receiver down. While walking to collect Felix from his playgroup she sometimes rehearsed what she would say if an Italian voice answered the phone. She felt that all her Italian had deserted her and that maybe she should even write out what she wanted to say, but then she would maybe sound like The Queen reading out what bills her government proposed putting through in the coming session at the State Opening of Parliament. She was truly devastated that she would never see Robin again. She somehow had always imagined that she would be walking along a street somewhere and, with Jungian synchronicity, he would be walking on the very same pavement and she would see him. After years and years of this stupid habit, she had given up, realising that this owed more to the last few frames of David Lean's *Dr Zhivago* than to her reading of the Collected Works of Carl Gustav Jung. Finally, one morning, when she was alone in the house, she took a deep breath and dialled.

'Pronto, Da Giacomo,' said a voice at the other end which she recognised immediately as Giacomo himself, unmistakeable still, after so many years. She decided not to try to give him the benefit of the connection and asked, in her best possible Italian, if Signor Belmont was available.

'Aspetta, signora,' came the reply and he disappeared for a moment.

There was the gentle clunking of the receiver being picked up once more and the voice said, 'Mark Belmont.'

'Mark, it's Julia, Julia McCallum. I'm so sorry to disturb you, but I heard from – I mean I heard from a friend about Robin. I'm so terribly sorry. I simply wanted to find out a bit more. I mean, not details about his personal life, but just where he was buried or cremated or whatever. I hope you don't mind talking. I rang Haverstock and they gave me your number.'

'No, that's quite all right,' Mark said. 'It was all very quick and quiet and his mother's no longer alive so a few of us, his old pals that is, did it. He was cremated actually and we scattered his ashes a few weeks ago.'

'Did you do that in England or in Italy?'

'In England. In London, well not quite, but good enough. He was always fond of the Isabella Plantation in Richmond Park, so we scattered his ashes in the Still Pond. He asked us to do it. And you? Are you well, Julia?'

'I'm fine thanks. I've got three children now, and you've obviously settled in Italy. You decided to give up the theatre then?'

'Yes, I burned my boats in London quite a long time ago, and let's just say Giacomo and I go back a long way.'

They had all assumed all those years ago back in Rossigno on the student drama trip that they were there in the Villa Marcella because Mark knew Count Lombardini and his glamorous wife. Now the final pieces of the jigsaw had fallen into place. This was Jungian synchronicity of a kind which she had certainly not anticipated.

'Well, that's so very kind of you, Mark,' replied Julia. 'I'm sure you must be very busy. It's an hour later than London in Italy so a restaurant at lunchtime is not a place where the proprietor should be having his time wasted on the phone.'

'Oh, it's really no trouble, and it's not wasting time. Are you in the phone book? I'll try to give you a call when I next come over. I'm Robin's executor so there are still quite a lot of loose ends to tie up.'

'Yes, we're in the book under C. L. Cavendish; we live in Borneo Road. It's not far from the river; Putney, that is, not far from where I lived when I knew Robin.'

'Yes, wonderful. I know that part of London. Lucky you. Well, goodbye, Julia.'

'Goodbye, Mark.'

Julia went out of the sitting room into the long cool hallway and stood silently with her brow pressed against the cool wall.

The following Saturday Maddy had to be dropped off at a party at Putney Baths.

Julia's husband, Charles, was away on business and so she decided to take the boys for a picnic. Felix was beside himself with excitement and kept running into the kitchen bearing all kinds of unsuitable toys that he wanted to take along. Rory begged to be allowed to take his bike, but Julia was adamant that it was not biking terrain.

'Yes it is!' he insisted. 'When Hugo's mum took us we went up and down a little road by the car park in Richmond on our bikes and then along a big flat path.'

'Well, that wasn't the bit I was going to,' Julia said, 'that was Pen Ponds. I think we'll go to a different car park and see a new bit of the park. You'd like that, wouldn't you?'

'Can I take a ball then, and what about my kite?' asked Rory.

'No problem, but you have to be responsible for your things. And we'll take lots of bread. We'll be able to feed the ducks and the swans. Felix, get down off that chair, darling, I've just finished packing the picnic in the cool bag.'

Felix was beginning to inspect the contents of the bag to find out if she had put any bananas in it and to peel open the sandwiches to find out if there was any Nutella on the menu.

'Felix, leave those things, please, come on, get down and let Mummy finish the picnic.'

She shoo'd the boys into the playroom and opened and shut a few more cupboards, checking if everything was there.

'Mummy dot lettuce with pwitty colours,' Felix said to Rory.

Rory was lying on his stomach playing with his soldiers.

'Don't be stupid, lettuce is green!' said Rory, and went on manoeuvring his little plastic fighting force on a makeshift battleground.

'OK, everything ready?' Julia called to them. 'Come on, jump in the car, and don't forget the kite, Rory.'

They clambered in and Julia strapped them into their seats.

Twenty minutes later they were inside the park and driving along the perimeter road.

'Look boys, there are some deer over there, can you see?' she said, as all the cars in front slowed down so as not to frighten the majestic animals grazing very near to the road. Most of the deer were does or Bambi look-alikes. However there were three very macho chaps with unfeasibly large antlers on the edges of the group, possibly acting as guards. The road climbed up a little hill and the boys craned their necks to look back at the deer. A few young women on horses cantered by and the boys got seriously excited about all the possibilities the park held for their own vigorous activity. Julia turned into the Broomfield Hill car park and found a shady place under a tree. The boys tumbled out, eager to get across the road to where there were a number of large fallen trees which made perfect natural adventure playgrounds. Julia carried the large cool bag plus the kite and held Felix's hand with the other hand, cautioning Rory as they made their way out of the car park and across the road.

A small tree on their left just beside the bridle track appeared at first to be laden with huge green and red fruit, and then, as they got closer, Julia realised, to the boys' delight, that there were about fifteen parakeets filling the tree and making their ugly squawking, screeching sounds. The number of birds were completely disproportionate to the small tree and they weighed down its rather delicate boughs. Julia found the perfect spot to eat a little further on, beside an enormous tree trunk which was lying across the grass. As well as providing some shade, it also meant that there was plenty for the boys to explore while Julia laid out the food. She handed out the fingers of carrot, crisps, the boxes of apple juice, chunks of ham, bread, little boxes of raisins for them all and the inevitable Nutella sandwich for Felix. At the same time as eating a smoked salmon sandwich herself, she chopped an apple into chunks and handed it out. There was also a big box of strawberries.

'Where's the lettuce?' asked Rory.

'There isn't any, sorry, Rory,' said Julia. 'But look, why don't you have these baby tomatoes instead?'

'Felix said there was coloured lettuce,' said Rory.

'Oh no, it's not lettuce, it's just a little bunch of flowers; I wanted them to stay cool,' said Julia, as matter-of-factly as she could. There was a slight pause and then she picked up an acorn off the ground. 'D'you know, boys,' she said, 'that there used to be wild turkeys in this park? About three thousand of them! Can you imagine that? They used to eat acorns just like this one. Look Felix, this is what an acorn looks like. Those big trees grew from little seeds just like that.'

Felix looked at it for a moment, then lost interest.

'Come on, let's put all the rubbish away,' said Julia, 'and we can go down the hill over there. It's a really magic place, like a little forest. It's called the Isabella Plantation. I've kept some bread for the ducks. There are moorhens and coots on the island at the bottom, and we may even see a heron if we're lucky.'

Once they got inside the high gate of the Isabella Plantation, they took ages to wend their way down along the banks of the stream with all its little bridges and stepping stones which Felix insisted on crossing. Most of the azaleas had finished flowering but there was still the odd splash of colour from plants that had been on the shadier sides of the bushes. At the bottom of the Plantation, they threw their crusts to the mallards in Peg's Pond, and Rory, for the first time, saw a black swan hiding in the sedge. Julia realised that all that was now left was to make one small pilgrimage.

'Let's go back up a different way,' she said. 'We might even see some rabbits. D'you know there's a big tree up there somewhere where there are tawny owls nesting? A friend of mine has seen them sitting in a big hole near the top. Wouldn't that be amazing if we saw them today?'

As they picked their way through bits of the bog garden, Rory revelled in hiding behind the massive gunnera leaves which looked like giant rhubarb, and pretended he was lost in the Amazon. Felix got fed up with trundling about in the rushes and ferns and demanded to be carried. The Isabella Plantation was alive with birds and butterflies. Little goldcrests hopped about on the ground, Julia noticed several greenfinches and tree creepers, and blackbirds seemed to be auditioning for the "Feathered Singer of the Year" contest. When they got back almost to the exit gate Julia turned right and walked towards the large pollarded oaks with their hollow calloused trunks and showed the boys how, in some cases, an unusual multi-stemmed beech seemed to be embracing an oak tree. And then they were finally there. The Still Pond, surrounded by irises, was like a large dark mirror reflecting the foliage of the azaleas and rhododendrons growing all around. Julia put Felix down on the ground and checked that Rory was not getting into any serious mischief, and she rummaged about inside the cool bag. Felix had found a large tree stump and was climbing on it.

'What Mummy doing wiv dat lettuce?' he asked, as he saw her taking the flowers out of the little polythene bag.

'I just want to leave them here to keep all the other pretty flowers company, darling,' she said, taking his hand, and with that laid the small bunch of sweet peas gently in the shadow of a large fern.

'Come on, Mummy, hurry up,' shouted Rory. 'You promised me we could go and fly my kite!'

At Roundfire we publish great stories. We lean towards the spiritual and thought-provoking. But whether it's literary or popular, a gentle tale or a pulsating thriller, the connecting theme in all Roundfire fiction titles is that once you pick them up you won't want to put them down.